Sleet Banshee

Book Three of the Sleet Series

S. J. Tilly

Sleet Banshee
Sleet Series Book Three
Copyright © S.J. Tilly 2021

All rights reserved.

First published in 2021
No part of this book may be reproduced, stored in a retrieval system or transmitted in any form or by any means, without the prior permission in writing of the publisher, nor be otherwise circulated in any form of binding or cover other than that in which it is published and without a similar condition, including this condition, being imposed on the subsequent purchaser. All characters in this publication other than those clearly in the public domain are fictitious, and any resemblance to real persons, living or dead, is purely coincidental.

Cover: Lori Jackson Design
Editor: M. Penna and Brittni Van Author Services

This book is dedicated to every woman who makes the choice to be unapologetically authentic. Let your inner Banshee out. Own it. Flaunt it. Wear whatever the fuck you want. Then toss a pair of middle fingers in the air and tell the patriarchy to go suck a dick.

Chapter 1

Meghan

"Remind me again why the fuck I'm here? And where in the hell we're going?" I ask from the backseat of Jackson's SUV.

Sitting in the passenger seat is Katelyn, aka Kitten, Jackson's fiancé and my oldest friend. I don't know our destination. All I know is that I was told to *dress warm*.

I know right? What a load of shit.

So here I am, wearing my favorite pair of jeans. And when I say "favorite", I mean my most tolerable pair of jeans. I don't know anyone who actually loves wearing hard pants. Maybe skinny bitches? But skinny bitch, I am not. For me, jeans are worn to look good, and to stand in. Sitting in tight jeans is probably on par with waterboarding. I'm fairly certain it's listed in the Geneva code as torture. So, I'm suffering through this car ride sitting in tight jeans that I have tucked into my warmest fake-fur-lined boots. I lost count, but I'm pretty sure I have about three layers on my top half. I know I put on a bra, which is another item that will get ripped off along with the jeans the second I get home. Over that, I have a long tank top to keep cold air from sneaking up my back. Then a thick, long-sleeved white shirt, and finally my rainbow-colored Mexican poncho hoodie. To top it all off, I wore my black feather earrings. They've sort of become my calling card, and I have a pair in every color.

Since the moment they picked me up, the girls have been giving me crap for looking like a Rastafarian Eskimo. Whatever, those bitches are going to freeze and I'm going to be nice and toasty. End of October in Minnesota is no joke. I'd rather be warm than sorry. I did forget my mittens at home, but I'll just shove my hands in my hoodie pocket to keep them warm. Or better yet, I'll find a sexy man to warm me up.

"You're here because you love me, and you want to support me. And you know damn well that I have no idea where we are going. Ask Jackson," Izzy replies.

Jackson turns up the music to drown out our voices. Katelyn's shoulders shake in laughter.

"Don't play all innocent!" I shout over the music. "Kitten, you traitor, I know Jackson told you!"

Honestly, I'm surprised that Izzy invited me to come along to this. Her new slice of man-meat invited/asked/begged her to come out tonight for some sort of birthday celebration. But with Katelyn and Jackson already here I have a feeling I'm going to be third wheeling all night.

But I guess I'm here as a buffer between Izzy and Zach. She's been fighting the attraction like crazy. Or, well... she has been since the week after their one night stand, when she found out he's the newest player for the Minnesota Sleet, our local professional hockey team. I don't understand why she won't just go for it. He's hot as fuck, he's into her, and - with a name like "Zachary Hunt" - you *want* to swoon.

Yeah, okay, so Izzy's dad also happens to be the head coach for the team, but you can't fix that. Of course I know why she's resisting. The night she first met Katelyn and Steph, Jackson's sister, they had a big long talk full of rational reasons as to why she shouldn't date hockey players. Who would've known that conversation would backfire so spectacularly?

Anyways, I've made it clear that I think she should give Zach a chance. She won't listen, but bringing me here tonight is opening Pandora's Box. Because if I get a moment alone with him, you bet your ass I'm going to give him some insider information. It's what any good friend would do.

Snapping out of it, I look out the window into the darkness. Seriously, where are we going? I feel like we've been driving into the country forever.

That's when I see it. The sign for *Visceral Village*.

I don't even try to play it cool. "Oh my gods, yes!" I laugh, while bouncing in my seat and clapping my hands.

Can't say I'm surprised when Izzy tries to put up a fight about going. Jackson obviously knew the plan, so no amount of complaining on her part will get him to turn around. Honestly, this place was a brilliant move on Zach's part. Izzy is going to spend the entire night clinging to his side. I'll make sure of it.

Chapter 2

Meghan

My many layers of clothing are going to all be for naught when I catch a cold from walking around all night with damp panties. Because *holy heart attack*, Zach's friends are stupidly-attractive. I should've assumed they'd be, since Zach is hot and Jackson is hot. But even if I'd tried to prepare myself, I wouldn't've been successful, because Zach's friend Sebastian, aka "Ash" LeBlanc - star goalie for the Sleet, is in a league of his own.

I know I've seen photos of him. And I've seen him play. But seeing him up close and personal has my ovaries short-circuiting, releasing a bucket-load of hormones straight into my thong.

Zach's already distracted by the beautiful Izzy, so I guess I'll just stand here staring since no one is doing introductions.

I'm an average five-foot-five, so Sebastian towers over me at around six-three. The man is the epitome of Tall Dark and Handsome. His last name sounds French, but his olive skin, black wavy hair, strong jawline, and five o'clock shadow deep enough to crawl into, make him look *all* Greek. I don't know much about the Greek, but I do know they make finger-licking good food. So throw this man on a platter and call him a snack, because I. Am. Salivating.

His *player* reputation is well known, but - whatever, I'm no saint. And I want a taste.

The sun's dipped below the horizon, and the descending night makes his brown eyes look almost black. He's wearing jeans and a dark grey sweatshirt. But even with the hood up, his black, shoulder-length wavy hair is visible around his face. His clothing hides the sinful form of his body, and since I've seen photos of Sebastian without his shirt on, I know his clothes are hiding his full sleeve tattoos. I don't care who you are, sleeve tats on a burly Greek god are always a *Yes, Please*!

I'm not sure why I'm surprised to see Sebastian here; he obviously knows Zach, but I hadn't realized they were friends. Not that I would've dressed any differently had I known he was coming, but maybe I would've worn thicker undies.

Izzy's scream pulls me out of my ogling. I'm not even sure Sebastian knows who I am, but I have plans for tonight and standing here won't get Izzy into Zach's arms.

"Let's get this party on the road!" I call out, turning toward the entrance.

Striding ahead, I make a point to be aware of my surroundings. I might be excited about being here, but that doesn't mean that I won't scream like a little girl the first time something jumps out at me. I have a real love-hate relationship with haunted houses. I love them. I hate them. I scream. I swear. I smile when it's over.

The one part I always forget about is having to wait in line. Somehow Katelyn and I got into a wedding planning conversation with the wives of Zach's college buddies, so I'm surprised when I see that we're up next.

Izzy looks like she's about to bail. Or puke. She spots me looking at her and grips my arm so hard I'm afraid her nails are going to cut my skin. As casually as possible, I shift our stance until I'm the one holding her arm. The lady in charge gives me a nod. So, without giving Izzy time to protest, I pull her into the haunted Santa's Workshop.

I saw one of the Santa characters walking around earlier, and he resembled the Sleet Yeti mascot more than a childhood happy memory. I'm equal parts excited and terrified to do this.

Right before we pass through the door, I look back to make sure Zach is right behind us. Catching his attention, I throw him a wink. I really hope this stud has some brains and knows what I'm getting at. If he doesn't step in, Izzy is going to kill me for this next move.

The door slams shut behind us, and Izzy screams.

I feel like the worst friend ever, but it's now or never. I let go of her arm and sprint ahead into the dark.

I hear another scream and hope that Zach takes his cue.

Except this is the part of the plan I didn't really think through. Because now I'm walking through this creepy Christmas slum by myself.

Oh, boy this was a bad idea.

Having no one and nothing to grab on to, I tuck my hands into the end of my sleeves and bring my covered fists to my mouth. Hopefully I'll be able to muffle my own screams so I can pretend calmness when I make it out the other side.

The first room I walk through is nightmare inducing, but nothing has jumped out at me yet. From past experiences, I'd bet they're waiting for a friend to catch up. Most people don't do this shit alone.

In my peripheral vision I see someone, or something, rush towards me, so I scream and take off into the next room.

I know you aren't supposed to run inside here, but I need to find a buddy like right-the-fuck now. The consensus is in; I can't do this alone.

I push through some rubber flaps to enter the next room and suck in a deep breath. Body parts... everywhere.

I keep my eyes on the ceiling and not on the gore sprawled across the floor. If I can't see it, it can't scare me.

Thinking this is the best idea ever, I release the breath I've been holding. Then, with my eyes still up, a pair of bloody Santa legs drop from the ceiling.

Right in front of me.

I stumble back tripping over some unknown lump.

I'm going down.

My instincts are torn to the point of inaction. The fright part of my brain wants to cover my eyes. The smart part of my brain tells me to reach back and brace my fall. Instead, my arms flail out to the side, achieving neither goal.

With a scream stuck in my throat, all I'm able to do is clamp my eyes shut and pray for death.

As I tip past the point of no return, my shoulders hit a hard surface... and a pair of strong arms circle around my waist.

The sudden contact releases the scream that was snagged in my vocal cords.

"Hush. I got you, Baby," a deep voice rumbles into my ear.

The octave is so low that I feel the vibrations dance across my scalp like a mating call. It's a voice I've heard before. One that I've already started to fantasize about.

"Sebastian?" I croak out.

Real fucking sexy, Meg.

"Nice to finally meet you." I can tell he's chuckling from the way his chest is shaking against my back.

A loud bang startles another scream out of me, causing Sebastian to laugh outright.

He may be hotter than anyone I've ever met, but that doesn't mean he gets special treatment. I elbow him in the ribs and wiggle free from his grip.

Forcing my face into a scowl, I turn to look at him.

Fuck me, this man is my new wet dream.

His hood is still up, making it nearly impossible to see his face. But the hint is enough. His hotness causes my brain to lapse, and I forget what I was about to say.

"Come on, we gotta keep moving before they catch up." Placing his large hands on my shoulders he turns me to face forward.

I'm still so stunned by this change of events that I go along for a few steps before I realize that he's shoving me into the next room ahead of him.

Spinning around, I grab a hold of his sleeve and pull. "Look here, jackhole. You are *not* sending me in first like a sacrificial lamb. Get your big sexy ass in there and clear the way."

Sebastian grins as he strides past me. "You think I'm sexy?"

I just roll my eyes. With a voice like his, you don't even need to see him to think he's sexy.

Long legs mean long strides, and before I know it, he's half a room ahead of me.

Maybe this is a good strategy? Maybe the creepy crawlies will go after him first?

"Pretty girl!" a high pitched voice screeches right behind me.

As I scream, my body automatically rotates to look for the source of the voice. I don't want to turn around. Seeing the source of this voice is honestly the last thing I want. But I can't stop myself. I'll have a stern talk with my body about this reaction later, when this image keeps me awake tonight.

Bracing, I find myself face-to-neck with a beheaded woman.

I know it's fake. I know that's a prosthetic neck, placed on the head of a short person who's covered in a cloak. I know all of this, and it's still the scariest thing I've ever seen.

The voice cackles, and the bitch steps even closer.

Finally my body responds, turning and running for dear life. Sebastian is still standing in the middle of the room, laughing his stupid sexy ass off.

"You twatwaffle! I hate you!" I shout, as I rush past him.

"No running!" is his response.

I want to ditch him, but I know that's more of a punishment for me than him. He seems unmoved by any of this, so I decide to do the smart thing and wait for him to catch up.

"Okay," I say when he steps through the doorway to join me. "We're going to go through this together. You'll go first, but you won't ditch me like you did back there."

"Why do I have to go first?" Sebastian asks.

"Because you're bigger. There's more of you to go around if the zombies decide to attack. Now come on."

I'm positive I'm trying his patient exterior as I tug on the front of his sweatshirt.

"I have a better idea," he says, before spinning me around. "You go first."

He keeps his hands on my shoulders and starts to push me forward.

"What?! No! What the fuck is wrong with you?" I'm shuffling my feet, trying to fight the forward momentum. "Take one too many pucks to the head or something?" I hiss over my shoulder at him.

He leans in closer. "You're pretty feisty for a cute little thing, aren't you?"

Cute? I'm honestly not sure what to think about that. Yeah, sure, "cute" is a compliment. But it's not the sort of compliment I want to hear from the demon sex god standing right behind me. Hot, stunning, sexy - take your pick. But *cute*...?

"Cat got your tongue?" I can hear the smirk in his voice.

"Lookie here, buckaroo-"

That's how far I get before a half-dead elf pops out from a hidden panel in the wall.

"What kind of Santa titty-twister hell hole is this?" I shout at the elf's face.

And Sebastian is back to laughing. I'm glad this is all so damn amusing for him.

Grabbing my hand, he steps past me and pulls me forward.

Finally, he's going first!

I surprise myself when I have enough wherewithal to register the feel of my hand in his giant one. His palm is warm and dry and entirely consuming mine. He's tall. Not a giant, but his hands seem giant-like. And I can't help but wonder, *does Sebastian have a giant dick to go with these oversized mitts?* God, I hope so. Even if I don't get the pleasure of experiencing it myself, I hope he's big. For his sake. It'd look really strange to wrap monster hands around an average-size cock.

And just like that, I'm imagining him jerking off. And it's hot. Like - turning me on, my hand is gonna start sweating, *hot*.

I must've been fantasizing for longer than I thought, because I suddenly find myself standing outside. The exit for the Santa House of Horrors behind us.

"You alright?" Sebastian asks.

He's standing next to me and has yet to let go of my hand.

"Huh? Me?"

He smiles. "Yeah, you."

"I'm fine." I shrug, then I hope the movement doesn't jostle his hand enough to remind him that he should let go. I don't want him to let go.

"Well, you cried like a baby for the first half of that house, then you walked through the rest without a single flinch." He raises an eyebrow at me.

Out here, there's enough light that I can see his facial expressions. And it's dangerous.

"I was..."

I was what? What am I possibly going to say? *I was distracted wondering if you have a donkey cock.* Yeah, I don't think so.

"You were...?" he prompts.

"I was thinking." There. Good enough.

"Thinking about what?" He smirks, like he knows.

I huff. "What does it matter?"

"Well, I'm just wondering what could've possibly distracted you so greatly that you'd suddenly stop noticing all the things that frightened you so terribly just moments before."

Frightening me so terribly. This prick.

"You really want to know? You're that damn curious?"

"Yes, I want to know." His voice, *ugh*, it's so sultry. So confident.

Time to put him through the Speak Your Mind Test.

"I was thinking about the size of your cock. Wondering if it fits in your big hands or if it's teeny-tiny and you have to daintily grip it every time you whack your weenie." Smiling sweetly, I let go of his hand and skip away.

Score one to Meghan.

I think.

Chapter 3

Meghan

I WAS HOPING to let Sebastian stew on my dick bomb for a moment, but rather than getting into another long line, Katelyn leads us all to the corn maze.

Oh goodie, a scary jacked-up corn maze to add to my nightmare rolodex.

At the first fork in the path, the group fractures off in different directions.

With the exception of Sebastian and me, our group is made up of all couples if you count Izzy and Zach as an item. So - with no great options, I grumble to myself and start down the path that Katelyn and Jackson took.

"You're coming with me." Sebastian's voice is so close it startles me.

I spin around to face him, but before I can yell at him for sneaking up on me, he takes my hand and tugs me in a different direction.

"Umm, none of our friends came this way," I tell him, trying to pull my hand free.

"I know."

That's all he says - *I know.*

"But..." I can't think of a way to argue with his non-answer.

"Come on, Meghan, live a little."

My name, said in his voice, does things to me. *Naughty things.*

Wait.

"You know my name?" I hate how surprised I sound.

This stops him in his tracks.

Sebastian tilts his head questioningly as he turns to face me. "Of course."

"What do you mean, *of course*? We've never met before -" The *duh!* strongly implied in my tone.

He reaches out and pinches one of my wild red curls between his giant-size fingers. "You're hard to miss."

The honey badger that lives inside of my chest just rolled over, and is showing her soft underbelly to Sebastian. The gentle feel of my hair running through his soft grip sends tingles straight from my scalp to my girly bits.

My mouth opens, but my brain momentarily forgets the English language.

A chainsaw roaring to life nearby snaps me out of my mesmerized state.

"Run!" I whisper shout.

"What?" Sebastian's face scrunches up, making him look stupidly adorable. A face that causes spontaneous orgasms should *not* be adorable.

"Come on." I start pushing him. "It's the Chainsaw Guy. I can't deal with Chainsaw Guy."

"The Chainsaw Guy?" His tone is so condescending I would punch his perfect man tit if I wasn't so frantic to get away.

"Yes. Now move!" I push against his chest. "What the hell

are you made of?!" I'm full-out yelling now. He's immovable. Made of stone. "I'm leaving you behind."

I go to dart around him, but he snags me with an arm around my shoulders.

"Okay, okay!" Sebastian pulls me into his side while he guides us down the path. "Can't you distract yourself thinking about my teeny-tiny weenie again?"

A giggle hits me and I'm defenseless to stop it. His deep sensual voice saying *teeny-tiny weenie* has got to be the funniest thing I've ever heard. Replaying it in my head, my giggle turns into a laughing fit. I feel tears pricking my eyes as my whole body shakes, and if he lets go of me I'm sure I'll topple over.

"You sure know how to make a guy feel special." He's trying to sound mad, but I can hear the smile in his voice.

I lean into him, wiping the corners of my eyes. "I'm sure your ego can take it."

Sebastian just hums his reply, and I'm finally able to catch my breath.

Unfortunately, my laughter prevented me from hearing the approaching danger. We must have gotten turned around in this godforsaken maze, because rounding the corner right in front of us is Chainsaw Guy.

I instantly still.

"He found us!" I whisper, all traces of humor gone.

I *Hate* Chainsaw Guy.

I try to turn away, but Sebastian's grip on my shoulder tightens.

"Face your fears."

"What?! Are you insane?"

"Come on Megs, you can do this."

His marble body shifts, and he's somehow brought me directly in front of him. One of his large, muscular arms wraps around my upper chest. I feel him crouch down a little before his other arm crosses lower around my waist.

I want to melt into the embrace, but then the Chainsaw Guy revs the speed of his killing tool reminding me where we are. My pulse kicks into overdrive, but it's the feeling of Sebastian laughing against my back that sends me over the edge.

I start to thrash. "Let me go you dick-bag!"

The asshole just laughs harder.

"Sebastian, I'm real fucking serious right now. I don't want to hurt you, but I will."

Chainsaw Guy is approaching, and my flight reflex is firmly shoved into high gear. I know it's fake. I know there's no real danger, but I can't help it. I need to flee.

Sebastian's grip on me tightens. Bringing my whole body flush with his.

"Baby, you're gonna want to stop wiggling that sweet ass against me if you don't want to find out just how *not* teeny-tiny I really am."

I think I might die. This is how I go. My body is so overwhelmed with fear and lust that I'll probably combust. I'll go up in flames, and in the process singe the arms of the best goalie the Sleet's ever had. And then someone will graffiti *Bitch cost us the season* on my tombstone.

I close my eyes and focus on his words, while trying not to hyperventilate.

"Don't call me Baby," I whisper.

Sebastian's warm breath tickles my ear as he nuzzles my hair. "Why not, Baby?"

"Because - in my experience, only douchebags and controlling assholes call girls *Baby*. But then, based on our current situation, I'm guessing D-bag might be a perfect description for you!" By the end of my mini-rant my attempt at calm slips and I'm back to struggling.

Sebastian's grip is so firm, my struggle is more of a wiggle.

And *Oh. My. Giant dick. I think he's getting hard!*

I think the perfect specimen known as Sebastian LeBlanc is getting a boner from being pressed against my ass. I mean, it's a good ass, if you like big round asses. Which apparently Sebastian does.

Sebastian's hard dick is pressed against my ass!

My eyes reflexively close, so I force them back open.

And I'm staring straight into the eyes of Chainsaw Guy. Who, a second later, revs his murder weapon right in front of my face.

I release the Mother of All Screams.

Sebastian throws his head back laughing, causing his grip to loosen enough that I'm able to break free and dart away.

I have no idea if this is the way out, but it's away from Chainsaw Guy and that's all I care about.

A few turns later, I find myself at a dead end. A real dead end. The path leads to a solid wood fence.

Shit.

My heart is still beating too fast to be safe, so I walk up to the fence and lean my back against it. It looks solid, no visible trap doors, so I don't think anything can pop out of it.

I'm clearly stuck in the far back corner of the maze, where only the idiots end up. And with that thought, I look up to see Sebastian rounding the corner.

This sexy idiot.

"*You!*" I accuse, pushing off the fence to stand straight.

"Me." He smirks, not slowing his approach.

"You have some nerve. You don't even know me."

"Let's change that."

With one more large stride, Sebastian's body is covering mine. I step backwards, but find myself pressed against the fence.

I open my mouth to ask him what in the hell he's doing, but my question is stopped. With his mouth. On mine.

Sweet baby corn maze, Sebastian LeBlanc is kissing me.

Wait! Who the fuck does he think he is? I shove at his chest and he releases the kiss, leaning back enough so I can look right into his eyes.

He just kissed me. Without asking.

I slap him.

Oops.

My eyes widen. I can't believe I just did that.

Sebastian, the demented bastard, *grins*. "I think I'll call you Banshee."

"Wha..."

He waits for me to get halfway through the word, then he takes advantage of my open mouth again. His lips are back on mine, his tongue pressing in to invade. He still didn't ask, but this time my brain stutters, and my greedy vagina takes over.

I kiss him back.

Sebastian's hands start by gripping my sides. Holding me hard enough that I can feel the tips of his fingers through my sweater. And *fuck*, I love it.

We both must feel the same surge of lust, because our kiss grows more frantic and one of his hands slides around to my back, pulling me in tighter.

I let him lead when his lips dance over mine. But when his tongue slips into my mouth, I bite down. Gently. Sort of.

Sebastian smiles into our kiss, sliding that hand down my back to squeeze my ass.

This man is a bit of a freak. And it turns me on so damn much.

I release the groan building in my chest.

My sound is apparently the green light that Sebastian was waiting for because he turns the kiss up to 11.

With his hand palming my ass, he pulls me hard against his body. I swear this kiss has only lasted for a matter of seconds, but time's become a blur. However long it's been, the hard length pressing against my belly tells me that there's indeed *nothing* teeny about this man.

Oh Heavenly Father of Dicks, I want to feel this one inside of me.

I press harder against him. He's too tall for me to be able to rub my pussy against his erection, so I settle for rocking against him. Searching for a friction I won't achieve.

It's Sebastian's turn to groan. Only - with his deep voice, it sounds more like a growl.

My hands have found their way up to his neck. In one motion, I pull his hood back and sink my fingers into his long waves. His hair is soft, and a complete contrast from the heavy stubble on his cheeks, rubbing against the smooth skin around my mouth.

I know I'm going to look like a ragged mess when this is over, but it's an acceptable cost.

When I sweep my tongue into his mouth, he nips at the tip. My grip in his hair tightens, and I give it a little tug. Sebastian moans, and grinds against me.

I smile, and pull harder until he tips his head back enough for me to taste his neck.

Releasing his hair, I scrape my nails down the back of his head and place an open-mouthed kiss on the side of his neck. Something about this spot on a man just does it for me.

Licking and biting my way up and down his throat, I'm distracted from his movements until he's cupping my breast, with nothing but my bra separating his palm from my tight nipple.

My head drops back.

"Fuck - " we both moan the word at the same time.

I have large boobs. Large enough that they are usually more a pain than a pleasure. But Sebastian's giant hands are my titties' Goldilocks; they're just the right size.

Taking advantage of my exposed neck, he starts at my collar bone and licks a trail all the way up to my chin.

His tongue... his hand gripping my ass, the other working its way under my bra. It's all too much.

"Sebastian... what... *shit*..."

"You feel so good, Banshee." He punctuates his statement with a bite to my earlobe.

I squirm. "Banshee?"

"Mmm."

"Isn't that like a crazy screaming lady?"

"Basically," Sebastian agrees before moving back to kiss my lips.

"What?!" I find myself shoving at his chest, again.

The push dislodges his hand from under my shirt, and I shiver as the cold air rushes in to take its space.

He smirks. "You got a problem with *Banshee*?"

"Obviously! What the hell sort of name is that?"

"You told me not to call you 'Baby.'"

"Wipe that smug look off your face, twerp. That doesn't give you free reign to call me something like *Banshee*!"

He laughs. "I think it's the perfect name. Look at you, all feisty and riled up. Toss in your lips looking freshly-fucked, and your eyes looking like they want to slice me in two." He grins. "I think Banshee is the perfect name for you."

I narrow my eyes.

"Just tell me one thing before you run away..." He leans in close, his deep voice lowering. "Are you as wet as I imagine you are?"

I slap him. Again.

Chapter 4

Meghan

I'd feel bad about slapping Sebastian and taking off, but I can hear his dumbass laughing behind me. There's *definitely* something wrong with that man.

"Little Banshee, you're only proving my point - " he calls after me.

Lifting a middle finger high over my head, I continue to pick my way back through the maze. His voice rolls over the cold breeze. I want to hate him for being a big dumb animal, but even the sound of his chuckle turns me on.

I'm not embarrassed about what we did. We're both adults. We both consented. We're both sexy creatures.

But there's this stupid little bitch of a voice in the back of my head telling me he's out of my league. I mentally toss her the middle finger too. So what if he looks like the cover of a smut novel? So what if he's a rich famous hockey player? So what if he could have any girl he wants? I'm sexy. Usually. When I try. Maybe I wouldn't consider today's choice of an oversized striped hoodie as sexpot attire, but hey - it worked. Dressed like a teenaged stoner, I still got felt up by the hottest man I've ever met. So that goes in the win column. And yeah, my pant size might be in the double digits. But not all guys crave runway models. There's just more of me to love. And touch. And fuck. Ugh, I kinda hate Sebastian right now, but I really hope I get to experience him biblically. Like *Oh God, Oh Jesus, Oh God* -biblically.

Needing to get out of this maze, I turn what I'm hoping is the last corner. And would you look at that, Chainsaw Guy is standing halfway between me and the exit.

My hands ball into fists. This is the home stretch. I'm almost there. I can stand here and wait for Sebastian, or I can suck it up and deal with this demon head on.

Chainsaw Guy spots me. And I swear I have a *Whoville* moment where my lady-balls grow three sizes.

"No!" I shout, pointing a finger at him.

He doesn't listen and takes a step towards me.

I take a step towards him.

"I said No!" I feel like I'm yelling at a dog. So, when in Rome - "Go home! Go on, Get! We don't want you here!"

I think I'm winning.

Then Chainsaw Guy cocks his head, and it's officially the scariest thing I've ever witnessed.

My finger is starting to tremble but I keep it pointed at him.

"I said No!" My voice cracks on the word *no*, and I know that I've lost.

Chainsaw Guy takes another step in my direction. I take a step back. He steps forward. I step back. And right into a hard body.

"That was a good effort, Little B." Sebastian's voice rumbles through my body.

I instantly feel a little more confident, then I berate myself for feeling like I need a man to protect me.

Chainsaw Guy guns his weapon and starts sprinting in our direction.

Somehow, I manage to not throw up. Instead I spin around and bury my face in the warm hard planes of the asshole hockey player's chest, my hands fisted together underneath my chin.

"There, there, sweet girl," he pats me on the head with one hand while the other hand spans my back, holding me in place. "I'll protect you from the scary high school kid with the gardening tool."

It's a good thing my voice is muffled by his sweatshirt. If he could hear the things that I'm saying about him, I'm sure he'd toss me to Chainsaw Guy with a smile on his face.

"Megs, we gotta move our feet a little bit here if we want to get out of this maze."

"No shit, Sherlock. But I'm going to wait here until *he* passes. Obviously. Idiot."

Nose pressed firmly against his warm body, I take in a deep breath in through my nose. He smells divine.

"Okay, Mumbles. I think you called me Sherlock *and* an idiot. You're throwing out mixed signals."

I pry an arm free so I can flip him another bird.

I feel something warm and wet on the tip of my finger, right before teeth close down just above my top knuckle.

My head jerks up and my knees nearly give out at the sight of my finger still firmly locked in his bite. His lips turn up in a smile as his tongue darts out to lick the tip of my finger.

I think my vagina just drooled.

Then the *very near* chainsaw sound pulls my attention away.

Sebastian's teeth release my finger. "Looks like we're doing this my way."

"What do you mean, your way?"

Instead of answering, Sebastian bends down, lines his shoulder up with my stomach, wraps an arm around the back of my thighs, and stands. With me. On. His. Freaking. Shoulder.

I have died and gone to firefighter heaven. This is every house burning fantasy, mixed with every pro athlete dream, mixed with every bad boy crush I've ever had. I can't even pretend I don't like this. Yeah, the feminist in me is outraged, but she'll also be imagining this moment while she flicks the bean later, so she can keep her thoughts to herself.

"You alive back there? Did I finally find a way to shut you up?"

Oh, well, that kills the fantasy. "Shut me up? Really?"

My coordination is put to the test, hanging upside down like this, but I'm able to slip my hands up the back of his sweatshirt. Where I find nice warm, muscly skin, with my freezing hands.

He flinches. "Ahh! What the hell?"

"Mmm, you're so warm..." I coo.

"Get your icy claws off me, Banshee!"

I spread my hands out, getting the most possible contact. He really is quite warm. And firm.

When I slide my hands around to his sides I can feel his quick inhalation. A sharp smack lands on my ass and I withdraw my hands with a jolt.

"You did not just..." I sputter.

"Oh, I just. Put your frozen talons back on me, and I'll spank you again."

Well, when he puts it that way... I slide my hands back up his shirt.

Sebastian laughs, as he bends forward, placing me back on the ground.

Using the back of his hand, he brushes a lock of hair away

from my face. "They always say the most dangerous things come in the prettiest packages."

Oh. Wow. I like the word *pretty* better than *cute*.

Standing inches apart, we start to lean in towards each other, but a voice calls out my name.

"Meghan! Oh my god, this place is Hell." Izzy steps around a cluster of bodies, heading our way. She has Zach, Katelyn and Jackson with her and somehow they all missed Sebastian carrying me. I'm hoping to keep whatever is going on between us a secret; tonight Izzy needs to focus on Zach.

"Come on, I need to find the bathrooms," Izzy says, grabbing my arm.

Chapter 5

Meghan

Dear Diary,

I don't even know where to begin. Tonight was... something. Kissing Sebastian LeBlanc was like nothing I've ever experienced. I mean, *obviously* - you've witnessed all my make out sessions. But this one. Ugh. Pretty sure Honey Badger is still fanning off her lady parts.

Sebastian's just so... fucking hot! But he's more than just that. He's tall, dark *and* handsome. Kidding. Well, not kidding, but you know what I mean. Even when he was torturing me, it was easy to be with him. Too easy. Normally there's some awkwardness when I'm around a new person. There's the weird silences and the boring small talk where you end up discussing the dumbest shit. But there was none of that tonight. Maybe it was the setting? Maybe the heightened fear made all that other bullshit fade away? I don't even know how to describe it. It was just... right.

Which is a totally lame thing to think after one short evening together. One *evening*, not even a date. Plus, I've heard enough about Sebastian's trail of broken hearts to know I shouldn't read too much into this. He's a "ladies' man". Wait, do people even use that phrase anymore? Whatever, that's probably why it was so easy to talk to him. He's used to flirting. And kissing. Not that I'm judging. I like to date. I like sex. I'm no blushing virgin. Not for a long time. But hot damn! When he had his tongue down my throat, and his hand on my tit, he got me blushing. Everywhere.

So Diary, you need to remind me to not get attached. I'll need to play it cool when he's around. I mean, I know he's interested. The python in his pants was a firm sign of his interest. And the kissing. And the tossing me over his shoulder like I weighed nothing. *Swoon.*

Anyways, we stayed near each other for most of the night. I swear I wasn't trying to cling to him, but I also wasn't going to avoid him. I was pleasantly surprised when he asked for my number. I gave it to him, duh. Not that I expect him to call, but you never know. He also told me that I can call him Ash if I want... I'm not sure how I feel about that. I know that's what people call him, friends and fans alike, but there's something about calling him Sebastian. I like it. It feels special.

Omfg I want to punch myself for writing that!

Oh right, then there's the whole "Banshee" thing. My friends get nicknames like Kitten and Sugar. And I get *Banshee*. #NotFair - I looked it up. Apparently, the real definition is a wailing, shrieking female spirit who warns of death. Oh fucking joy.

Most importantly, when Izzy went to the bathroom, I finally got my chance to corner Zach. I had like 2 minutes to lay out my plan, but he's game. I knew he would be.

And I've decided to keep the Sebastian Situation to myself until Izzy admits that Zach is the man for her. But they're way too perfect for each other, so that shouldn't take long.

So in honor of all the budding lust, I'm dubbing this month Dick-tober. Fingers crossed I get some D, of the LeBlanc variety, in the near future!

XoxoX

Chapter 6

Meghan

"No - trust me, Mrs. Johnson, I know how to handle this. That's right. I have a much better - and safer - form of entertainment lined up. No, no, don't worry. I'll take care of it." Pushing through the front door of BeanBag, I let my eyes roll as I hang up the call.

Instead of sounding a chime, the movement of the door opening sets off a small rain stick filled with coffee beans. The sound is nostalgia wrapped up in the delicious scent of roasting caffeine. And just one more reason why this is the best coffee shop in all of Minnesota.

"Hey, Meghan! Looking fabulous, as always."

"Thanks, Benny. You're looking hip." In his favorite pair of tight overalls, I can't help but tease him a little for being *such* a hipster.

He smirks. "You want the usual?"

I come in here pretty often. Regularly. Okay, basically every day. BeanBag is just a few blocks away from my office. And by "office," I mean my apartment.

Running my own event planning business means I spend a lot of time on phone calls and computer work, but I spend just as much time meeting with caterers, rental companies, and clients. And since I'm the only employee of Meghan's Moments, I get to do things however I please. And it pleases me to be surrounded by coffeehouse smells, secondhand furniture, and local artwork. Plus, being in the middle of downtown Minneapolis means there's always people coming and going. Even if I'm the only person posted up at a table, it's always good people watching. I do my best thinking when I'm people watching.

"Ya know what," I say, approaching the counter, "I'm gonna go with a triple shot Fluffer Nut latte."

"Your wish is my command." Benny performs an elaborate bow. "Long night last night, or coming up tonight?"

"Both," I sigh. "I did this haunted house thing last night and nearly died. Then I kept jolting awake every time I'd finally nod off. Freaking Satan Santa flashbacks." I shiver at the memory. "And the coffee I had earlier is not doing the trick."

Benny nods as he loads up the espresso machine. "Well, if a triple shot doesn't do the trick, you could try one of those giant syringes full of adrenaline straight to the heart."

I grimace. "Hard pass, Benny. Hard fucking pass."

He shrugs as though it was a serious suggestion.

"Anyways..." I continue. "I'm working with this law firm to put together a surprise retirement party for one of the partners. The dude's a huge wrestling fan. Like the TV type of wrestling. You know, *Finish Him!*" I use my deepest voice to yell the last two words.

Benny raises an eyebrow. "Uh, pretty sure that's Mortal Kombat."

"Right."

"No, Meghan, that's a video game."

I look skyward and let out the biggest sigh ever. "Oh my god, Benny. I don't care."

He tosses his hands up. "My bad. Wrestling, classic video games, what's the difference?"

I ignore his sarcasm. "Exactly. So, this old guy likes wrestling, and turns out someone knows someone, and they were able to get The Polar Bear to agree to come to this party."

"No way! For real?" Benny's eyes widen.

"Yes, for real. Do you seriously know who that is? I had to Google him."

It's Benny's turn to roll his eyes. "Of course I know who The Polar Bear is. He's a goddamn legend."

"Okay, sure." I shudder. The videos I found online were not what I'd call appealing. In his heyday, the dude's humongous body was covered in thick body hair that he had to have dyed white. I blink away the image. "Well, some jackass thought that Mr. Johnson, the retiring guy, would love it if The Polar Bear jumped out of a cake and tackled him."

"Sweet!"

"No, *not* sweet! You're just as bad as the rest of those fools!" I hold up one finger. "First, Mr. Johnson is 79 years old... he's like 130 pounds, and he has chronic heart problems."

"Oh."

"Yeah, *oh*." I raise another finger. "Second - you say you know The Polar Bear. Pray tell, how do you suggest I get his gigantic ass into a cake? And come on, no one really does that!" Another finger goes up. "Third. The Polar Bear is no longer in what you'd call *fighting form*. I saw a recent photo, and - let me tell you - there is not a single person attending this party that wants to see that man in his white fur speedo. I sure as fuck don't. I enjoy having the gift of sight. And if I see *even a hint* of his wrinkly dangleberries falling out of their fur

Sleet Banshee

sack, I'll have to pluck out my own eyeballs and set them on fire."

Benny's bent over with his forehead on the counter, shoulders shaking.

I continue - "Thankfully, someone told Mrs. Johnson the plan. How these idiots thought they'd be able to pull this off without telling me, *the event planner*, is a mystery. So, I just got off the phone with a hysterical wife, who's afraid that this hairy man-bear-cake is going to kill her husband."

The rain stick starts singing it's tune, forcing Benny to stand.

He uses an honest-to-god handkerchief to dab away the tears in his eyes. "Seriously, the mental image of *dangleberries* is going to be seared into my brain now."

"You're welcome." I smile.

He hands me my drink, shaking his head.

Benny goes to help the new customer, and I snag a seat at a table in the corner.

As I fire up my laptop, I think about the brunch I had with Izzy today. She told me all about how much she likes Zach, which is obvious to everyone, but then she went on with all the reasons why she can't date him. I get it. I do. I'd agreed with the whole *no hockey players* thing for her, too. She's the coach's daughter, so yeah, don't date the team. But that was before Zach fell into her lap.

She even asked me to help her arrange some dates. She wants to meet someone new to "get Zach out of her head." Like that will ever work. But since setting people up is one of my favorite pastimes, I couldn't say no.

Of course, I agreed knowing full well that I'd be sabotaging these dates by feeding the info to Zach. Now I just need to find the perfect date for Izzy.

Glancing up, I catch sight of Benny talking to a guy that

looks just as young and hipster as he does. I'm pretty sure Benny's in his seventh year of a four year college degree. He's fun, chill, and probably has a ton of friends just like him. Friends that would be totally inappropriate for Izzy.

An idea unfurls in my mind. And, oh boy, this is gonna be fun.

Chapter 7

Meghan

"Please, pretty, *pretty* please, tell me those aren't our dates," Izzy pleads.

Ha. I'd be offended if I'd picked her a date that I thought she'd actually like, but the whole plan is to set her up with some rando she's not interested in. Then Zach can swoop in and work his magic.

Benny might be a goofball, but he pulled through. Watching him and his friend, Zander, stroll haphazardly through the bowling alley, I know this night is going to be hilarious. I'll simply sit back, wait for Zach to show up, then watch the comedy unfold. Poor Zander won't get a second date with Izzy, but he'll get to meet a famous hockey player. So there's that.

"Hey, Meghan!"

I greet Benny with a hug, hips back to minimize touch points. He knows tonight isn't a real date between us, that I just needed someone to do a double date with Izzy. But he's a chill guy, so it shouldn't be a chore to play nice for an evening.

The first few minutes are a little awkward, but - after a

round of drinks - everyone seems to be having a surprisingly good time. And it helps my mood that I'm winning by a long shot. I may have failed to mention that I'm a kickass bowler.

Benny's cute and funny, and being around him feels like I'm hanging with my little brother. He'll never be my boyfriend, but I could definitely see us being friends outside of BeanBag. Maybe I'll help him find a nice little hipster girlfriend, and I can be the godmother to their future flannel-wearing children.

I can see it now: my business, Meghan's Moments, can have a side hustle - Meghan's Matchmaking. I could do dual-sided business cards. My current awesome design on one side, and the flip side can be pink with shiny gold hearts and tiny little stick figures banging each other. *I really need to write this down.*

Shaking myself out of the daydream, I glance around the alley wondering when Zach is gonna get here. We've been bowling for quite a while, and I told him what time we were starting. *Dude better hurry up.*

And that's when I spot him. Only my eyes don't snag on Zach. No, my eyes are glued to a different hockey player. Sebastian.

What the fuck?

And of course, Sebastian looks hotter than ever. His hair's mussed and wavy, and he looks freshly-fucked. He's wearing worn jeans, has a black t-shirt plastered to his body, and a zip-up slung over his shoulder. Like he's too warm to wear it, and too cool to carry it.

And freaking hell, his short sleeves leave his tattooed arms on full display. From the wrist on up, both of his arms are a colorful mess of art. He looks like sin. The good, yummy kind that goes straight to your thighs. I press my lips together, making sure my mouth isn't hanging open. No one should look that good at a bowling alley for shit's sake. It's annoying.

It's not until they start setting up a few lanes down from ours that I even notice Zach.

Izzy's up on the polished wood floor taking her turn, and I know the second she sees them. Her spine goes rigid in surprise.

Walking up to Izzy, I watch as a waitress places her hand on Sebastian's bicep and laughs at something he says. A feeling flashes inside my gut, and my honey badger picks up her baseball bat, smacking it into her palm menacingly.

"What's he doing here?" I say before I can stop myself.

Izzy shrugs. "You're asking me? I have no idea why Zach is here."

"Zach?" I ask.

"Uh, yeah. Who were you talking about?" Izzy looks at me like I've lost it.

Duh, I'm an idiot. I need to get my head back in the game. "Oh, um, yeah. What's Zach doing here?"

"That's what I'm wondering."

"And since when did he become buddy-buddy with Sebastian?" I really can't help myself. I wasn't prepared for him to be here.

"Huh?" Izzy seems confused. "Oh, you mean Ash? I don't know, but he was at the haunted house thing, remember? I think they're friends."

I reply with a super ladylike grunt as I chastise myself for the flood of bitterness that crashes over me at the sight of him. He never did use my number after asking for it last weekend. I mean, I figured he wouldn't, but still. *Come on.* He couldn't spare a single text? He found time to have his hand up my shirt. And he spent several hours flirting with me. It's not like I slipped him my number, he *asked* for it. And he didn't give me his, so it's not like he can claim the old "phone works both ways" bullshit.

Ugh, *whatever*, fuck him. I know I'm not everyone's cup of tea. If he doesn't want me, that's his loss. But I'll be damned if I'm going to sit over here acting like I'm pining over him.

—

Take it from me, it's shockingly hard to pretend to be into *one* guy, while keeping a side-eye out for *another* guy you are super into. This task is made harder by the fact that I'm the only sober person in our little bowling group. Like a dumbass, I agreed to be the DD for the night. Why, in a world of rideshare apps, did I make that offer? With a warm blanket of alcohol, this situation would be more tolerable.

Benny's well on his way to drunk, so he's constantly leaning in closer than necessary and laughing louder than what's called for. It's a little annoying, but his behavior does make it look like we're actually on a date and not just a couple of friends.

I don't know if it's in reaction to us, or if it's just his normal resting bitch face, but Sebastian looks pissed. I can't imagine that Sebastian would ever feel jealous of a guy like Benny, but it's worth a shot.

"Meghan, this was such a great idea!" Benny says as he drops into the seat next to me. "You're up. Please don't get another strike." He puts his palms together in prayer and pouts out his lower lip.

I laugh. "Suck it up, Bennycup. You're going down."

I can hear him crack up as I walk up for my turn. Guy has the mind of a 14-year-old.

I nail another strike.

Smiling, I step off the alley and glance over to find Sebastian watching me. On impulse, I decide to give him something to look at. I toss him a wink before walking over and sitting down on Benny's lap.

"I told you not to strike!" Benny exclaims as he puts his arms around my waist.

I gotta hand it to him. He's good at going with the flow. Playing it perfectly, as though this isn't the first time I've placed my ass on him. Must be the alcohol.

Annnnd fuck. Now I feel like I'm being a sexual predator. The older woman taking advantage of the innocent drunk college kid. I also worry that I'm going to make his legs go numb, since he's about half my size.

"Oh man, he's going for it," Benny whispers while pointing.

Following the motion, I see Zander standing with Izzy up by the lane, giving her bowling tips.

I shake my head and mutter, "Zach is going to eat that little boy alive."

"What was that?" Benny asks.

"Oh, nothing - " I wave it away.

Together, we watch Izzy and Zander fumble through a demonstration about the perfect toss.

In my peripheral vision, I see Zach and Sebastian both stand, facing our way. When Zander gets right up behind Izzy, I'm not surprised to see Zach striding over.

Oh baby, here we go! I have to stop myself from clapping.

Shit. Sebastian is coming with him. Why?! Go back and play with the balls by yourself, you stupid man.

It takes everything I have to pretend that I don't notice them, until Zach walks right in front of me as he goes straight to Izzy. The gig is up. They're here.

"Holy shit, Zachary Hunt came over here!" Benny's voice is full of pure excitement.

I know he saw that the *hockey gods* were here earlier, because he damn-near squealed when he saw them, but he obviously wasn't expecting a personal meet-and-greet.

I follow Zach with my eyes and smile to myself as he waits for the perfect moment to interrupt Izzy and Zander.

"Banshee."

I startle at Sebastian's deep velvet voice right behind me, and slowly turn my head in his direction.

I saw him walk over with Zach, but I didn't think he'd come all the way into our space to talk to me. His radio silence made it clear that I hadn't been on his mind. And that reminder reignites my aggravation.

Ignoring how entirely hot he looks, I treat him like any other guy. "Hey, Scuttle."

He narrows his eyes.

"Oh fuck! You're Ash LeBlanc!"

I roll my eyes at Benny's enthusiasm.

"Oh, right!" I slap my palm to my forehead. "*Sebastian.* I *knew* it was one of the Little Mermaid characters..."

Watching Sebastian's jaw work, I'm not sure if he's biting back a smile or a snarky response.

Benny pats my hip, signaling for me to get up. Sebastian's eyes lock on to the movement, and his gaze becomes murderous. *Interesting.*

Unaware of his own impending death, Benny keeps his hands on my hips as he helps me rise from his lap.

As soon as I'm up right, Sebastian grabs onto my elbow and pulls me a step towards him, and away from Benny. His hand is still gripping me, but Sebastian's attention is focused on Benny. I was a little worried about what Zach might do to Zander, but it appears I should've been more worried on Benny's behalf.

"Hey man, I'm a huge fan." Benny says as he stands.

He holds out a hand. Sebastian waits a beat before finally taking it. Without saying a word, or cracking a smile, he shakes Benny's hand. *Awkward.*

Benny nods to where Sebastian is still holding my arm. "Uh, so I take it, you know Meghan, too?"

At the use of my name, Sebastian's grip tightens.

Oh for the love of cavemen. I yank my arm away, breaking his grasp.

"Sebastian and I go way back." I reach out and pat Sebastian's chest. "Although I'm pretty sure you're breaking the restraining order right now. This has got to be closer than 100 feet." I cock an eyebrow at Sebastian.

"Cute." Sebastian deadpans.

"Umm..." Benny is clearly, and rightfully, confused.

I let the crackling silence ride. I'm curious what'll happen next.

Unfortunately, Zach interrupts our drama. "Ash, the fuck you doing, man?"

We all look over to see Zach, Izzy, and Zander mirroring our uncomfortable threesome. Zach gives a head nod towards Zander, clearly indicating that he wants him gone.

I feel ya Zach. I wish a head nod was all it took to get rid of unwanted men, too.

Sebastian takes the hint and motions Zander to come over. Zander seems too starstruck to care about the fact that these Sleet guys just took over our little double date. Zach's a new rising star on the Sleet, but *Ash* has been a fan favorite for years.

I shouldn't be ticked off right now; I arranged this whole ambush, but I am. I am, because I didn't arrange for Sebastian LeBlanc to show up and charm the pants off everyone in a five mile radius.

After a few uncomfortable minutes, Benny asks if he and Zander could take a photo with the players. Which yours truly has the pleasure of taking. I think about cropping Sebastian out of the picture, but I don't want to disappoint Benny.

Then the law of unintended consequences decides to take over. Apparently, half the people here tonight are hockey fans, and seeing the first group photo unlocks the floodgates. It's a non-stop flow of group photos and signed napkins, and our bowling time is officially over.

Benny and Zander are enjoying the nearness to fame, so here we all sit, ten feet away from the ever-growing fan club. *Shoot me now.*

"Thanks for planning this date. Sorry it got sabotaged," Izzy whispers into my ear. "I appreciate the effort, but I'm going to take Zander aside and tell him that it won't work. I don't want to lead him on, and I don't want him to ask for my number in front of you guys and have to turn him down. That'd be embarrassing for everyone."

"I gotcha. It was a blind date, so no hard feelings. I'm pretty sure the excitement of seeing *real live Sleet players* will help to dull his heartache," I tell her.

"True. Okay, I'll be right back."

I watch as Izzy walks off with Zander. I should feel bad about using him and Benny in my plan. But I was probably correct in assuming that meeting Zach and Sebastian would make their week.

Ugh, Sebastian. I want to look away. I don't want to watch him smile at that pretty blonde. But for the life of me, I can't stop staring.

It's like he put on a whole different personality between now and when he first stepped into our evening. He was all scowls and brooding darkness before, but now he's all grins and laughs and leaning in close for selfies with a pair of co-eds.

What a poser. And a jerk. And I can't believe he called me Banshee tonight. The nerve on this guy. He gives me that nickname. Then he ignores me. Then he uses it again while acting all Alpha. I was afraid his next move was going to be whipping out his dick to pee on me in a show of claiming. Then, ten minutes later, he's back to pretending I don't exist. What an obnoxious twat.

The blonde scampers off, with a lingering look over her shoulder. Sometimes I hate being body- and sex- positive. Because I'd love nothing more than to loathe her for her beauty and call her a whore. But I won't.

When Sebastian starts walking in my direction, I realize he's caught me watching him. And there's no point in pretending otherwise. Benny's sitting next to me, at the table we claimed after closing down our lane, but he's on his phone texting his dad about meeting hockey players. So yeah, I'm just sitting here, silently staring.

Sebastian smirks. *Damnit.*

He turns his attention to my table mate. "Benny, come here for a minute."

I thought Benny was too distracted to hear the world around him, but he pops out of his seat in a flash.

"Yeah, sure!" He sounds like the eager puppy that he is.

Sebastian puts his arm around Benny's shoulders and steers him towards the bar, away from me.

I watch, dumbfounded. The motherfucker just stole my date. Still sitting.

Mouth agape, I wonder what the hell is happening to my life. Right as they reach the pair of open stools at the bar, Sebastian looks back at me, and winks.

Why, that little, giant, sexy, dick of a man.

"Where's Izz?" Zach's voice cuts off my inner tirade.

I turn to face him. "You mean Sugar?"

"Cute. Where is she?"

"Why did you bring Ash with you tonight?" I say *Ash* with maybe too much venom. I don't know what he told Zach about the haunted corn maze, but I feel like calling him Sebastian will sound too familiar.

My question seems to catch him off guard. "Because Ash is my friend. I couldn't very well show up at a bowling alley by myself. Looking like a complete loser isn't the goal."

"Hmmm." I guess that makes sense. But shit, why Sebastian?

"Meg, where's Izzy?" Zach looks around. "And where's Zander?"

"They're not here."

That gets his attention. "What do you mean they're not here?"

"Cool your man-pecs" I sigh. "Izzy asked Zander to walk her to the restrooms."

"Why the fuck would she do that? Isn't it usually you girls that always go to the bathroom in packs?"

"Nice generalization." I roll my eyes. "If I had to guess, I'd say she wanted a moment to talk to him alone."

"Why?"

"Oh my God! Men are such thick-headed morons sometimes!" I've had enough of these idiots for one night. I get up and walk away, looking for a place to sit that's hidden in a corner where no one will bug me. As soon as Izzy's ready, we're getting the fuck outta here.

Chapter 8

Sebastian

So, in hindsight, I could've handled that better. There's just something about Banshee that throws me off my game. I knew she'd be here. She's the only reason I agreed to come tonight. I like Zach and all. We've managed to become good friends in the past couple weeks. But it takes the promise of amazing tits and a fiery attitude to get me into a bowling alley on one of our few free weekend nights.

When we met at the haunted house, Meghan seemed surprised that I knew who she was. But I've been itching to meet her since the infamous Kiss Cam game last year. She was at that game with Jackson's fiancé. They weren't engaged at the time, but Jackson was already smitten. So when he told the team that his woman's friend wanted high-fives from the team as we came down the ramp, I complied. Jackson's a good guy, he's my captain, and he never asks for anything. No harm in giving some girl a slap on the hand. Some girl named Meghan.

When I came down the ramp, she was bent so far over the railing I was worried she'd topple over. I know I should say it was her smile, or her eyes, that first caught my attention. But it wasn't. It was her hair. Her wild, dancing-flames mane of hair. I instantly pictured her in front of me, on her knees, hair wrapped around my grip, mouth wrapped around my cock, and I got a freaking half-chub. On my way onto the ice. For a game. Needless to say, she left quite the impression.

Obviously, I couldn't say *Hey, Jackson, I really want your girl's bestie to give me a blow job. Can I have her number?* Now, I might've been able to say that to *Zach*, but I didn't have to. He walked me right to her.

The media always blows things out of proportion. I'm not a complete man-whore like they say I am, but I'm no monk either. Somewhere in the middle.

I like women. I like sex. I like casual. I don't have some strict code of one-night stands -only, but I don't want to deal with labels, such as *girlfriend*, and all the bullshit that goes along with that. I'm always up front. I'm always honest. And if a girl doesn't believe me when I tell her what I want, or if she starts getting too attached, I end it. It's just who I am. How I'm built. And it works for me.

I wasn't celibate over the past year, but I never forgot about Meghan. So when Zach asked me to come along to his birthday outing, mentioning that Jackson and his fiancé's friends would be there, I said yes. That's also when I found out about Zach's recent history with Izzy. Shocked doesn't even begin to describe my reaction. Izzy's a beautiful girl sure, but Zach's got bigger balls than I do, because I never even considered touching her. But after seeing it for myself, I get it. They're great together. Turns out, Banshee and I are great together too.

Right from the start, I could tell that Meghan was one of a kind. She's feisty and funny and more than a bit of a wildcard. I don't even know how to describe her style; whatever it is, it works for her. I'm so used to jersey chasers who wear as little as possible, which yeah, I don't hate, but it *is* getting a little old.

And Meghan definitely didn't throw herself at me. Just the opposite. Banshee made me try. Hell she made me more than try. She fought me tooth and nail from the moment we first collided. The crazy little nutball even slapped me. Twice. And being the sick fuck that I am, I loved it.

And shit, the feel of her curves in my hands. The way her mouth melted into mine when we kissed. The sounds she made. It was an intoxicating combination. Had she not slapped me the second time, I'm pretty sure I would've tried to fuck her right there in the corn maze. And had I tried, she would've either let me or she'd have slapped me. Honestly, it's a tossup, and that unknown factor turns me on, too. Add it to the list of reasons why I need a therapist.

When I asked for her number, I fully intended to use it. I did. But then I couldn't stop thinking about her. Every day over the past week, I've thought about her. And it kinda freaked me out. Even when I'm sleeping with a girl, I don't think about her this much. So, I second-guessed calling her.

The more I think about it, I'm pretty sure that sleeping with Banshee will help to get my brain back in check. It's my working theory. But honestly, I'm not sure I want the chase to end.

I was still debating about texting her when Zach asked if I wanted to go bowling with him. My first answer was, of course, *fuck no*. Because bowling sucks. But then he told me that Meghan messaged him about the double date and that he needed a buddy to go with him to crash it. Jackson and I are the only players that know about him and Izzy. Maybe Luke Anders, the co-captain, too. But since Zach just moved back to the States, he doesn't really have any other friends. I can pretend I came just to be a good friend, but the truth is he had me at *Meghan*.

I do feel like a bit of a dick for not telling him my intentions, but - if I tell him now - he might tell me to leave Meghan alone, afraid I might fuck things up for him and Izzy. And that's a totally valid worry. But I'm a selfish bastard, and I do what I want.

I am also a dumbass, and didn't put it together that a double date meant that Meghan would have a date, too. And since I didn't think of it, I didn't ask Zach for any background. Is this her boyfriend? Did she have a boyfriend last weekend when I was feeling her up? Is her date some stranger?

But I didn't ask. I spotted them before they spotted me, and I felt the anger roll over my body. Whoever the fuck he was, the sight of him sitting next to Banshee made my blood boil.

I did my best to focus on bowling, waiting for Zach to decide when to strike, but my eyes kept tracking over to their lane. To her beautiful face. To her mouthwatering ass. To her date's stupid little hands getting way too close to her.

Then she winked at me.

It was so unexpected that my brain slowed down, trying to process what it meant. But when she sat on his lap, it all snapped into place. She was fucking with me. She was trying to torment me. For what, I didn't know. Not calling her? Maybe. If I knew what women were thinking, I'd be a much richer man. No matter her motive, her date was looking far too comfortable with the situation.

I got to my feet before I even knew what I was doing. Izzy's date was riling Zach up in much the same way, and he stood at the same time. When Zach started striding over to the girls' lane, I knew I'd be going, too. No way was I going to just sit back and let this shit happen.

It was my pleasure to get within reach and startle Banshee with my greeting. She probably thought I wouldn't come over. She thought wrong.

I'll hand it to her though, she played it pretty cool. I

couldn't pry my eyes away from hers, until the movement of that punk's hands on her hips stole my attention. The wave of possessiveness that rolled over me was so strong, I was gripping her arm and tugging her towards me before I even realized what I was doing.

The red-headed firecracker had me on my toes right from the get-go. Her *Little Mermaid* comment had me biting back a smile. I could tell she was pissed at me though, so I figured I'd match her fight for fight. She didn't disappoint, tossing out that quip about a goddamn restraining order.

I could see that her date actually considered it for a moment. I know what I look like. Women might find me attractive, but I also look like a classic *bad guy*. Muscles and tattoos and scowls. I'll admit to being an asshole, but I'd never do anything to earn a restraining order. Especially not to a woman. I might not want anything serious, but I still treat the females in my life with respect. My mom would smack me upside the head if she ever heard how I talk to Banshee.

She might've been mad at me, but sparring with her had me half hard. I was about to toss her over my shoulder again, hoping we could continue the tongue lashing elsewhere and with far less clothing, but then Zach called out and cock-blocked my whole plan.

It only took a couple minutes with Hipsters One and Two to recognize the opportunity. If I could keep them talking, specifically Benny, then Meghan no longer had a date. And without a date, she'd have no one to rub against, driving me crazy.

Once the idea hit, I switched on my *Public Ash* persona, laying on the charm. Zach's seen the switch before, and he told me it was - and I quote - *creepy as fuck*. Whatever, I play hockey for the sport, not to be a public figure.

Basically, my usual attitude isn't quite appropriate for

public appearances. I can accept this as true. Like I said, I'm an asshole. And I love being a goalie - it's what I was made to do, but - with the highs come the lows. The stress of every loss weighs heavily on my shoulders. Yeah, it's a team sport and my teammates never rag on me for missing a save. But none of that is a comfort after a lost game. The worst parts of my personality take over and I become a surly piece of shit. It's unhealthy and I'm working on it. Or, I *will* work on it. Some day.

Luckily for everyone, the Sleet PR team is extremely talented. And they've spent many hours coaching me on how to imitate a pleasant person. So, I pulled those skills out and put them to use. The look of jealousy that covered Banshee's face as she watched a couple of chicks openly flirt with me bolstered my game plan.

I was impressed that she didn't pretend to look away when I caught her staring, and I started to wonder which one of us is more stubborn. That thought prompted me to steal her date for a drink at the bar. The fact that Benny leapt out of his seat to join me pissed me off. Pissed me off on Meghan's behalf. He was supposed to be there with her. Yeah, I'm famous and blah blah whatever, but he came here to be with her. So it might have started as sabotage, but I figured I was doing Banshee a favor by removing him from the equation.

What I didn't count on was actually liking Benny. He turned out to be a super funny kid. And it didn't take long to get him talking about Meghan. He told me how she's a regular at his work. That they're friends. That he knows he has zero chance with her. That this whole date was just a way to get his friend to go out with her friend.

The relief I felt at his words was a bit unnerving. I didn't realize how tense I was about the idea of her having a boyfriend. I shouldn't care. It's none of my business. I mean, I wouldn't've felt great about what we did in the corn maze if she'd been in a relationship, but if she did have a boyfriend it'd be a good reason to walk away.

But I can't walk away. Walking away from something I want isn't my style. Grabbing on with two hands is.

When I decided to drop the games and go talk to her, all I caught was a glimpse of her bright red hair as she jogged out the exit. She's nothing if not unpredictable.

So now, here I lie, alone in my bed, staring at an open text box on my phone. My reaction to Banshee tonight should be a red flag, scare me away, make me delete her number. It should. But - like I said - I'm a selfish bastard. And I won't feel settled until I feel every inch of that wild woman surrounding every inch of me.

Fuck it.

I type out a text and hit send before I second-guess myself.

Me: Goodnight, my feisty little Banshee.

I wasn't sure if she'd reply, but she responded immediately.

Meghan: I'm sorry, this number does not accept text messages from giant douche holes. #unsubscribe

I laugh out loud into the darkness of my room. I should've known she'd come back with something full of sass.

I kinda love it.

Chapter 9

Meghan

Dear Diary,
    Men are so dumb. So, so dumb.
    XoxoX

Chapter 10

Meghan

Last night I was able to keep my mind busy with the retirement party for Mr. Johnson. (Thankfully no one died of a heart attack or self-inflicted eyeball wounds.) But today's a different story.

Last week I landed my biggest job ever: The International Calligraphers Convention. I'm not sure why, but they changed cities at the last minute, and they'll be here in just three months... which means I have a ton of work to do. But I've organized my tasks from now until the night of the event, and somehow I'm already caught up.

Being on schedule is usually good, but I need to keep my mind off of *Fucking Sebastian*. He was a dick to me at the bowling alley, then he sends some stupid goodnight text, then he doesn't reply to my response. For two days! *Who does that?*

Guys always complain about girls giving mixed messages, but Sebastian takes the damn cake. I mean, yes, I was technically out with another guy when he saw me. But he could've tried to charm me. Show me what I was missing. Instead he acted like my date was a personal attack against him. I didn't even think he'd be there!

Hold up...

I didn't think Sebastian would be there, but he had to have known I'd be there. There's no way that Zach didn't lay out the plan for him. *No freaking way.* Sebastian doesn't strike me as the type to go bowling for the hell of it. But... does that mean he came out just to see me?

Ugh, wow, way to be egotistical Meghan. He was probably just being a good friend to Zach. Probably. Maybe? Hmmm...

Well now I don't know what to think. If he was coming because of me, then yeah, I can maybe get why he'd be mad I had a date. But I told Zach that we were going on a double date.

"Uuuggghh!" I groan and tug on my hair.

Why is this so complicated? I'm tempted to ask Zach if Sebastian's said anything about me, but that sounds so *middle school*.

My ringtone chimes and I scoop up my phone, glad for the distraction.

"Hey, Izzy."

"Hey! How's it going?"

I sigh. "Oh, fine. Just pretending to do work. You?"

"All good here. Just wanted to let you know that I have the tickets for tonight. Katelyn and Steph are coming too." I can hear the smile in Izzy's voice. "I'll text you your ticket in just a moment."

"Awesome, thanks!"

"Oh for sure! I think everyone's just planning to meet there. I have a meeting at the end of the day, so I'll stay downtown."

"Works for me. I just want to get there early enough to grab one of those giant pretzels before the game starts."

"Mmmm, yes. Great plan," Izzy agrees. "Okay, I'll see you tonight!"

"See you."

True to her word, Izzy sends my ticket a moment later. This isn't my first time attending a Sleet game, but for some reason I feel nervous. Stupid Sebastian, I know it's his fault. And it's not like this is even the first time I've seen him play. This might be their first game this year, but I'm pretty sure he was in goal for every Sleet game I went to last year.

Being from a true Minnesotan family, I grew up surrounded by hockey. All three of my brothers played through high school. They were alright. And since our parents were big on family bonding, I got dragged around to all their games. I even played one year myself. I was in sixth grade, and I hated it. None of my friends were on the team, and when I found out that the girls would never be allowed to check I wanted to quit right then and there. My parents made me play out the season, but that was the last time they forced me into organized sports.

Glancing at the clock, I see it's already mid afternoon. Fuck it, I'm not going to get any more work done today. I'll go take a long shower, shave every inch of my body, and tame my hair into nice smooth curls. I don't actually think I'll be getting any action tonight, but feeling sexy will help put me in a better mood.

Chapter 11

Meghan

TONIGHT'S GAME nearly gave me a heart attack. It was bad luck that our home opener was against Utah, the reigning Cup champions.

The normal stress of watching my team lose was compounded by Sebastian being in front of the goal through it all. He's not to blame. Hockey's a team sport.

My younger brother played goalie, and I heard my parents repeat that line to him every time his team lost. They're right. When the Defense is strong, the puck doesn't get a chance to make it near the goalie. Of course that's in a perfect world. Tonight was not a perfect world. Tonight was a combination of our team messing up, the refs making bad calls, and the other team performing well. It's not Sebastian's fault, but the hang of his head as he skated off the ice said it all.

The only part worse than watching his reaction after missing a save was seeing him punch that guy.

I don't think I've ever seen a goalie get involved in a fight before. But Sebastian most definitely did. The player he hit was a prick who'd taken a cheap shot after the puck was already in

Sleet Banshee

Sebastian's control. Zach saw the asshole move and was the first to go in, fists flying. But that's *his* thing. It's not Sebastian's thing. Not at all. When I saw him push into the fight, my honey badger wrapped her claws around my throat and started squeezing in terror. I wanted to scream, but I couldn't get my vocal cords to work.

I don't know how Izzy deals with watching her man throw down all the time. I'm a fucking hot mess over that fight and no one even swung at Sebastian. I want to thank Zach for being such a good Enforcer, but I think that'd probably embarrass all parties involved. Maybe I'll just bake him a cake. Or tell Izzy to give him a blowjob.

I take a deep breath, in an effort to chill out. This is not Sebastian's rookie season. He's a professional. This isn't the first game he's lost, and it won't be the last.

It doesn't help. No matter how many times I tell myself that he's fine, I can't shake the image of him skating off the ice looking defeated. I need to see him. I need to make sure he's okay.

And that's how I ended up here, in the guts of the arena, outside the locker room.

Izzy's going out with her dad, Steph's left with her mom, but Katelyn said she'd be coming down here to meet up with Jackson after the game. When she mentioned it, I asked if I could join her. It was an impulse, but once the words were out I couldn't take them back. Katelyn didn't ask me why. She probably assumed I wanted to get a look at some of the players up close and personal. And really - that's not a bad idea, because these boys are *built*.

"Be right back." Katelyn taps my arm.

I spot Jackson walking out into the hall, talking with his friend Luke. Izzy already wandered away looking for her dad.

"Take your time," I say, still leaning against the wall. "Actually, don't worry about me. I'll just hang for a few more minutes, then I'll find my way out."

"You sure?" Katelyn asks.

"Yeah, yeah -" I wave her off. "Go attack your man."

"Okay, bye!" She grins and gives me a quick hug.

I roll my eyes as she races off towards Jackson. Those two are the real deal. They both knew it from the initial meet. Sure, they had a few bumps in the road, but - once they declared their love for each other - they've only gotten closer. They're like a fine wine: better with time.

Me? I'm like an *open* bottle of wine. I get bitter and turn to vinegar when left untouched.

Thankfully, there are lots of other people down here for me to blend in with. Some of them work here, but the rest look like family members of the players.

I'm dressed casually, and I fit in fine with the crowd. I'm sporting tight jeans, knee-high black boots, a *Wilder* Sleet jersey that Katelyn gave me last year, and my blue feather earrings. The time I spent on my hair earlier paid off; for once, my locks are in perfect Disney Princess curls. I remind myself that I look good, hoping to bolster my confidence against the nerves churning in my belly.

Try as I might, the nerves are winning. This was a mistake. Sebastian won't want to see me. I should leave.

Just as I push off the wall to make my exit, Sebastian walks out of the locker room. He's wearing black pants and a white button up, with the sleeves rolled to his elbows. His hair is still damp from his shower, and he looks sexier than I've ever seen him before.

I really shouldn't be here.

Before I can sneak off, Sebastian looks up and locks eyes with me.

We stare at each other for a few seconds before he tears his gaze away to glance around the hallway. Presumably wondering who I came down here with.

Looking back at me, he takes a few steps closer.

"Uh, hi -" I kinda croak out the words.

Yeesh. I really should've planned what I was going to say. I'm usually so confident, even when I shouldn't be. But this just feels so awkward. I knew I should've left.

"Hey." Sebastian stops, close enough for me to touch.

"Hey." My smile probably looks more like a grimace.

I'm about ready to sprint down the hall away from him. This is embarrassing.

"What are you doing down here?" His brows draw together in confusion.

I hear ya, man. What the hell am I doing down here?

"Um, well. . . Katelyn was coming down to meet up with Jackson and I've never been, so I wanted to check it out." I shrug." She took off the second her big slice of man appeared. So, umm... " I cut off my rambling. I waited down here for him. I should just say what I came to say.

I grab a hold of his sleeve and pull him a little further down the hall, away from the other lingering people. I figure the sleeve is less personal than grabbing his hand. Skin to skin contact might fry what's left of my brain.

Sebastian's deep chuckle Plinkos through my body. "Banshee, if you're trying to sneak me into an empty closet to have your wicked way with me, you're going the wrong direction."

I turn back to face him. "I'm not even going to ask how you know that."

A smirk is all the answer I get. *Gross.*

"Well, if you're not here to ravage me, then what *are* you doing here?"

My cheeks puff out with my exhale. "Right. Okay. So, I just wanted to come down here to... see you. See if you're okay?"

His smirk is replaced with a mask of indifference as I speak those last four words.

"See if I'm *okay?*" he repeats back to me, slowly.

"Yeah. I just know how tough losses can be. Especially as a goalie."

I didn't realize I was still holding onto his sleeve, until his other hand comes up and pulls on my wrist, causing me to release my grip.

"Oh, you know how tough it is?" The ugliness dripping off his tone prickles at my skin.

Mayday! Mayday!

Mortification starts to creep over me, and I grip my hands together in front of my stomach. "Umm, one of my brothers was a goalie, my other brothers played too, but I'd always hear my parents talking to them after a loss. They'd remind him that it's a team sport, ya know. It's not all on one player to win or lose. But still my little brother would always take each goal personally. And that's just not right. And then watching you tonight, I was worried..." I cut off my next thought as Sebastian takes a step forward, nearly closing the distance between us.

But the vibe is not sexy. It's hostile.

"That's all very touching, *Meghan.*" The emphasis he uses on my name makes it sound like an insult. "I'm sure your little brother tried very hard. And I'm sure his high school put the same pressure on him as I have on me. But how I feel, or don't feel, is none of your goddamn business. And pity from some puck bunny is the last fucking thing I need tonight."

I'm stunned. Completely and utterly stunned.

I knew I shouldn't have said anything, but I never expected him to respond with this level of cruelty. I know I was stumbling through my explanation, but I meant well. I was just trying to help.

I take a small step back. As a toxic combination of humiliation and hurt flares in my cheeks.

Worst of all, I feel my lip start to tremble. I bite down on it to keep it steady.

This was dumb. I was dumb to come here. I don't actually know him. What am I doing?

I take another step back.

I can see the moment when Sebastian realizes the effect his words have had on me. The look on his face twists. Anger is still there, but now it's mixed with something else. Something I can't read.

Everything about this was a mistake. I need to get out of here.

Swallowing hard, I force the lump down my throat. "Okay." It comes out as a whisper, but I know he heard it.

I don't give him any time to respond, or to insult me further. I only know the one way to get out of here and that's back the way I came.

As I move to step around Sebastian, I see him reach out towards me.

No. Fuck him. Fuck this.

I cross my arms tightly over my chest, away from his outstretched fingers, and rush past.

I keep my eyes on the floor as I pass through the remaining people in the hallway. I'm glad that Katelyn is gone, because I'm sure she could read my face like a book. I want to scream. I want to hit something. I want to crawl into hole and cry.

Chapter 12

Meghan

DEAR DIARY,
 I need to find a new sport to watch. Hockey is the absolute worst. It's full of asshole shitbags. They think they're the hottest thing since snack-size Nutella. Well, they aren't. They're the Nature Valley Granola Bars of snacks.
 Fine. Fiiiine. That's not entirely true. Jackson and Zach are great. They're handsome and sweet and obsessed with their women. But my player? Mine is a scrub. He's rude. A total dick. And he only cares about himself.
 I can't believe what he said to me tonight.
 Can. Not. Believe.
 I was honestly worried about him. I hate when someone witnesses me failing, and he had a whole arena watching him. I looked it up; that's nearly 20,000 people. And that doesn't even count the people watching on tv or the bums who just watch the highlights online after a game.
 I've always liked hockey. I've never been a superfan of the Sleet, but my family is pretty die-hard, and I pay attention.
 Fucking Sebastian. He ruins everything.

No, fuck that, he's *Ash* now. Since I'm just like everyone else to him, I'll call him what everyone else does. Ash the... dash. Ha. I bet he cums in under two minutes. He probably has no idea where the clit is. Every puck bunny he's banged has probably faked it. I bet he calls out his own name when he blows his load.

Daaaammnit! I need to get laid. It's been way too long. Next weekend I'm logging back in to every dating app I have. And if anyone even looks like Ash then I'm swiping them straight into the garbage.

XoxoX

P.S. Why the hell did I react that way to him? I have thicker skin than that. People have said worse to me. What the hell is wrong with me?! Just more proof that I need to avoid Ash the Dash LeBlanc.

Chapter 13

Sebastian

"I know, Ma" it takes all I have not to groan into the phone. If I show any sign of distress, Mom will get in her car and head over. No matter that it's nearly midnight. "I'm fine."

"Promise me, Sebastian." She's using her stern voice now.

"I promise, Ma" I say while rolling my eyes.

"Now say it again, without rolling your eyes."

"What the hell?"

"Language!" Mom says like she's shocked at the curse. All her kids swear like sailors, but she still acts surprised each and every time.

"Sorry. I promise that I'm okay. I'm not upset. I won't cry myself to sleep tonight. If I do, I'll dry my tears on my spun-gold sheets."

"No one likes a braggart," she chastises me.

"I'm fine. I promise."

"Okay, son. I love you. Now get some sleep."

"Love you, too, Ma. Goodnight."

Hanging up, I drop my phone onto my nightstand and scrub my palms over my eyes.

I wasn't lying. I *am* fine. I just always need a little time to get out of my own head after a loss like tonight. I know all the usual pep talks. My parents have been giving them to me for decades. The problem is, it doesn't matter how much logic and reason you throw at a problem like this, none of it helps. So-and-so could've blocked. So-and-so could've scored. But - ultimately - *I* was the one who let the puck into my net. I failed at the one job I have. I don't like failing. I like perfection. I just need time. And my mom knows that.

I just wish Meghan had known that, too.

As soon as the words were out of my mouth, I knew I'd fucked up. Banshee isn't a puck bunny. She's not even fucking close. She's a feisty little goddess. Every interaction I've had with her has been full of spunk and fire. Except for tonight.

Even before I went off on her, I could tell there was something different. I couldn't place it until afterwards, but she was nervous. She was nervous because she wasn't sure how I'd react to her concern. I already felt like the biggest piece of shit when I saw how my words hit her. The downcast eyes, the tremor in her lip, the whispered response. I don't think I've ever been more disgusted with myself than I was at that moment. Never, until a moment later when I put it all together and realized she was uncomfortable before she even spoke. And what did I do? I played straight into those fears. I became the bully. The bad guy. That's not a title I ever want, especially not with my Banshee.

So, yeah, I told my mom the truth. I'll be fine about the loss. It's the way I treated Megs that has me wanting to peel my skin from my body.

I've upset women before. Not from being deliberately mean, but from ending relationships, and things like that. I've even made women cry before. It's not something I enjoy. I always feel bad. I try to set the right expectations on the front end, but sometimes it doesn't work out. But tonight... It doesn't make sense. We aren't anything to each other. We aren't even casually hooking up. I shouldn't care what she thinks or how she feels.

Maybe that's it though. Banshee didn't hunt me down for a quickie. She wasn't looking for me to invite her back to my place. She wasn't looking for anything. She was just concerned. About me.

Fuck. I don't know what we are, but I know I messed it up.

Chapter 14

Meghan

A PATHETIC SOUND leaves me as I toss my purse into the cart. How do I have 78 items on my grocery list?

I do a grocery shopping trip every week, which means I cleared the list 7 days ago. Scrolling through the items listed on my phone, I see the problem. I have peanut butter on here six times. Avocados - four times. Three types of coffee. I really have lost my mind recently.

Rolling my eyes, I mutter to myself - "You stupid bitch."

A gasp startles me, and I spin to see a 70-ish year old woman selecting a cart from the row next to me.

"Oh, not you," I say, using my thumbs to gesture to myself. "Me. I'm the bitch."

She huffs again and jerkily swings her cart around, heading into the store.

"Okay, correction," I grumble, "maybe you *are* the bitch. You old hag."

Admittedly, I've been in a bit of a mood. I hate that I'm in this funk, and I know the source of the problem, but I'm not going to think about *him*. It's embarrassing that I'm still so cranky when that stupid hockey game was nearly a week ago.

No. Nope. Not going there. This is my Casual Friday. I'm caught up on work so I'm going to spend my day baking and feeding my soul. Plus, tonight is going to be amazing because one of my friends is throwing a sex toy party. I've invited the usual suspects, but I've also invited Zach. He thinks that Izzy is going on another date and I am literally giddy about seeing the look on his face when he walks into the room to find zero dates and dozens of dildos. It's going to be epic.

Wandering my way through the produce section, I occupy my mind by feeling and squeezing every fruit and vegetable I can get my hands on. This grocery store is my happy place, and I can already feel the tension leaving my shoulders.

The store is huge, glorious, a touch expensive, and I'm mentally prepared to be here for a while. It's not my neighborhood store, but it's worth the drive. And the deposit check from the Calligraphy Convention cleared, so it's time to treat myself.

I'm sniffing the bottom of a pineapple when I feel a presence stop behind me. I'm not blocking the whole display. They can move around me, or they can wait.

I pick up another pineapple to sniff.

"What on earth are you doing?" the voice behind me says.

That voice. That sexy, masculine, piss-me-off voice.

"Keep walking, Dickhole," I say as I pick up another pineapple. The last one was perfect, but I'm not turning around now.

At the sound of a familiar gasp, I glance over.

Oh great, the old hag is back.

"Look, ma'am, I already told you - you're not the bitch. You're not the dickhole either. But don't push it."

I hear a choke of laughter turn fake cough behind me.

"Well..." she sputters. "I have never..."

"I'm sure you haven't," I say. "This guy here is with the complaint department," I toss a thumb over my shoulder. "Please take it up with him."

I drop the good pineapple in my cart and strut away.

Chapter 15

Meghan

I CAN NOT BELIEVE the nerve of this guy. Who the fuck does he think he is? He was a complete piece of shit to me the last time I saw him. Then today he just walks right up to me. Does he seriously think I'll talk to him?

Argh! I want to scream! But that'd probably get me escorted out of the building, and I really need to refill my cupboards.

Hopefully that nosy old bitch will keep him busy with complaints. Then he can scamper over to the cooler section, find some bags of blood (which I'm sure he drinks for dinner), and get the hell out of here.

Might as well get back to my list. No way he'll track me down after that outburst.

Pulling my cart to a stop, I look around and see I'm in the condiment aisle. Perfect. I need to replenish my mustards. An uncultured child might think that one type is enough, but they'd be wrong. Yellow is great for your classic all-American dishes. Honey mustard is perfect for turning a panini into something fancy. And spicy brown is wonderful in vinaigrettes.

With that thought, and a small pile of mustards in my cart, my hand trails down the shelf until I find the large array of vinegars. Some people are purists, but I'm all about flavor. I have several at home already, but hmmm... This cinnamon pear aged vinegar has my gears turning and my mouth starts watering just thinking about the possibilities. Placing it next to my mustards, I start to think that one new bottle isn't enough. I should get a second.

When I think, I have a habit of wiggling my toes. Wiggling my toes now, my gaze moves to my feet. My feet, clad in sandals, despite the nearly freezing, nearly November weather. This was meant to be my low-key self-love day, so I dressed accordingly. A wash of dread starts at my bare toes and rolls up my legs. The Greek idiot ex god just saw me. *Like this.* My footwear is made of worn, brown leather and is what my friends refer to as my *Jesus sandals.* They expose my toes, each painted a different fall color. And it only gets worse as you go up. I'm wearing a pair of very snug, and very comfortable black leggings. Those aren't too bad. My sweater is a bit much, though. It's an oversized cardigan, and it's tie-dyed. By me, I might add. It's a flurry of green and purple with the original shade of tan peeking through. It's glorious, and completely *yikes.* But the shirt under the cardigan is the real cringer. It's a white wife beater with "I like big Bundts" screen printed across the chest. Complete with an image of a Bundt cake. After that, who cares about my mass of red curls tossed into an extra messy, messy bun. I look like I walked away from a 21st century Woodstock, and the purple feather earrings just confirm it.

Movement at the end of the aisle catches my attention. Bracing myself for the worst, I turn and see the bane of my existence. And he's heading towards me.

Quickly, I decide I'm done with the condiments. If he

needs to buy something from here, he can buy it without company.

Refusing to make eye contact, I spin my cart around like a contestant on a reality shopping show and escape.

In the brief glance I took, I saw he was just carrying a basket, so he can't be here for much. He better fill 'er up fast because I don't want to spend my whole time here fleeing him.

Deciding distance will make me safer, I dart past several aisles before randomly selecting one. Pulling to a stop halfway down, I take out my phone to consult my list. Checking off my mustards and pineapple, I still have a long way to go.

Okay, deep breath. I will not let Assface ruin my self-love shopping vibe. I close my eyes and force myself to take several deep breaths. Aware that I'm in public, I chant silently, moving my lips but not making a sound.

I do not care what that man thinks of me. I do not care if I'm dressed like a total goober. I do not care if said man is hot-as-fuck. I do not care if his voice sets my libido off like a match soaked in gasoline. I do not care. I do not care. I do not care.

With a final exhale, I open my eyes. And shriek.

My hands fly up to cover my mouth, attempting to trap in the sound.

I'm face-to-face with Ash-hole. And he's grinning.

"Hey, Banshee. What just happened there?" He gestures at me, as if I wasn't sure what he was referring to. "Was that a meditation, or some sort of seizure?"

"It was none of your damn business!" I fume. "You'd probably be thrilled if I keeled over, so what do you care."

I grab hold of my cart so I can push past him, but he stomps his foot down, blocking the front wheel.

I turn my stormy glare on him, a little surprised to see that his grin is gone.

"What?" My hostility is clear in the word.

He sighs. "I'm sorry."

I roll my eyes.

"I am - " he takes one step towards me. "I shouldn't have said those things to you."

Knowing that he's referring to our last encounter, my emotions rise back up as if it just happened. But I won't let him get the best of me this time. *I don't care what a man thinks of me.*

I do my best to sound calm. "You're right, Ash. You shouldn't have said those things, but you did."

His eyes narrow. "You've never called me Ash before."

"Yeah, well, I figured if all the other slut bunnies call you that, I should too."

He breaks eye contact, and I use the opportunity to push past him.

"Meghan!" he calls after me.

I don't stop.

"Please - " his voice comes out quieter.

Damnit!

I stop.

I keep my back to him but listen to his footsteps. I hold a deep inhale, releasing the breath when he stops next to me. I want to keep staring forward, but I've always tried to face my fears straight on. And for some reason, part of me is afraid of this confrontation. I can't imagine he's following me around just to be mean to me again, but the mind isn't always rational.

Slowly, I turn to him. Mustering all my inner courage, I put my hands on my hips and wipe the nervous expression from my face.

Making eye contact this close, his dark eyes show more emotion than I think he realizes. I can read his worry and hesitation, and it makes me feel a little more at ease. He *should* apologize to me, but I definitely wasn't expecting him to. And I don't know if I should believe whatever's about to come out of his mouth.

As we stand here, watching each other, a bit of his unruly black hair falls across his face. And I have the absurd urge to reach out and brush it away.

"I just... I need to explain." He runs a hand over his always-there shadow of a beard. I can hear the scratch of it against his palm. "You were right."

My eyebrows shoot up. Well, that's a good start.

He continues, "I was upset. I don't do well when we lose. It pisses me off and puts me in a shit mood. Everyone knows it, so everyone leaves me alone after a game like that. They know that I need time to cool off. Otherwise I'm a total asshole."

I make a humming sound in agreement, and he gives me a half smile, half cringe.

"I'm not sure why you were down there, but I wasn't expecting it. I know you were trying to be nice." He looks away from me. "Honestly, when I saw you, I thought maybe you were there to try to hook up. Then you started talking about losing the game, and your brothers, and I just didn't know what to think. I didn't want to talk about it, and the fucked up part of my brain figured that being a jerk would be the quickest way to end the conversation."

"If that was your goal, it worked," I reply bluntly.

With his eyes back on me, he gives me a slight nod.

I keep my hands on my hips. "I'm not some jersey chaser. Just because my friends have found hockey players to be with, doesn't mean I have some delusion that I'll find my happily-ever-after on the team. I'm not after you because you're an athlete." Realizing how that sounds, I add, "I'm not after you at all."

"I know. I do. And as fucking dumb as it sounds, I think that's why I called you... *that*. It was the most ridiculous thing I could think of." He runs a hand through his hair, serving only to mess it up even more. "I'm an idiot."

"Yes, you are." I agree.

"Do you forgive me?"

When I don't answer, he squats down, putting us eye level with each other. His expression is so earnest that I find myself wanting to believe him. I know how much of a mindfuck losing can be, and I can only imagine how much worse it is to deal with when you're at his level. But I don't want to just be another one of those bimbos who lets a man push her around just because he has a hot face and a heavy bank account.

At my continued silence, Sebastian raises his eyebrows, looking hopeful.

"I'm thinking," I say. "You really were a prick. A giant asshat."

He nods. "Don't forget dickhole."

I fight against the urge to smile. "How could I forget?"

"That old lady sure won't. She had quite a bit to say about you."

"Seems to be going around," I reply.

He winces. Then, to my surprise, he drops to his knees. Clasping his hands together in front of him, he literally begs me for forgiveness. "Please, Meghan. Megs. Banshee. My Fire Goddess of Wisdom and Kindness. *Please* forgive me. I'm so sorry for the things I said. I'm a major dickhole and I'll owe you a life debt if only you'll accept my apology."

"Oh my god! Get up, lunatic!" I motion with my hands for him to rise.

"Not 'til you forgive me. I take it all back. You're no bunny. Never were. Never could be. You're a Banshee."

"Fine. Fine! You're forgiven."

As soon as the words are out of my mouth, he knee-walks forward and wraps his arms around me. He's so tall that even kneeling, his face is level with my chest. With his cheek pressed against my boobs, his arms tighten around my waist, pulling me in for a hug.

I can't help the laugh that bubbles out. This man is not what I expected.

My honey badger is standing on two legs clapping her paws. The dirty bitch likes this show of submission.

Tugging at his shirt I whisper-shout at him, "Get up!" His response is too mumbled for me to understand. "Get your face out of my tits. I can't hear you." I grab a handful of hair and tug until his head is tilted back. The smile on his face is entirely wicked.

"I like having my face in your tits." I use my free hand to flick his forehead. He just laughs. "Plus, I'm not getting up until you agree to call me Sebastian again."

"What?"

"You heard me. You can call me Ash when you want to, but not out of spite. I just can't have that," he frowns.

"Okay, *Sebastian* - " I hiss out his name. "You're forgiven. I'll call you whatever you want. Just get the fuck up!"

Pulling against the grip I still have on his hair, he tilts his head back down so he's looking right at my chest. "What can I say, I've been dying to bury my face in your Bundt."

An extra-loud gasp stops me from reaching out and slapping Sebastian. We both turn our heads to see that the old hag is back and glaring at us. Before I can say anything, Sebastian turns back and starts to nuzzle his face into my cleavage. The old woman is saying something as she storms away, but I can't hear her over my own laughter.

"Seriously, get up you maniac!" I choke out. "If you get me kicked out, I'm going to take back my forgiveness. I need to buy food!"

Releasing his grip on me, Sebastian rises to his full height, looking smug and sexy. I refuse to acknowledge how wildly my body reacted to his attention. I've tried to forget our make-out session in the corn maze, but my body didn't forget. It didn't forget at all.

"Okay. Let's go shopping," he says, putting his basket on the bottom rack of my cart.

"Umm, what?" I ask.

"Shop-ping..." he drags the word out.

"I'm familiar with the term, thanks. But what do you mean *let's*? We aren't grocery shopping together."

"Why not?" Sebastian asks, like I'm the crazy one.

"Well..." I don't actually have a good reason. "I have a lot, like *a lot* a lot, on my list. It's going to take me a while."

"I got time," he shrugs.

I toss my hands up. "Alright, weirdo, let's shop together."

Grabbing my cart, I look through the grate at his basket and see that it's empty. "Where's your list?" I ask.

"Huh?"

"Do you have a list of what you need?"

"Uh, no. I'm just here to get lunch. I've never been to this location before, but I figured it'd have a good deli, like the other ones I've been to."

"Hmm." Guess that explains why I've never seen him in here before. "Why are you here if this isn't your usual store?"

"I had a sleepover in the neighborhood."

And just like that, my heart drops. This guy really is a player. He spent last night in bed with some woman, and the next morning he's on his knees in a grocery store motorboating my tits.

"*Ah*," is all I can manage. We're not dating. We're nothing. I have no right to feel upset.

I take my phone out, and once again check what I need.

"Did you need anything from this aisle?" Sebastian asks.

I finally take note of where we are standing, and I have to stop myself from doing a literal face-palm. We are in a sea of adult diapers, pads, organic tampons, a large selection of vegan lube, and of course, pregnancy tests.

"No." I go back to pushing the cart.

"Are you sure?" Sebastian easily keeps stride with me. "I did find you, talking to yourself, before you had a chance to grab anything."

I glance up and see that he's smirking down at me.

"I was trying to get away from you. And talking myself down from my plan to murder you via an eggplant shoved down your throat. It seemed like a good idea."

Sebastian laughs. He's smart enough not to comment on the fact that I'm leading us back to the produce section. I wasn't done when I rushed away from him earlier.

Opening a bag of red grapes, I gently squeeze a few.

"What are you checking for?" He opens his own bag.

"Just to see how firm they are. I like the crunchy ones. Squishy grapes creep me out."

"Huh." He watches as I go through and select the perfect bag. When I pick one, he reaches over and plucks one of the grapes off the bunch and pops it in his mouth. I watch him chew. His jaw flexing, his throat working with a swallow. It's disturbingly attractive.

We wander through the stands silently for a few minutes. I can feel Sebastian's eyes on me as I sniff through a pile of peaches, selecting the ones that are just a day or two shy of perfectly ripe.

I'm digging through a pile of garlic bulbs when Ash startles me by saying, "My brother."

"What?" I turn to look at him.

"My brother, Curtis, lives over here. I stayed at his house last night."

"Oh. Okay." I try to keep the relief off my face. "I didn't ask."

"Uh huh, you were *not asking*... very loudly."

I make a noncommittal sound. "You guys must be close."

"Yeah, I guess," Sebastian says as I move on to the bananas. "He has the cutest little twins. They're... I dunno, like eight months old now. Curtis's wife left last night for a much-deserved girls' retreat, and he was freaking out a little about being home alone with little Anna and Raymond. But - of course - he couldn't tell the Mrs. that he was losing his shit, so I offered to stay the night."

"That was awfully nice of you." My honey badger is swooning against my ribs and her eyes are little cartoon hearts, imaging Sebastian with an armful of babies.

"Nah, not that nice. I pawned him off on my parents for the rest of the weekend. It was nice hanging with my brother for a night, but I'm not looking for a whole weekend of parental duty. Plus, I have today off, but it's back to the grind tomorrow."

"That's right. You guys have a home game."

"Sure do. You comin'?"

"No. I have a birthday party. Or, well, a foundation's birthday party."

"Am I supposed to know what that means?"

I chuckle. "It's for work. I'm an event planner, so I have to be there to make sure all the details run smoothly."

"Event planner." He gives me a slow once over. "I can see it."

"Oh shut up," I smack his chest. "I can be professional. This is my weekend no-one-I-know-is-meant-to-see-me look."

Sebastian smiles. "I like it."

"Yeah, I'm sure." I roll my eyes.

"What? I do - it's fun. Just like you."

I'm glad he's walking behind me as I finally lead us away

from the produce. I'm pretty sure my cheeks are pink, and my smile could be described as dopey.

I snag some bacon on the way to the baking section because every home needs a proper bacon stash.

Pausing in front of the flour, I take a deep breath. This is my mecca. I start piling items in my cart. I'm low on just about everything, and I need to make more of my coffee cakes.

"Don't you have a co-worker you could switch shifts with?"

With a bag of pecans in each hand, I face Sebastian.

"Switch shifts?"

"For tomorrow. So you could come to the game." If I didn't know better, I'd say he's being a little bashful.

"Oh, right -" I smile proudly. "It's just me, there are no co-workers. I run my own business."

"No shit? That's cool. Color me impressed." His words seem genuine.

"Yeah, I'm pretty fucking impressive," I laugh, tossing the nuts in the cart.

"How long have you had your company?"

"A few years now."

He nods approvingly. "Is owning your own business what you always wanted to do?"

"I started it not too long after I finished college. I got my degree in business management, because I had no idea what I wanted to do. Then the first office job I got, I ended up being tasked with planning their annual sales meeting. Then their Christmas party. Then the summer picnic. And it just kinda became my thing. I was good at it, if I dare say so myself, and it got my gears turning. I ended up leaving that job for a low-level position at an event planning company. Spent a year there learning as much as I could, then went out on my own. I bartended to pay the bills until Meghan's Moments became big enough to sustain me on its own. Which actually didn't take as long as I thought it would. So, I've been working full-time for myself for about four years now."

"Congratulations."

I shrug, pawing through the sugar selection.

"I mean it. That's really awesome. You had a goal. Set a path. And succeeded. Not many people can claim such a thing."

"Thanks." I turn to face him. "I've always been a bit…"

"Stubborn."

I glare at Sebastian.

"Hard-headed?" he suggests.

"Not what I was going to say," I respond. "Maybe *annoyingly persistent*? Oh, wait, no. That's you."

He just smirks.

I move to the flours, and I can hear him digging around in my cart.

"Who needs this much sugar? What do you do with it all?"

I spin around and swat at his hands. "Keep your grubby man paws off my stuff."

"Alright, alright - " Sebastian puts his hands up like he's trying to calm a wild animal. "Seriously, though. What do you do with all this stuff?"

"Uh, bake things. *Duh.*"

"But why do you have so many types?" He looks honestly perplexed, pointing to the bags.

"Have you never seen brown sugar before?"

"You have three! And they're all different!"

I laugh. "What'd you do, grow up under a rock? I have light and dark brown sugar. The third is Turbinado." He gives me a blank stare, so I continue. "I'm getting more powdered sugar, too."

He holds up the large bag of granulated sugar. I find myself rolling my eyes again. "Okay, and that too."

"Seriously. What do you do with this?" Sebastian's starting to look concerned.

"I repackage it and sell it at the farmers market." I deadpan.

"Really?"

"*Ohmygod.*" How is this smart man so dense? "No, you fool. I use it. Cookies, cakes, breads, whatever. I do *normal* things with the sugar."

"Hmmm." He stares into my cart for a long moment. "You must be a good cook. Baker. Whatever."

I dump an armful of chocolate chips into the cart. "I do alright."

"I bet you do more than alright," he traces a finger along the edge of the bacon packaging. That shouldn't be any kind of sexual, but a tingle runs along my arm as if it were my body he was touching. His eyes come up to meet mine. "Cook me dinner tonight." He doesn't say it like a question.

I'm about to say yes, when I remember I have plans.

"I can't."

"Why?"

"None of your damn business." I meant to say it sternly but thinking about the sex toy party has the corner of my mouth pulling up.

"Why does that sound nefarious?"

"Me? Nefarious? Never!" I say, aghast.

"Do you have a date?"

I snort. "Oh, yeah. I'll definitely be getting a dick tonight." I pause and tilt my head. "Well, technically, I'll be buying it."

"What?!"

Deciding I've gotten what I need, I grab the cart handle and start to push.

From behind, Sebastian reaches around, one arm on either side of me, grabbing the handle. His grip halts my forward motion.

He takes a step closer, pressing the front of his body against the back of mine.

"Banshee. You had better not be paying for sex."

God, he's way too easy to rile up.

I tip my head back until I'm looking straight up into his eyes. "You got a problem with that, *Ash*? Because I'm pretty sure I'm free to do whatever, and whoever, I want."

He growls.

He honest-to-god *growls*.

And my panties go damp.

He stares at me for a long moment before breaking the silence. "You're fucking with me."

"Not tonight..." I bat my eyes.

"Meghan."

"Sebastian," I tease.

He ducks his head, putting his face in the crook of my neck. I can feel his chest rumbling, so I know he's talking, but I can't understand the words that he murmurs against my skin.

I reach up and pat the top of his head. "Relax, caveman. The dick I'm buying tonight is silicon."

Another rumbled word comes out and I'm pretty sure it was *what*.

"My friend is throwing a sex toy party. So tonight is gonna be a bunch of drunk, horny chicks, buying playthings."

His head slowly rises until he's making eye contact. "And do you already own some of these *playthings*?"

"Several. But there's still room in my drawer for more." I wink.

The corner of his mouth twitches. "Thank you."

"For what?" I ask.

"For all the new material that just went into my spank bank." He bends down again, only this time he bites my neck.

I yelp and elbow him in the side.

Sebastian chuckles, but releases his grip on my cart, so I hurry to put some distance between us.

"I don't know what it is, Banshee, but something about you getting all violent just fucking does it for me," he says from a few paces behind me. "Come on, Babe. Hit me, again. Just one more time."

"Pretty sure it's a form of erectile dysfunction if getting smacked in the face stirs your cock. Diagnosis heavy on the *dysfunction*."

Sebastian just laughs.

We carry on through the rest of the store, talking about food and needling each other. And I have to admit, shopping with Sebastian has been fun. You never can tell where a day will take you.

Stopping in front of the ice cream coolers, I search for the one I need. Spotting the high-end vanilla, I open the door and reach for it.

"Hold on," Sebastian stops me.

"What?"

"Two things. First, with all your crazy food selections, why the hell are you picking out boring-ass vanilla ice cream?"

Letting the cooler door shut, I step back. "If you must know. I currently have several *crazy* flavors already at home. I need the vanilla for my balsamic and peaches."

Sebastian looks horrified. "Balsamic. As in vinegar? On ice cream? What's wrong with you?!"

I dig the bottle out from under my pile of sugars. "This." I show him the cinnamon pear label. "Mixed with sautéed peaches, on top of *boring-ass vanilla ice cream* is one of the best things you will ever put in your mouth."

He looks torn between disgust and lust as he slowly shakes his head. "I doubt that. Very much."

"Well, you'd be wrong. What was the second question? Thing. Whatever."

"Oh, right. Secondly," he starts to push me away from the ice cream. "Buy the frozen stuff later. Otherwise it will melt."

"Melt?"

"Yeah. Since you're ditching me for a bunch of dildos tonight, you're having lunch with me. Here. Now."

"Uh, okay, my turn for two things - " I poke a finger into his chest. "First, I'm not ditching you. I hadn't even planned on seeing you today. Or honestly, of talking to you ever again."

"Hmmm. Fair enough." He nods. "And secondly?"

I drop my hand. "Secondly, what if I already had lunch?"

He raises a brow. "Then you can just sit and watch me eat. But since it's..." He looks at his watch, "just after 11:00, I doubt you ate lunch before coming here."

"Fine," I huff, acting put-out.

But secretly, I'm a bit excited. Fuck it, I'm ecstatic.

I went into today hating Sebastian's existence, but after the past hour together I'm ready to give him another shot. He's just so damn easy to be with. Today was just like the haunted hell place. Only grocery shopping is about as mundane as you can possibly get, so making it fun... yeah, takes a special type of person.

We split up in the massive deli section, each making our own lunches. I can never decide what to get when I come here, so my container has a little bit of everything off the hot bar. Then I fill a soup cup with bread pudding. Because... bread pudding.

Chapter 16

Sebastian

W*HAT THE FUCK is wrong with me? Lunch?*
Lunch is too... *something*. Too intimate? Too comfortable? Too much like a date you'd go on with someone a year into a serious relationship? But can it really be called a date when it's at a damn grocery store and it wasn't planned?

Scooping more grilled chicken onto my creation at the salad bar, I realize just how far off script my day has gone.

When I left my brother's house this morning, the plan was to stop here, grab a pile of food big enough to last the day, then go home and veg out. Today is the team's rest day and I usually take full advantage of that. Though I can't really claim that walking around the store for the past hour with Banshee has been taxing. It hasn't. It's been... nice.

Fuck, I'm such a tool. If people could hear my inner monologues, they wouldn't think of me as a smooth-talking player.

But today *has* been nice. And I feel like a weight has been lifted off my chest. Honestly, I haven't felt right since I snapped at Banshee after our loss a week ago.

I've picked up the phone to call her so many times, but I

always backed out. I'd been such a dick, and I didn't know how to ask her forgiveness. And - with my overly strong attraction to Meghan - I honestly wasn't sure I wanted her to forgive me. I want her more than I should. More than I should want anyone. I'm happy with my life the way it is. I need to focus on my game. I can settle down and do the whole domestic bliss bullshit when I retire. But even telling myself that, I couldn't let go of the guilt that I felt.

I spotted her the second I walked into the store. There she was, sniffing a pineapple, and I knew I had to go to her. I needed her to understand how much I regretted the words I said to her. I needed her to forgive me. I needed to feel *right* again.

And I was immediately reminded why I call her Banshee. Meghan earned that name with her spitfire personality, take-no-shit attitude, and infectious wild energy. I may have dulled that during our last interaction, but today she came at me full-fucking-force. Calling me a *dickhole* and startling a cranky old lady. She had every right to be mad at me, so I had to hold back the laughter that wanted to burst out. I needed to take her insults. It was the least that I deserved.

When I was finally able to get her to stop and listen to me, it was easier to find the right words than I thought it would be. She just opens something up inside of me. For whatever reason, I feel like I can be honest with her. So I was. Dropping to my knees and pressing my face into her glorious tits was an improvisation. But it worked. And it felt great.

Thinking about the feel of her against me has me reaching down to adjust myself. *Wow, I'm disgusting.* What sort of sexual deviant has to pause at a salad bar so they can rearrange their hardening dick?

I'm putting the finishing touches on my lunch when I see Meghan pushing her cart my way. She's so cute in her oddball hippie outfit. Cute, and sexy-as-fuck. Not sure how she accomplishes both, but I won't question it. I'll just enjoy it.

"Ready?" she asks.

"Yep." I see her lunch container on top of the pile in her cart. I reach for it. "I'll buy our lunches."

She jerks her cart away from me before I can grab it. "What? No. I can buy my own lunch. Actually, you should just put yours with mine. I have to check out anyway."

"Uh..." I think my brain misfires, because I can't think of a single thing to say in response.

I don't think a woman has ever, like never-ever, offered to pay for my meal. I'm not saying every girl I've been with has been a gold-digger, but this is a brand-new situation for me.

While I try to remember words, she tugs the container out of my hands and puts it in her cart.

She's already in line, unloading her groceries onto the conveyor belt, when I snap out of it and catch up.

Meghan glances up at me and smirks. "Did you decide to do some mediation back there, or were you having a seizure?"

This girl doesn't miss a damn beat.

I gesture back to where she'd left me, "I was suffering from a system reboot. I guess a pretty girl offering to pay for my lunch causes my speech program to shut down."

She rolls her eyes at me for the hundredth time before handing the cashier her stack of cloth bags.

Watching the total tick up, I start to feel guilty about letting her pay for me. "Okay, Banshee, I appreciate the gesture, but let me at least buy my own lunch."

"Sebastian, it's already rung up. That ship has sailed. But if it'd make you feel better, I was planning to grab a coffee from the kiosk over there." She nods towards the coffee counter I spotted earlier. "You could get that while I check out here."

"Deal!" I perk up like a goddamn puppy, now that I have a task to focus on.

I start to walk away before realizing that I don't know what she wants. I spin around to see she's watching me with a knowing smile.

I try not to show how dumb I feel. "So, was that just a normal coffee?"

Meghan nods. "Dark roast with a splash of cream, please."

I give her a slight bow. "As you wish, my little B."

She snorts.

Adorable.

Chapter 17

Meghan

Dear Diary,

Can you get whiplash from a person? Specifically a guy? Specifically a super-hot guy named Sebastian? I have no idea what's going on between us, but I can't stop thinking about him. Our time together, at the freaking grocery store, was more relaxing and enjoyable than should be possible.

And his apology... who could have resisted that?! Part of me hates myself for giving in so easily. But really, isn't forgiveness a virtue? And I tried to resist! I swear I did. But I have a weak spot for that giant stupid man. He's just so cute. Obviously, he's hot-as-sin, but his personality is just... *cute*. When his walls come down and he's being himself, he's irresistible. I'm a little afraid that he might be just as batshit as I am, but that just adds another level of excitement.

And then lunch... lunch at the grocery store. WTF, amiright? It should've been weird, but it wasn't. I don't know if bumping into someone can be considered a date, but - if it was - then it was maybe the best date I've ever been on. And it wasn't because of the food (*although, yum!*), it was the company.

Sleet Banshee

Why is it so easy with him?!?!

We talked the entire time we ate. He even reached over with his fork and tried bites of all the different items I selected. I did the obligatory "pretend to be outraged" reaction, but the move just endeared him to me even more. He offered to let me try his salad, but we both knew that my food was better.

Then we sat there talking more while I finished my coffee. He asked about my brothers, remembering that I'd said they played hockey. (Even though he'd been a dick after I told him, apparently he was still listening to me.) I told him all about my older brothers, Miles and Max. And my little brother, Marvin, who was forced to play goalie until it just stuck.

Sebastian grinned after hearing that all our names start with the letter M. I'm not sure if he knows my last name... I never told him. But I'm sure he'd love that it's Morris. And that both my parents have M names. Yep, we're *that* family.

And can we please take a moment of silence to remember the story about his niece and nephew twins? I almost asked if he had any pictures of himself holding the babies, but I thought that might be a little weird. And I don't even really like kids, but there's still just something about seeing sexy AF men holding babies.

We didn't talk too much about his family, but I found out he has a second brother. And - I'm not sure why, but - I was surprised to learn that he has a little sister. I think her name was Annabelle? I'd have teased him about being a middle child, but I'm a middle child and I've heard all the stereotypes. Yeah, yeah. We're a bunch of freaks.

But the cherry on our non-date sundae? The ice cream.

We parted ways after we finished lunch, with a smile and a wave, going in separate directions to our cars. I was putting the last bag of groceries in my car when Sebastian came jogging over. Carrying the *boring-ass vanilla* ice cream that I forgot to go back and buy.

When I opened my mouth to say thank you, he crashed his lips to mine in a searing kiss that lasted for barely a moment.

That devil-man knows exactly what he does to me. He kissed me, torched my blood, ruined my panties, and then he stopped. Just fucking stopped, and stepped back, with a big dumbass grin on his face.

Before turning around he said, "I'll be tasting your dessert soon."

Then he winked, spun around, and strode away.

Needless to say, I bought a new vibrator at my sex toy party tonight. And I named it SmAsh.

XoxoX

Chapter 18

Meghan

"Hey, Hoe - " I say, holding my apartment door open for Katelyn.

"You're such a bitch!" she laughs, before taking a large inhale through her nose. "But you're a bitch that can bake."

"All true," I agree.

Katelyn hands over the quiche she brought and makes herself at home.

Today is our Sunday Brunch Day. Even though Katelyn's life changed after meeting Jackson - falling in love, getting engaged, and moving in together - we still keep our monthly binge brunch. No matter what.

Pulling out my tray of pumpkin cinnamon rolls, I slip Katelyn's pan into the oven.

"How's your morning going so far?" I ask.

"It's fine," Katelyn sighs. "But I already miss Jackson. I hate these long stretches when they have a bunch of away games in a row."

When they first started dating, Jackson left town for a multi-day trip and all hell broke loose. Not his fault. It was all his stupid viper of an ex. That was a year ago now, but Katelyn still dreads every time he leaves.

"I know." I give her a half smile, purposely ignoring the fact that I've missed Sebastian in the few days since our grocery store run-in.

Someone should slap me; I'm being ridiculous. We aren't even talking about me, we're talking about Katelyn. The only one here who's in an actual relationship.

It's gotta be tough being with a public figure. Because of Jackson, my bestie ended up in the tabloids. Who has that happen? Oh, right, professional athletes.

Could I deal with that? Getting involved with Sebastian wouldn't just mean seeing photos of us online, it'd mean comments about me and speculation about him anytime he's seen anywhere, even *near* another woman. I can be pretty chill. Sometimes. But I also know that I could potentially be a raging jealous bitch of a girlfriend. Just the thought of witnessing some floozy putting her herpes infested hand on his arm makes me grit my teeth.

"Earth to Meghan? What the hell is wrong with you?"

"Huh?" Oh, shit. I unclench my fists, sure that I look like a crazy person. "Nothing. Sorry, I spaced out there. What were you saying?"

"I was wondering..." She looks at me like I might be mentally deficient, "if you're free on Friday?"

I think for a second. "Pretty sure. Why?"

"There's an opening night party at this place called Puck Off. It's a sports themed night club type of place. The whole Sleet team has to attend, so obviously I'll be there. And so will Steph."

"Sure, I'm down." I reply as nonchalantly as possible, when really my slut of a honey badger is doing the happy dance inside my rib cage. Because Sebastian will be there.

"Eek! Yay!" Katelyn claps her hands together and bounces around my living room. "I'm going dress shopping this week. I want to find something that will make Jackson's tongue hit the floor when he sees me."

I laugh at her excitement. "Count me in for shopping - I could use some retail therapy."

If I can find a dress to make *Sebastian's* tongue hit the floor, it better slide across my clit on the way down.

Fuck, I've got to focus. And charge up the new vibrator I just bought.

"I imagine Izzy will be there, too - " Katelyn cuts into my dirty daydream.

"Oh, I'm sure she will be. If the team knows, then I bet Zach's already asked her. She's finally given up her fight and has given in to his charms." I smile, because they really do make a great couple.

"Steph told me how adorable they were together at that sex party!" Katelyn coos.

I make a face. "Uh, yeah, it was a sex *toy* party. A *sex party* is an entirely different thing."

"Whatever, you know what I mean." She waves me off.

"But yeah, they were super adorable. And I can't believe how easy it was to get those two to fall for each other. They're going to make the most adorable little hockey-obsessed babies." I give Katelyn a pointed look. "Speaking of stupidly-attractive couples, when are you two gonna set a damn date?"

Katelyn sighs as she falls dramatically onto my couch. "We're working on it. Life's just so busy right now. Jackson is bogged down with usual team stuff, and my company just took on a handful of new authors, so I've been editing my damn fingers off. I know we need to just do it and pull the trigger, but that would require focus. And planning. And fancy clothes. And let's face it, naked time is just too much fun."

I groan. "I liked hearing about your sex stories when you were first hooking up, but now that you're engaged, it's just gross."

Katelyn laughs. "Oh, shut up. You're just jealous."

"I am," I agree.

"Who have you been seeing recently?"

"What? What do you mean?" My heart rate picks up. She can't know about Sebastian. I've been so careful.

"I mean, you normally don't go this long without telling me about some loser date. And I can't really count that bowling thing you and Izzy did, since you weren't actually trying to date that guy."

I shrug, feeling like a complete asshole for not telling her about Sebastian yet.

I should've just done it on the ride home from the haunted house. *Hey guys, I made out with Sebastian LeBlanc in the corn maze.* What'd be so hard about that? But I didn't. I didn't because... Fuck, I don't even remember my reasoning. Something about not wanting to distract Izzy from Zach. But now she's all-in with him. So that means I should tell them now. Right? But I know how that will go down. It'll go down like an epileptic hooker with braces. So, not good. Not good at all.

I'll get the third degree, just like I'd do to them, asking how I could keep this a secret. Or rather - *why* I'd keep this a secret.

And really, what is *this*? This is Sebastian and I making out like rabid teenagers. This is Sebastian being so rude to me after that game that I nearly burst into tears like a lovesick tween. This is Sebastian accosting me at a grocery store, forcing me to accept his apology, and then spending all morning shopping and eating lunch together. This is feeling way too comfortable and attached to a person I've only just met. This is us kissing again. In a parking lot. In broad daylight. This is us not having a single conversation about dating, or relationships, or sex, or anything else adults who are interested in each other might talk about. This is us being mutually attracted to each other, without a single goddamn plan about how to continue.

"I've been in a bit of a funk," is all I say, and it's true.

The timer goes off, and I'm saved by the bell. I take my time turning off the beeping alarm, then over-mix the glaze for the rolls, making as much noise as possible. By the time I'm done pouring the sugary wonder-sauce all over my cooled rolls, the next timer is going off and the quiche is coming out of the oven.

Katelyn has busied herself pouring coffee, and my new goal is to steer the rest of today's conversations away from my dating life.

Chapter 19

Sebastian

I'm the world's biggest pussy. I've been pining over a firecracker all week, but I've been too chickenshit to text her. Oh, I think about it, but then I *over*think about what the fuck I should say ...

Hey babe, I had a great time grocery shopping with you!

Hey babe, I know we hardly know each other but I miss you!

Hey babe, I'd like to do more than kiss you next time I see you.

Hey babe, my balls packed up their little sperm buddies, told me they were going out for cigarettes, and never came back. Wanna cuddle?

World's. Biggest. Pussy.

"Come on, Ash. Let's turn this party up!" Luke Anders, teammate and pain in my ass, shouts as he pushes past me.

I roll my eyes, but this place looks like it could be a good time.

Stepping through the entrance, I see the club is pretty packed. We're a little late getting here, but we just got back into town. Zach beelines away from us, eyes locked on to his new lady. The rest of the team doesn't know about him and Izzy yet, but I've had to listen to him blather on about her for the past several days. It was annoying. And made me think about Banshee, which made it even more annoying.

Stepping off to the side, I survey the room. The digs, and clientele, are pretty swanky. Coach told us to dress nicely, and I mostly listened. My dark jeans and fitted black long sleeve shirt blend in well enough with the crowd.

I'm turning to head for the bar when I spot her.

Banshee.

I'd hoped she would be here, but I didn't have the balls to ask. But lucky for me, Meghan's hard to miss.

The bright red curls tumbling down her back shine like a beacon, drawing me in. I'm walking towards her before I even realize I've moved. She's on the dance floor: arms up, head tipped back, with her mouth open in what looks like laughter.

As I near, the lights dim, and the volume of the music goes up. The nighttime vibe just went into effect. Meaning I got here just in time.

Megs does a slow twirl and I finally get a look at the entire package. And my cock springs to life.

She's wearing a clingy, dark-purple dress. The long loose sleeves tease at being conservative, but the severely-plunging neckline screams sex appeal. The dress cinches at her waist then flares out into a tantalizingly-short skirt. It's hard to see her feet through the blur of bodies, but she's definitely taller. The mental image of her heel-clad feet wrapped around my back has my cock hardening even more.

A flash of light draws my gaze toward her face. She's traded in her usual soft feather earrings for long, jewel-encrusted ones. It's hard to tell for sure, since she won't keep still, but they seem to be shaped like a feather.

I bite back my smile. Even decked out in club wear, my favorite girl still shines through.

I don't wait for her to see me. I don't wait for permission.

Slipping through the mass of people, I time my moves with Banshee. When her back is to me, I step forward, pressing my body flush with hers. I feel her muscles tense for a split second before she picks up the beat again. I don't allow my mind to race with thoughts of her doing this with a stranger. Instead, I place my hands on her hips, grip her tight, lean down, and graze my teeth over her exposed neck.

The music is loud, but with my mouth this close to her throat, I can hear her moan.

One of her hands goes over mine, securing my hold on her. The other hand reaches up and grabs a hold of my hair. Banshee grabs tighter than would be comfortable, for a normal person. But me... I love it. She gives it an extra tug as she grinds her ass back against my erection.

"Hi, Sebastian." Her voice is husky.

A low sound gets trapped in my chest. I love that she knows me by feel.

"Hi, Banshee."

The song changes, and Meghan leans harder into me as she moves to the beat. The heels she's wearing make her taller, but she still only comes up to my chin. From my position behind her, with her pressed up against me, I have a perfect view straight down the front of her dress. This dress, her tits... it's so sinful I'm prepared to die a happy man if I can just get my face *there*.

With every sway and shake of her hips, her breasts rise and jiggle and bounce. Every movement is a combination of torture and pleasure. And I don't know if I've ever been more turned on.

Then she spins to face me.

Face-to-face, Meghan places her hands on my abs and slowly runs them up, over my chest, and around my neck. I bend my knees slightly, so she can clasp her hands together.

Taking advantage of my new position, she straddles my leg. And grinds.

Fucking hell.

I grip her lower back, holding her tightly against me.

I can feel the heat of her core on my thigh.

I can feel her soft, heavy breasts pressed against me.

I slide my hands down until I'm cupping her ass.

We rock together like this for a few minutes, bringing me closer to insanity.

Goddamnit. I can't take it anymore. I need to be inside her.

"Follow me," I growl into her ear.

I don't give her a chance to question me or turn me down. I grab her hand and drag her through the crowd. Luckily, the place is still packed, so no one notices the obvious erection tenting the front of my pants. But time for embarrassment has passed. I'm on a mission.

We find our way to the back of the club, down the hallway with bathrooms, down another hallway, and out a back door.

I don't have a plan beyond getting us out of here. I'll find a way back to the main road where we can order a Lyft back to my place. I don't know how I'll make it through the car ride, but I gotta get her alone.

The door closes behind us, but it doesn't click shut. Someone who works here must use this for smoke breaks.

I hear people to the right, so I turn to the left, taking us deeper into the alley. We make it past a pile of crates before Meghan tugs on my hand. I ignore her, tightening my grip, and I hear her giggle.

"Sebastian!" she whisper-shouts my name.

I turn to face her and the smile on her beautiful face snaps the last cord holding me together.

I step forward and slam my lips to hers. I don't finesse my way in. I push my tongue into her mouth and claim her the way I wanted to on the dance floor. Banshee calls my kiss and raises me two hands fisted in the front of my shirt.

I feel frantic.

One of my hands goes to her hair, wrapping a handful around my fist. I tug hard enough to tip her head back, and she groans in pleasure. Seems like I'm not the only one who enjoys a touch of pain. And *fuck* that's hot.

My free hand cups one of her generous tits, squeezing.

"Damn, Baby. You feel so good..." I growl into her mouth.

Banshee bites my lip. Hard. "Don't call me Baby."

"Fuck - " I groan.

I walk us back until Meghan's against the alley wall, between two stacks of empty pallets. The stacks are taller than I am, but we're only hidden so long as no one walks past.

I still don't have a plan, but I need these out. I pull down on the front of her dress, until both her breasts are exposed. She's wearing a completely see through red lace bra. It's not doing much to hold her in place, but it is making me want to taste her. And I'm past the point of self-control.

I bend down and close my lips over one of her already hard nipples. Meghan gasps and digs her nails into my neck. While I lick and suck, I move a hand to pinch at her other peak.

"Oh shit... I... Holyfuck..." Banshee's words are starting to slur together.

Letting go of her hair, I reach down and slide my fingers up her inner thigh. I can feel her legs tremble. Just before I reach the sweet spot between her legs, I bite down on the nipple that's still in my mouth. As she pulls in a shocked breath, I move my hand up and firmly palm her pussy.

"Sebastian!"

She doesn't come, but I can feel her clench against my hand.

She's close. So fucking close. And I need to have her.

I step back, removing both my hands from her.

Meghan looks up at me in shock. "You motherfucker. If you think you can work me up like that and walk..."

Now she sees it.

The condom in my hand.

Her words cut off, and her mouth falls open as I unzip my jeans and pull out my rock-hard cock. My eyes stay on her, as her eyes stay on my dick as I rip open the package and slowly roll the condom on.

"Turn around." I growl.

She doesn't listen.

She's still staring at my dick. I grip the base and squeeze.

"Banshee." She looks up and meets my eyes. "Turn around. Hands on the wall."

She listens.

I step up behind her and pull her panties down. They're red lace just like her bra.

I guide her as she steps out of them.

Standing, I slide them into my pocket. These are mine now.

Grabbing the hem of her dress, I bunch it up around her waist, exposing her perfectly round ass. With her hands on the wall, she's slightly bent over, and I can see the glistening wetness on her pussy from here.

I keep a hand on her lower back, holding up the dress. The other holds my cock, and I run it along her wet lips.

We let out matching moans at the contact.

"Feet together."

"What?" She glances over her shoulder at me.

"Feet." I use one foot to tap the outside of hers. "Together."

She does as I say and I bring my body closer to hers.

"But.."

Her question turns into a scream when I bury myself inside her, with one hard thrust.

Fuck.

She's hot. And slick. And oh so fucking tight.

I mold my body over hers, allowing her a moment to adjust.

Just a moment.

Then I start moving.

Chapter 20

Meghan

HOLY. *Fucking. Shit.*

I think I just died.

I think Sebastian just killed me with his giant fucking cock.

With my mouth hanging open from my scream, I thank the Big Dick Gods that he's allowing my pussy a moment to adjust after ramming into me with his entire length.

Then he starts to move.

And *oh my holy hell*, this is the best thing I've ever felt!

With my legs pressed together, I can feel him everywhere. I can feel him buried inside me. I can feel him sliding between my thighs, along the curve of my ass, as he thrusts in and out. I can't even help it. I squeeze my legs together even tighter.

Sebastian growls. "Fuck, Baby. Do that again."

I squeeze.

Sebastian groans and slaps my ass.

Holy shit. I whimper in response. That's all I can do. Whimper and grip the brick wall in front of me.

My breath is coming hard and fast. I'm not even moving but I'm panting and more worked up than I've ever been. I'm being fucked in an alley and it's the hottest thing I have ever experienced.

"Oh... Fuck... Seb... Ash..."

He leans in and licks the shell of my ear. "You know my name, Baby. Say the whole thing."

"Don't. Call me. *Baby,*" I gasp out.

Sebastian chuckles against my neck, dragging a hand up between my breasts until he's holding my throat. His grip is gentle, but firm. *And holy shit I didn't know I liked this!* I feel the pressure all the way to my core.

"Do what I tell you to, Baby." His grip tightens slightly. "Say my name."

I swear I'm going to black out from need.

"Sebastian." His name sounds like a groan. "Sebastian." I say it again.

"Good Banshee," he rasps into my ear.

Then he picks up the pace.

Just when I think my mind is going to fizzle away into oblivion, I feel a firm pressure against my clit. It must be his fingers. I'd look, but my eyes are squeezed shut, trying to hold my sanity together.

I clench around him.

He hisses.

"Come," he says, fingers running circles, setting my nerves on fire. "Come for me, Baby."

I have no choice. My body obeys him.

Just as I start to tip over the edge, the hand on my neck moves to grip my hair. The sting of the tug has my eyes popping open. He's right there, over my shoulder. His gaze meeting mine.

That's how I come. With a cry on my lips, my eyes locked with his, and Sebastian's cock buried as deep inside me as it can go.

My shuddering orgasm sends Sebastian over the wave with me. His stare holds mine through the first guttural grunt of his release, then he throws his head back and I feel his cock jump inside of me.

Holy. Mother Fucking. Shit.

Chapter 21

Meghan

I CANNOT BELIEVE I just did that. I mean I can totally believe that I let Sebastian fuck me, because - well, he's hot. But I cannot believe that I let him fuck me in a gross back alley. Like seriously, what the hell? Who does that? Apparently, I do. And honestly, I'd do it again.

Sebastian nuzzles into my neck.

"Holy shit, Banshee." His breath is still coming in pants.

"Uh, huh." I mumble, my heart still skittering out a rapid beat.

I can feel his whole body shake with a suppressed laugh.

With a kiss to the back of my head, Sebastian starts to untwine himself from me. The feeling of him leaving my body seems nearly more personal than when he entered it.

The loss of his body heat has me shivering, so I quickly adjust the top of my dress, pulling the material back up to cover my boobs.

Turning to face Sebastian, I watch as he tucks himself back into his pants, spent condom in hand.

Standing in a dark alley, holding a used rubber... that

Sleet Banshee

should be disgusting, but it's so not. The sight makes my thighs clench.

Oh. Right.

"Uh, can I have my undies back?" I ask, blushing.

Why *that* has me blushing, and not the whole dirty-alley-sex, is a mystery. I'm sure I need therapy.

"No." He smirks as he steps back.

"No?" I follow.

"Yeah, no. I'm keeping those."

"That... what? You can't do that." I still can't think straight, so I'm finding it hard to form a full sentence.

"Finders, Keepers."

"Sebastian - " I scold. "I need those!"

"Why?" He sounds sincere.

I stare at him. "Because... they're mine." I gesture to his hand. "And you get to throw your orgasm away in that nice little package. My orgasm is messy and still between my legs. A layer of underwear would be better than nothing."

I watch as his eyes trail down my body and his chest expands.

"Well..?" I ask.

He seems to think about it for a moment. "I'm still keeping them."

Sebastian takes a few steps further down the alley and tosses the condom into an open dumpster.

I frown. Okay, now it's a little gross.

Sebastian turns back with heat in his eyes. "Want to come over?"

His question catches me off guard, and I feel my eyes widen. "Now?!"

"Yeah, little Banshee. Now." He grins. "I'm not done with you."

For every step he takes towards me, I step back. It's not

backing up because I'm not interested. It's just my natural reaction to being stalked by an oversized predator.

I open my mouth to reply when my back hits the stack of pallets. The contact causes the stack to shake and a cat leaps down from the top, hissing.

I let out an embarrassing squeal.

"Cranky little pussy," Sebastian says with a smirk.

I chuckle and place a hand over my still racing heart. "Okay."

"Okay?"

"Yeah. I'll come over. I just need to let my friends know I'm leaving."

Sebastian grabs my hand and we walk back to the door we came out of.

Stepping through, we find that everything has changed.

Chapter 22

Sebastian

I'm not sure what we missed, but something's definitely happened. With Meghan's hand in mine, I push through the bodies filling the back hallway. When we left, the crowd was on the dance floor, not back here. I don't know what's wrong, but we weren't gone that long. Not saying I'm a quick shooter, but frantic high-passion fucks aren't known for being long-drawn-out affairs.

Trying to focus, the conversations around us start to make their way into my awareness.

"I can't believe they arrested him."

"Didn't you see that other guy? He nearly killed him."

"So what? That fucker hit that girl first."

I can feel a prickle of awareness on the back of my neck.

"What's going on?" Meg asks from behind me.

I shake my head, since I don't have the answer.

I'm tall, and I'm walking ahead of Banshee, so I get to take in the scene first. The lights are up. The music is turned down. And my teammates are standing around a cluster of tables where Izzy is sitting on a barstool. With an ice pack against her face. Talking to a couple of cops.

What the fuck?

"What the fuck?" Meghan whispers.

I just shake my head, again.

"Izzy!" The alarm in her reaction is instantaneous when she sees her friend.

Meghan pulls her hand from my grip and runs to Izzy's side. I look around for Zach, but I don't see him.

Striding up to the group, I keep looking for him. "Luke, where's Zach?"

He cocks his head. "Where's Zach? Where the fuck have you been, if you're asking that question?"

I step into his space. "Not the time, dickhead. What's going on?"

Luke looks back at Izzy. "He got arrested. Some asshole hit Izzy, and Zach lost his shit. Beat him half to death before Jackson and I could peel him off the guy."

"Fuck." I drag a hand over my face.

"Yeah, *fuck* is right." Luke sighs.

I watch as Izzy gives Meghan a sad smile. She's the one that got hurt, but it looks like she's trying to comfort Meg. I might not know Banshee as well as I'd like to, but I know her enough to guess that she's feeling guilty. While we were out back fucking, her friend was in here going through a crisis.

My chest constricts when I see a tear streak down Meghan's cheek. She reaches up to wipe it off, and her eyes catch mine. She looks away quickly and swipes at another tear. My chest tightens another notch.

Goddamnit. I know that look. It's the look of regret.

I'm not done with Banshee, but I'm afraid she might be done with me.

Chapter 23

Meghan

Dear Diary,

What is wrong with me?! How could I let this happen? We were in *a club*. I knew that! And I still left Izzy. Girl code. Never go anywhere alone.

Fuck fuck fuck fuck.

If I'd been there. If I hadn't followed Sebastian out back like a horny puppy, I would've been there with her. I would've walked with her to the bathroom. I could've helped her fend off that piece of shit guy. Me being there might've been enough to keep him away. Creeps like that like to prey on lone targets. If I'd been there, she wouldn't have gotten hit.

Hit! Who the fuck gets hit? Like in real life, by a stranger?!

And if I'd prevented her from being hit, then Zach wouldn't have been arrested.

Fuck fuck fuck fuck. I'm the worst friend ever.

I wanted to stay at her house tonight, but she said no. I wanted to take care of her. Cook for her. Something. But I get it. She wants to be alone. Or maybe she just doesn't want to see me. I would get that, too. Even I don't want to see me.

I'm not sure if I've ever felt worse. Which is a bit of bitter karmic irony, because sex with Sebastian... I don't think I've ever felt better.

But clearly this is a message. The universe is telling me to stay the hell away from Sebastian. And I might not have many rules, but I listen to the universe.

No more Sebastian.

Here's hoping tomorrow is a better day.

XoxoX

Dear Diary,

Yet again, what is wrong with me? It's been 2 weeks since the alley/fuck/bar-fight incident, and I still feel like shit. More precisely, I feel heartbroken.

I know. What the fuck am I talking about?! I wasn't even dating Sebastian. I sure as Hell wasn't in love with him. So why should I feel like I've been through the worst breakup ever? It doesn't make sense.

He called me last weekend. I just stared at my phone until it stopped ringing, finally deciding I'd listen to his voicemail and go from there. Feel out his tone. Call him back if it felt right.

But he didn't leave a voicemail. He just hung up. And he hasn't called back since.

I should be grateful. It made my decision easy. But instead, it felt like an extra kick to the heart.

The salt in the wound... I never told any of my friends

about him. I can't very well tell them I'm suffering from a broken heart, without telling them about the man himself. And if I tell them now, then I'd have to tell them everything. And everything would include how I was fucking Sebastian while Izzy was getting hit in the face and Zach was getting arrested. Sure, everyone's fine now, but it was still an awful experience all around. Every time I think of that night, I first see myself pinned against the wall, having the best orgasm of my life, then I see the bruise on Izzy's face. Talk about a mind fuck.

I have got to find a way to shake this shit.

XoxoX

Dear Diary,

I'm messed up. A sadist. A crazy ass bitch.

The girls went to a Sleet game tonight. They invited me, and I turned them down.

No, that's not entirely true. I lied. I lied to my best friends. I told them I had a work event tonight. Which isn't true at all. I just couldn't go. I couldn't chance running into Sebastian. I couldn't chance him seeing me in the crowd. I know he probably wouldn't see me. But what if he did? Would he think I was there for him? Pining over him?

Gah! Look at me, I just lied to my fucking diary! I didn't skip the game because of him. I skipped because of me. Because *I am* pining over him. How? Why? WTF? His dick isn't made of gold. Yeah, it was nice. Big, thick, and talented. Okay, his dick is basically gold, but so what? Is that really what this is?

Am I just hung up on the physical chemistry between us? We only fucked once. Once! I'm acting like a goddamn Hallmark movie heroine.

Nope. Fuck all that.

I just need a new dick. Silver will do. Hell, I'd even be happy taking home the bronze. That's it. That's what I need.

And I need to stop watching his games. I may have ditched the girls, but I still sat at home in my sweats and watched the game. I sat there, chewing my fingernails in nervousness and cheering alone in my apartment at every save.

I suck so bad.

XoxoX

-

Dear Diary,

Welp, that was a new low for me. And you know me well enough to know that that's saying something.

I did it, I swiped. I found some tool to go out with tonight. He was cute. Maybe better than cute. And he was nice. Sorta funny. Not like enough to make me laugh but enough to make me smile. He was fine. He was totally fine.

And yet... When the date ended, I didn't even give him a chance to ask me to come over. Nope. You want to know what I did? As we put on our jackets and stepped out of the bar, I blurted out "I have a urinary tract infection!" He, of course, looked at me like I was a fucking lunatic. So I followed it up with "Sorry. Thanks for the drinks. Bye." And then I walked to my car.

Who does that?!? A crazy person, that's who.

I could've turned him down like a normal person. Or I could've just waited, since I was acting weird all night so he probably wouldn't have even asked me. But no, I had to blurt out the queasiest vagina thing I could think of without giving myself a fake STD.

Why did I do this? I'll tell you why. Because I'm the biggest fool alive. Because the TVs in the bar were all set to the Sleet game. Because I couldn't stop watching the game. Because I couldn't stop reliving all my moments with Sebastian. Because my mind wouldn't stop comparing New Guy to Sebastian. Because there is no comparison.

I tried. But riding a non-Sebastian dick isn't in the cards yet.

New tactic. No dicks. At all.

XoxoX

Dear Diary,

OMIGOD, whose brilliant idea was this dick drought???

It's been over 2 months since I've had a man-made orgasm. Er, well, like a literally man-made orgasm. Because Mr. Vibey has been putting in overtime, but it's not the same. Not the same at all. But you know what it *is* doing? It's making me into a royally-wicked bitch.

The girls are starting to notice. Or well, they're past noticing and they're starting to ask me if I'm okay. And it's fair because I've been... what? Down? Cranky? Dick-deprived? Depressed?

I mean what the fuck?! I slept with Sebastian once! 2 months ago! Why am I like this? Why is he still affecting me?

I haven't gone to a game with the girls since the one where Sebastian and I had that tiff in the locker hallway. And my new behavior is past obvious; I used to salivate at the chance to go.

And by not going to the games I'm missing out on much needed girl time. Katelyn's busy with Jackson. Izzy's busy being totally in love with Zach. Steph's busy with her own life, and games were the only time I really ever saw her. So by avoiding Sebastian, I've unintentionally forced myself into solitary confinement. I put on my best face when I see them, but I'm pretty sure they'll be staging an intervention soon.

I could pretend to be in a new relationship, act like that's what's taking up all of my time. But a new relationship should put me in a happy mood. Not a pile-of-bullshit mood. Instead, I pretend I'm swamped with work. It's not a total lie. Since I have extra time, I have thrown myself into work. I've grabbed up a few new events, but mostly I've been super focused on making the upcoming Calligraphy Convention off the chain. No detail is too small. No amount of overtime is unreasonable. It's still a month away, but I have plenty to do.

Once I wrap this project up, I'll find a new way to deal. Maybe I'll tell the girls everything. Maybe that will help.

XoxoX

Dear Diary,

I finally cracked and spilled last week.

I was at home for a family dinner and when the parents

went to bed, my brothers got me drunk. They knew something was wrong. They're idiots, but they can occasionally be clever. So they waited until we were well into drunk territory before the oldest asked *who's the dead man who broke your heart?*

I started to laugh, and then - to everyone's horror - I started to cry.

I tried to brush it off, but they weren't having it. My brothers might be giant dickholes sometimes, but they're also over-protective to a fault. Doesn't even matter that we are all in our 30's.

I did my best to keep things vague. They definitely don't want to hear details about my sexy life.

After yet another round of shots, my little brother pestered me for a name. Not really sure why, since - under normal circumstances - they'd never know the guy. But my life is not normal. And my little brother, who used to be a goalie, was questioning me while wearing a, I shit you not, Sebastian LeBlanc jersey. So my drunk-ass sighed and pointed at him. My equally drunk brother nearly shouted "you're in love with me?" with the most horrified look on his face.

And then I proceeded to fall off the couch. I was laughing so hard. *Idiot.* Once everyone's laughter faded, I jabbed my finger at the number on his jersey. "Him. Sebastian." When I was met with silence I clarified. "Ash."

It was almost comical how all their jaws dropped open. Since I have friends who are dating/engaged to Sleet players my statement was believable, so I didn't have to deal with any doubt.

Instead, their shock wore off all at once and they bombarded me with questions. I chose to ignore them all. Luckily "you're in love with Ash LeBlanc?" was drowned out by "holy shit, our sister banged Ash!".

What a bunch of morons.

But I have to say. It feels good to get it off my chest. Putting it out there makes it feel like it really happened. *It* being our short lived secret frenemy relationship.

I can't explain why 3 months later I'm still hung up on Sebastian. I don't want to think about it. I don't want to think about it because I'm afraid my brother is right. I'm afraid that, at least a small part of my heart, fell for him. But it's time to move on. I'm sure he has.

XoxoX

Dear Diary,

Holy shit I need to get laid!

At the Calligraphy Convention tonight, I was doing my typical rounds when one of the founders came over to dole out his praises. (Which were totally deserved.) But while he was talking to me he set his hand on my back, and I felt myself leaning into his embrace. This is not okay for a couple of reasons. First, I was there in a professional capacity. Secondly, he looked like fucking Mr. Miyagi from *The Karate Kid*.

Yikes.

But I'm home now. My big project is all wrapped. And I'm moving on to attempt 3 of bleaching Sebastian from my brain.

Tomorrow night I'm turning a new page. A new outlook. A new Sebastian-free existence. Katelyn and Jackson are finally having an engagement dinner. To be fair, they had one a year ago when they first moved in together, but I'm guessing they finally set a date.

I'll get to see all my friends. I'll be the old me again. It'll be fun.

XoxoX

Chapter 24

Meghan

"MEGHAN! Oh my god, it's been too long!" Steph jumps up from her seat to give me a hug.

"Hey, bitch! How've you been?" I squeeze her back.

This. This is what I've been missing.

"Sit by me - " she gestures to the open seat next to her.

Settling myself into the chair, I look around and smile. I got all my hugs in as I made my way around the table, and I already feel a million times better.

Katelyn rented out the back room at this awesome Mexican cantina place. The decor is rustic, the lighting is dim and it's the perfect vibe for a super chill dinner party. The tables already covered in chips, salsas, and pitchers of margaritas. So really, what more could a girl ask for?

Katelyn and Jackson are seated opposite me, along with Izzy and Zach. On Steph's other side is her mom, Mary. Luke Anders, Jackson's best friend, is at the end of the table to my right, but the two spaces between us are still open.

"I'm so glad you could make it," Izzy beams at me from across the table.

Sleet Banshee

Her new relationship looks good on her.

I grin. "Are you kidding? I wouldn't miss this for the world."

"I know. You've just been so busy at work recently. I wasn't sure if you'd have the night free."

I feel like such an asshole. I've been busy, but not as busy as all that. But I remind myself that I'm turning over a new leaf. I'm getting my shit together and I'm going to be more present.

"I actually just wrapped up my big convention last night. So I should have a lot more free time now." Not a lie.

Izzy squeaks and claps. "Perfect! Let's grab lunch someday this..."

I miss the rest of what she says because a deep rumbling voice just entered the room. A voice that I can feel in my bones.

He's here.

My eyes slowly pull away from Izzy, moving to where Jackson is standing from his seat, giving a bro hug to Sebastian.

Sebastian is saying something in greeting to Jackson, but his eyes are locked on mine. And he looks hungry.

My honey badger preens her fur coat.

I break the eye contact and look at the empty seat next to mine.

He wouldn't dare.

I try to act casual while I take a few deep breaths in an attempt to calm my racing pulse. This was not part of the plan for tonight. And I'm a total moron for not considering it as a possibility. This is Jackson's thing, not Zach's. I didn't think Sebastian and Jackson were close.

A hand grips the back of the empty chair next to mine and I clench my fists.

"This seat taken?"

I glance up, the voice is not Sebastian's.

I don't know this guy, but he looks familiar. He must be another teammate.

Before I can open my mouth to reply, a large hand lands on the man's shoulder.

"Dude, move down one." Sebastian's tone leaves no room for argument.

Dude rolls his eyes but moves down without argument and starts talking to Luke.

I refuse to show how stressed out his presence is making me. I also refuse to shy away, keeping my eyes on Sebastian as he noisily drags the chair out.

Smirking, he sits, and I watch as his eyes trail down my body. I'm seated, but he can see plenty from his vantage point. My grey cable knit sweater might seem demure, but it's stretched tight over my chest, and tucked into a burgundy leather pencil skirt. Sitting down brings the hemline up to a nearly indecent height, but the black tights I'm wearing keep all my skin covered. My hair is half-up, half-down tamed into a controlled mess. And I'm immensely glad I took so much care getting ready for tonight. I look good, and I know it.

Sebastian slowly reaches out, dragging a finger down my black feather earring. "Nice to see you again, Banshee."

Chapter 25

Sebastian

I KNEW BANSHEE WAS FEISTY, but now I know she's stubborn too.

I know she doesn't want to see me. I got that hint loud and clear when I didn't see her, hear from her, or hear of her, over the past three months.

I called once, but I refused to look desperate, so I stopped there. And I've been busy. You know, playing professional hockey. But the regular season is wrapping up, and this little firecracker is still on my mind. Constantly. I should be focusing on the upcoming play-offs, but instead I find myself daydreaming about Banshee. Wondering what she's been doing. Worrying about *who* she's been doing. I shake that last thought out of my head. The idea of someone else's hands on her fills me with possessive rage. I want to reach over and drag her onto my lap. Bite her neck. Mark her as mine. But I'm pretty sure that would get me slapped. Again. I smile at the memory.

She's done her damnedest to completely ignore me since I sat down. I gotta hand it to her. I've obnoxiously reached over her plate to grab chips, hot sauce, a spare napkin, all of which were available right in front of me. And not once did she so much as look at me. Pushing my luck, I let my arm brush against hers a few times. She stiffened, but that's it. Not even an elbow to the side.

Honestly, her reluctance to react is starting to turn me on. *I know, I'm a twisted fuck.*

Since tonight is a celebration, dinner is wrapping up with everyone getting a slice of chocolate cake. It's rich and delicious, and Meghan is making an obscene moaning sound with each bite she savors.

I can't take it anymore.

Leaning into Meghan's space, I put my mouth against her ear so every word has my lips brushing against her skin. "I'd rather be eating you for dessert."

Banshee slowly turns to look at me. I back up, slightly, but our faces are still only inches apart.

Finally, a reaction.

She gives me the most condescending once-over I've ever seen. "Even if you were the last man on Earth, I wouldn't let you put your mouth, or your fat sausage fingers, anywhere near my precious pussy. She has better taste than that."

This girl. I can't help myself. I love fighting with her almost as much as I love fucking her.

I smirk. "What's the matter, Banshee. Afraid you might fall in love with me?"

Her cool expression falters and I swear I see hurt mar her features.

That wasn't the reaction I expected. But before I can open my mouth to say something else, Banshee stands from her seat, picks up her glass and tosses the ice cold water in my face.

I'm shocked to shit, torn between laughter and apologizing.

Sleet Banshee

Clearly, I upset her, but Banshee's zest is so damn addicting. I love that I don't know what she'll say or do next.

While I sit here, brain stuck in a standstill, Meg steps around her chair and strides out of the room.

"Uh, dude, what the fuck?" Zach asks, snapping me out of it.

I shrug, needing to play it off. "Must've been something I said."

I use my sleeve to dry my face, glad she used water and not a salty margarita. Banshee might think she just slammed the door on me, on us, but she'd be wrong. She must've forgotten how much I like the chase, the fight, the challenge. Because instead of snuffing out the spark between us, she just threw gasoline on it.

You can run, little Banshee, but you can't hide.

Chapter 26

Meghan

MY EYES FLY OPEN, and I find myself in that confusing state between sleep and consciousness.

I can feel my heart racing in my chest, and with the suddenness of a slap to the face I remember the dream I was having. My hands scraping against a brick wall with Sebastian slamming into me, while all my friends stood there, lined up in the alley, watching. I blink my eyes to clear the image from my brain.

A floorboard creaks, and I sit bolt upright.

What the fuck was that? Is someone in my apartment?

I hear shuffling sounds, and jump out of bed. I grab my phone only to find it's totally dead; I forgot to plug it in last night. Fuck. I'm looking around my room for anything I can use as a weapon when I hear whispered voices. Picking up a large framed photo off my desk, I grip it like a baseball bat and hold my breath as the footsteps near.

"Meghan!" Katelyn's shout has me letting out a shriek.

"Jesus Fuck, Katelyn - " I attempt to yell, but my heart is beating so hard I can barely catch my breath.

Katelyn steps into my bedroom doorway just in time to see me lowering the picture frame.

She lifts an eyebrow. "Were you gonna beat off an intruder with that?"

"Seriously, what the fuck! Are you trying to kill me?" I set down the frame and rub my chest. "And don't say *beat off*. It doesn't mean what you think."

I hear a snort as Izzy and Steph step into my bedroom behind Katelyn.

"Good morning!" Izzy's being way too fucking chipper for just about giving me a heart attack.

Steph looks me up and down. "Hot."

I roll my eyes. "I'm assuming you're all here for a friendly interrogation?" I ask.

They respond with a mixture of smiles and glares.

I sigh. "At least let me pee before we start. You're lucky I didn't piss myself when I heard you in my hall."

Izzy's the only one to look even a little bit sheepish, and they all turn and make their way back to the living room.

I shouldn't be surprised. After my little show last night, I knew they'd be hounding me for answers. But I honestly wasn't expecting them to break into my freaking house at whatever-time in the morning to do it. Really though, I probably should've seen this coming. Katelyn has a key, and she knows me well enough to know that in-person is the best way to get me to spill my secrets.

Shutting the bathroom door, I let one more shudder work its way through my body. Waking up to the sounds of people in your home is terrifying. I may need some blood pressure medication now. And the lack of weapons in my bedroom is mildly concerning.

Not in a hurry to deal with the aftermath of my multi-month long deception, I take my time brushing my teeth, and look over my outfit. Steph was right, I do look hot. Kind of. To certain people. People that like a lot of tits and ass.

When I got home last night, I stripped down, got dressed for bed in the dark, and then hid under my favorite quilt until sleep took me. Which is how I find myself dressed in one pink sock, one blue sock, a pair of red lace boy-short undies that leave nothing to the imagination and a Sleet tank top. I bought the tank when I was in the mall one day and saw it on sale. I was in the midst of my self-imposed Sebastian ban, and feeling sorry for myself, but I'm a head case, so I bought it. And have since slept in it on a regular basis. It's small and cute and even with my boobs and hips spilling out all over the place, I feel sexy in it.

However, staring at the letters across my boobs reminds me why the girls are here. This is not going to be fun for me.

I pit-stop back in my room for a pair of sweatpants and a hoodie. Then take a deep breath and steel myself for what's to come.

"Hurry up, Bitch!" Katelyn shouts.

"Yeah, yeah." I grumble.

Shoulders back, I leave my room.

I find all three of them sitting on the couch, cups of coffee in hand. My apartment is decent sized, but not huge, and the only other spot to sit is in my yellow velvet high back chair. Which has been pulled to face the couch head on. Three on one. Here we go.

"We already prepped your coffee, so no need for you to delay in the kitchen," Steph gestures to the mug on the coffee table.

"You guys thought of everything," I mumble as I grab the mug and drop into the chair.

I take my time blowing on the steaming drink while the three wenches stare me down.

Izzy cracks first. "Oh for fuck's sake. Take a damn sip and then tell us what the hell is going on with you and Sebastian."

I can't help it. I smile. I love it when Izzy swears.

"Not uh - " Izzy shakes her head at me. "You don't get to laugh at this yet. We've all been worried about you, and you kept telling us you were fine. But clearly there's plenty you weren't telling us. Even though you had no problem shoving your nose into my business, feeding Zach information about my dates so he could crash them."

Oh, snap.

"Yeah, that's right. I've known for months." Izzy crosses her arms to punctuate her point.

"Huh." I figured she knew, but it's been so long I almost expected her to never bring it up. "In all fairness, you and Zach are now madly in love, so..." I trail off as her eyes narrow.

"Yeah, and that's why I'm not mad about what you did. I'm mad that even though you inserted yourself into my personal life, you kept me out of yours." She gestures down the couch. "You kept it from all of us."

My shoulders sag. "I know." I feel my throat tighten and the telltale burning behind my eyes, that warns of tears. "I'm sorry."

"It's okay," Izzy's voice is quieter now. "We're just worried."

"I know, I know..." I scrub a hand over my face.

"Are you okay?" Katelyn asks. "What happened between you two?"

I let out a huff. "A lot. *A lot* happened with Sebastian. And before I tell you everything, I just want to say that when I first decided to keep this all to myself, I thought it was the right thing to do. I was trying to get Izzy to see how great Zach was, and I was afraid that my drama with Sebastian might distract from that goal. It was a stupid decision, but once I realized it, I was already in too deep. Then it got complicated. Really complicated."

"I wish you wouldn't have done that," Izzy says, looking guilty. "We could've handled it all at once. Together."

I give her a soft smile. "I didn't intend for this all to snowball so much, but I don't regret what I did if it helped get you and Zach together."

"Wait - " Katelyn holds up a hand. "When did this start?"

I cringe. "At that haunted house thing."

"What?!" they all screech back. Even Steph. She wasn't there that night, but she's heard about it.

"Seriously?! What the fuck, Meghan? That was like four months ago!" Katelyn throws her hands up. "I'm sorry for whatever happened last night to cause you to throw that drink at him, but I'm glad it did. Because I'm pretty sure your stubborn ass would have never told us!"

I shrug. "I'm sure it would've come out eventually."

Steph barks out a laugh. "You're such a brat. Start spilling."

"And don't even think about skimping out on the details," Izzy glares at me.

"Really, Izz? You have your own man now. Do you really want to hear about Sebastian's dick?"

"You've seen his dick! Were you guys sleeping together?" Katelyn is about ready to launch off the couch.

The flash of memory brings me back to the alley. Back to the best sex of my life. Back to Sebastian asking me to go home with him. Back to the bar. To the aftermath of the fight. And any remaining humor leaves my features.

"Izzy, it's all my fault. If it wasn't for me, that fight wouldn't've happened. I'm so sorry." I carefully set my coffee down, my hands are shaking as bad as my voice.

"What are you talking about?" Izzy is looking at me with confusion.

"Holy shit!" Katelyn's eyes are wide. "Did you sneak off with Sebastian that night at the club? I remember looking and not being able to find you."

I nod. "Yeah. We, umm, we went out back." They stay silent in my pause, and I know I need to just come clean. "Sebastian and I snuck out the back door, to the alley. The plan was, well I'm not sure what the plan was, but, we... Well, we sorta did it in the alley."

"Did what exactly?" Izzy is smirking now, ignoring the part about me ditching her that night.

I roll my eyes. "Sex."

"In the alley?" Steph asks.

"Yeah," I admit with a small nod.

The three stooges break out into giggles.

"It's not funny. It's my fault Izzy got hit that night." I lock eyes with Izzy. "We went to that club together. I ditched you for a stupid man, leaving you alone, and then that asshole fucking hit you. I never should've left."

"Meghan, it's not your fault." She holds up a hand to stop my rebuttal. "It's. Not. Your. Fault. That guy was a prick. If not me, he would've targeted someone else that night. At least with me, Zach was there to beat the ever loving shit outta him. I know how you think. It's how we all think. And I can understand why you decided to drag all that guilt inward, but please, let it go."

I just stare at her. How can she be serious?

"Meg." Katelyn's tone matches the sad look on her face. "Have you been beating yourself up about this the whole time?"

I bite my lip. How could I fuck up so badly?

I drop my head into my hands. "I fucked up everything, didn't I?"

Katelyn lets out an exaggerated huff. "Well, we're here

now. You don't have to deal with this shit on your own. But if you think details like *we had sex in the alley* are gong to cut it, then you are sadly mistaken."

I part my fingers to look up at Katelyn's smile.

Her expression falters. "I'm sorry we didn't figure this all out sooner. I wish you would've talked to one of us. I know I've been busy with Jackson, but you could've told me."

"This isn't on any of you. I'm the idiot who thought keeping it all bottled up would be okay." I shake my head. "And if our positions were switched, I'd be breaking into your houses, too."

This gets a smile back on Katelyn's lips. "It's not breaking in if I have a key."

"Uh huh, sure." I feel a weight disintegrate from my shoulders. "Okay, you want details, we need to go back a ways…"

Chapter 27

Meghan

"Then he said, *'What, afraid you'll fall in love with me?'* And, as you all witnessed, I lost my shit and threw my water in his smug-ass face."

"What a prick! I can't believe he said that," Izzy says, disgusted.

Steph agrees, but Katelyn is oddly quiet as she chews her lip.

I've told them the whole story. Every encounter. Every kiss. Every detail from the alley fuck. And just like the story, their reactions were all over the place. Sebastian and I really did have a bizarre "relationship."

Katelyn is still sitting with that *look* on her face, and I can't take it anymore.

"Alright, spit it out!" I demand.

"Well, I'm just thinking... " she trails off, but has everyone's attention. "Okay, so - hear me out. Guys can be really dumb sometimes, right?"

"Riiiight..." I reply.

"Well, it sounds like he liked to rile you up. And since you cut him off cold turkey for all those months, he probably thinks that you hate him. And being dumb, he probably figured that suggesting you might love him, *rather* than hate him, would get a reaction out of you."

"Yeah. And it worked. Because he said it like us being in love was the most ridiculous thing he could think of."

"Exactly," she nods. "And this hurt you *because* you have feelings for him, which is why you reacted so strongly."

"Again, yeah. What are you getting at?"

Katelyn grimaces. "So, let's say that you didn't love him."

"I don't love him." I snap back.

"Okay, sure. Keep telling yourself that. Anyways... let's say that you didn't love him. If he made that comment to you, and you didn't have feelings for him, what would you do?"

I just stare at her.

"I'll tell you what you'd do. The Meghan I know would just roll her eyes and laugh in his face. Because you would also find it the most ridiculous thing ever."

I mull it over and hate to admit that she maybe has a point. I groan and my shoulders drop.

"We already established that she flipped because she still likes him," Izzy says. "I feel like there's a part two that you don't want to say," she says to Katelyn.

"I... Okay, don't freak out on me, but I think your reaction might've told him exactly how you really feel. Even though you didn't spend a ton of time together, it sounds like he gets you." I feel dread start to creep into my belly as Katelyn talks. "I don't know him well enough to guess how he'll react, but I think it's safe to assume he now knows that you still have strong feelings for him."

Fucking Hell.

"Question." This comes from Steph. "What's his reputation like?"

Izzy cringes and answers quietly. "He's only ever been nice to me," her eyes dart over my way, "but I've heard he's a bit of a player."

The dread in my stomach turns into a ball of tar. "So, you're saying that he'd be super excited to find out that some girl he banged once, three months ago, is still hung up on him." I aim for sarcasm, but I just sound pathetic.

"That's just what I've heard. You never know how people really are," Izzy says. "He also has a rep for being a miserable jerk sometimes, but from your stories it sounds like he's a nice guy. And funny."

"Don't forget hot-as-fuck – " Steph helpfully includes. "Pretty sure I'm going to make my next hookup bang me in an alley. That shit was hot."

"Sounds kinda dirty," Izzy makes a face. "And not in the good way."

"Ha. Says the girl who got off in a photo booth in the back of a bowling alley. Right, *Sugar?*" Katelyn laughs.

Even with the ill feeling I have over last night's ordeal and potential repercussions, I feel more like me than I have in months. *This* is what I've been missing. Friendship, love, comradery. Why did I isolate myself for so long? I'm such an idiot for waiting.

"Oh, speaking of!" Steph bounces in her seat. "These damn hockey players seem to have a thing with nicknames..."

I think she says more but I can't hear her over my choking. Of course she'd ask this question, and of course she'd do it while I'm taking a drink of my coffee.

"Uh, that's a yes," says Katelyn, with a giant grin on her face. My silence makes her grin grow even bigger. "What is it? I bet it's great!"

When I don't respond they start guessing.

"Pumpkin."

"Red Hot."

"Princess."

"Puddin."

"Flower."

"Candycane."

"Goddess."

"Oh my god, stop!" I hold my hands up, biting back a smile. "This will show you how much of a dick Sebastian can be." I nod to the girls in turn - "You got Kitten. You got Sugar. Want to know what I got?" I cross my arms over my chest. "I got fucking *Banshee*."

There's a beat of silence, and I wonder if they heard me. Then all three of them break out into peals of laughter.

I slump back into my chair. "I need new friends."

Chapter 28

Meghan

DEAR DIARY,

I feel like a weight has been lifted off my chest. The breaking and entering, turned intervention, turned girls' day, was exactly what I needed. And exactly what I should have done *months* ago. I've officially learned my lesson. No more trying to deal with shit on my own.

The girls made me promise that I'd start going to games again, which is hardly a hardship. And - clearly, I'll see Sebastian at Katelyn and Jackson's wedding. But I honestly don't know what I should do when I do run into him again.

Sounds like over the last few months, while I was pushing my friends away, Zach and Sebastian were wedging themselves deeper into the inner circle. So no matter what, I'll be seeing him on occasion. That'd be an easier pill to swallow if I hadn't showed my straight flush of emotions by reacting so strongly to his *love* comment. Katelyn was right. I put my heart on my sleeve whether I meant to or not.

At least now I have something to occupy my mind for the

next couple of months. Katelyn dropped that bomb right before they left my apartment. She wants me to plan their wedding!!!

I couldn't be more excited!

And since rich people (aka Jackson) can't do anything *normal*, they're giving me all of two months to plan the thing. They picked a Friday night in the beginning of April, and they have the venue booked. And it's at the coolest place imaginable - the Science Museum. Apparently Jackson has an in with someone who works there. I'll meet with the guy this week so I can do a walk through and start planning out the details.

On face value, it sounds super nerdy, but it's going to be amazing. It's been a while since I've been, but they have everything from giant dinosaur skeletons to an anatomically correct human heart big enough to walk through. The wedding will be after business hours, so we'll have free rein. And an endless budget. I told Katelyn I'd do it for free, but she said Jackson insisted on paying my usual fee. And since he makes millions (plural) every year, I feel zero guilt at charging him the full rate.

This gives me two months.

Two months to plan a wedding.

Two months to get back in touch with the old me.

Two months to prepare for another meeting with Sebastian LeBlanc.

XoxoX

Chapter 29

Meghan

HAPPINESS FLOWS through my body as I stride into the Science Museum. This was one of my favorite places growing up, and I can't believe I get to plan a wedding here. *Eek!*

The lobby is large; full of screaming children, frazzled parents, and school field trip groups. Typical crowd for a weekday afternoon.

My gaze sticks on the life-size whale shark replica hanging from the ceiling. With the walls and ceiling covered in ocean murals, the entire lobby is meant to look as though it's underwater. And I love it.

I let out a contented sigh. I'm going to spend as much time here as possible during the planning process.

Shifting focus to the customer information center, I exhale and switch on my professional persona. Jackson apparently knows someone that works here, named Samuel, and he'll be helping me get the lay of the land. I don't know anything about him other than his name, so I'm treating this as I would any other New Client meeting. Once I get to know a client, I'll let my walls down a bit, but I don't want to scare off some prude with the *Full Meghan* if they aren't ready for it.

To go with the pro attitude, I dressed in my usual business casual: black skinny jeans (that stretch, obviously), a flowy cream silk top, a black blazer, my black feather earrings, and hair somewhat contained in a low pony. Knowing that we'd be walking around, I stuck with flat-soled black ankle boots. And because I don't like hauling a giant purse everywhere, I tucked my essentials into my totally awesome blue velvet backpack that's currently slung over my shoulders.

"Miss Morris?" a deep, but somehow vibrant, voice catches my attention.

Turning, I spot a handsome man with a wide smile walking in my direction.

I smile back - "Please, call me Meghan."

The man is tall, so it doesn't take long for his strides to reach me. Taking my hand, he shakes it vigorously. "Meghan. A pleasure. I'm Samuel. Jackson described you perfectly. A stunning redhead I was sure not to miss."

This guy oozes charm, but in a non-creepy way, and my smile grows.

Standing about a head taller than me, Samuel is slender and polished. He has jet black hair styled back from his face. His eyes are a fascinating shade of hazel. He's clean-shaven, and his royal blue Science Museum polo shows off his sleeve of watercolor tattoos. Something about the design seems familiar, but I don't want to stare. The shirt might be part of a uniform, but Samuel is all style with it tucked into his designer dark wash jeans, and matching polished brown leather belt and shoes.

"It's great to meet you, Samuel. I'm so beyond excited to be coordinating an event here."

Releasing me from his grip, Samuel brings both hands to his

chest. "I know, right? This place is to die for! And those love birds are the most disgustingly-adorable couple I've ever met."

I laugh as I roll my eyes. "I know. They're the worst. I don't think Jackson told me how you two know each other..."

Samuel waves away the implied question. "He knows my brother. *Who cares.* I want to know about you! I hear you and that precious Kitten have been friends for ages."

The way he said Kitten made it sound both sexual and endearing. I can tell that I'm going to like Samuel a lot. And I think it's safe to be myself around him.

Chapter 30

Meghan

"Shut up, you did not?!" I'm dying for breath as I laugh at Samuel's latest tale.

I don't know how we got on the topic of PDA, but he's telling me the story of getting caught with his college boyfriend, mid thrust, by his mother, in his childhood home, and it's fucking hilarious.

"Hand to Jesus, they were supposed to be at the cabin all weekend." He shakes his head wiping away his own tears of laughter. "I couldn't look my mother in the eye for months. *Months!* I mean, she's one of the most open-minded people you'll ever meet, but - gay, straight, or otherwise - no one wants to see their son balls-deep in a stranger, bare ass glistening with sweat, wearing a leather vest and cowboy hat."

I clutch my stomach as I let out another laugh. "Seriously? Why the outfit?!"

"You think mine was bad. Crazy Eugene had one of those rubber horse masks on."

A strange sound falls out of my mouth, and I have to close my eyes and cross my legs to stop from peeing myself.

"Not my choice, okay!" Samuel pleads for me to believe. "It was his idea! Something he'd always wanted to do, and who am I to deny a man his dream?" He sighs. "He was weird, but he was a sexy, sexy man."

I open my eyes to peek up at him. "What did you do when your mom walked in?"

Samuel gives me a *look*. "I sure as fuck didn't finish."

I break up again.

"You try keeping a woody with the sight of your mother's horror burned into your retinas. She didn't even say anything. She just opened the door. Screamed. And ran down the hall. Thankfully, I dismounted immediately, since the next thing I heard was the sound of my dad running towards the commotion."

"*Dismounted?*" I choke out.

He smirks.

God, why does that smirk look so familiar?

"Well, we were really wedged in there... " Samuel shakes his head. "That lower bunk was not as spacious as I remembered it being."

"For real, stop. You did *not* do this in a bunk bed?!"

"True statement. My twin and I shared those bunks growing up. Once we hit high school, we both moved down into the basement, but for whatever reason my mom kept that room the same." He raises a hand. "Don't ask, okay. I don't know why Eugene wanted to try out his little horsey fantasy in my old bed. If I overthink it, I'll get weirded out."

"Yeah, because *that's* the weird part." I dab at my eyes and straighten up. "Okay, I need to find a bathroom before you tell me another story and I pee my pants."

"Can't have that. Follow me." He grabs my arm, guiding me down the hall. "Now tell me, have you ever been caught?"

"Thankfully no. And I hope to keep that track record."

"Oh, come on. That's no fun."

"Hey, I have plenty of fun! The last time I had sex was actually in public. Not my fault that no one found us."

Samuel grins as he looks me up and down. "When you say public..."

I make a face. "Uh, it was in an alley, behind a club."

He bursts into laughter. "Damn girl! That's some kinky shit."

I snort. "So says the horse fucker."

After leading me to the ladies room around the corner, Samuel promises to wait for me in the hall. Then we'll go up to the main ballroom space where the dinner will be held.

Washing my hands, I check my makeup in the mirror. All my laugh-crying has smudged some of my eyeliner, so I use the tip of my finger to fade it into a smoky look.

Staring at my reflection, I try to figure out why it feels like I've met Samuel before. I know I'd've remembered him if we'd met before. There's just something about him... I dry my hands and shake off the feeling.

"Alright, I'm ready to see the crowning jewel." I state, striding up to Samuel.

"*Fabulous -* " he rubs his hands together. "You're going to love this space."

As we walk to a private elevator, Samuel tells me all about the event space on the top floor. "With the right set up and lighting, you can turn the room into literally anything you want. I've seen everything from a circus-themed fundraiser to a black tie gala, and they both fit perfectly in the space." Samuel hits the up button. "We have a list of vendors for you to choose from, but - since I am the general manager here..." He buffs his knuckles on his chest, "I can look the other way if you have some special connections that you'd rather use."

I smile. "It's all about who you know."

Sleet Banshee

The elevator arrives, and we step in. Samuel swipes his employee card, selecting the top floor. "I'll gladly be your secret insider, Baby."

I smirk at his use of the word *Baby*.

Samuel looks like he's about to say something else, but the doors slide open and his eyes widen. He holds a finger up to his lips.

There's a man standing a few yards away with his back to us. His head is down, and his shoulders are hunched forward as if he's looking at something on his phone.

Quietly, I follow Samuel's lead, but it only takes me two steps before I recognize that broad frame, that mane of black wavy hair, that perfect ass, currently clad in worn jeans.

I freeze.

Samuel is quickly and silently sneaking up on Sebastian, while I'm stuck in a frozen state of shock.

Why the hell is Sebastian here?

And what the hell is Samuel doing?

For half a second I wonder if maybe Sebastian's gay, but then I remember his fascination with my tits. Okay, not gay. Maybe, bi? *Oh my god, is Samuel one of his lovers?*

Samuel throws an arm around Sebastian's neck and drags him down into a headlock, exclaiming, "Baby brother!"

Chapter 31

Meghan

B*ROTHER?*

"Brother?!"

At the sound of my voice, Samuel turns to face me, pulling Sebastian with, still trapped in a headlock.

"Babydoll," Samuel says, mussing up Sebastian's hair, "allow me to introduce you to my sweet, darling little brother."

"Sebastian." I don't mean to whisper his name, but that's how it comes out.

Sebastian hooks an arm around Samuel's waist, crouches, and reaches his other arm behind Samuel's legs. Sebastian stands, now holding his brother in a bridal carry, forcing Samuel to release his headlock.

Samuel tosses his head back laughing. "You're such a goddamn brute!"

Sebastian's eyes are locked with mine. "Hey, Banshee."

That stops Samuel's laughter. "Wait, what?" He looks back and forth between Sebastian and me. "Meghan is your Banshee?!"

His Banshee? He's talked about me to his brother?

Sebastian drops his hold on his brother, and I'm more than a little surprised when Samuel sticks the landing. This must not be the first time they've done that particular move.

Samuel walks up to me, placing a finger under my chin, pushing up. Effectively shutting my mouth, which I didn't realize was hanging open.

My eyes follow his arm. His tattoos. I look over at Sebastian's forearms. His hoodie sleeves are pushed up and bunched around his elbows, exposing the decorated flesh. Well, I'll be damned. The whole cuff of their tattoo sleeve is the same, only Samuel's is done in watercolors and Sebastian's is more graffiti in style.

Sebastian steps closer until they're standing side by side. And fucking hell. *Twins.* Not identical, but pretty damn close.

Samuel is slender, where Sebastian is buff. Samuel is clean-cut where Sebastian is tousled. Samuel's eyes have that touch of green, where Sebastian's are all dark. It's like having life-size versions of those angel and devil characters that you see in cartoons sitting on your shoulder, murmuring ideas into your ears.

"Did she just call you the Devil?" Samuel stage whispers to Sebastian.

Fuck, did I say that out loud?

"Wouldn't doubt it. She did toss that drink in my face."

"That was her?!" Samuel laughs and slaps his thigh. "This is total gold!"

I shake my head. "What... I feel like I stepped into a Bizzaro World."

"It's too much LeBlanc hotness in one location, right?" Samuel says with a wink.

A laugh bubbles up my chest, and I try to hold it back, but that just causes it to come out as a squawk. I give the universal *give me a moment* hand signal and walk away to gather myself.

This is just. freaking. perfect. Of *course* my new contact, at the best venue in town, is the twin brother of my... My what? My lover. My ex-lover. My tormentor. The man who goes from hot to cold, to hot, to frigid. The man I'm fighting not to fall in love with.

I shake my head to clear it. I'm not gonna try to figure out what we are to each other. I'm just going to carry on like I'm cool. Like I'm totally fine with all of this.

Continuing my stroll around the space, I work to take in the details. The room really is fantastic. Two walls boast full-length windows looking out over downtown St. Paul, and one wall of windows looks down into the museum. From here you can see part of a dinosaur skeleton, a full-size model of the Wright Flyer, and a three-story pipe organ. Then there's the ceiling, or lack thereof. The entire roof above the room is glass, currently showcasing a bright sunny sky, but I can just imagine it at night. Nothing but stars above while you dance on the hardwood floors. It's perfect.

"Meghan." Sebastian's voice is soft behind me. "Sorry, I didn't mean to catch you off guard like that."

I slowly turn to face him, one brow arched.

"Okay, so maybe I did. But..." He shrugs. "I wanted to talk to you."

"You have my number," I remind him.

"Yeah, and I'm nearly certain you wouldn't have picked up my call."

I purse my lips as I pretend to think about it. "You're probably right."

He gives me a slow smile. "It was nice seeing you last week." He steps closer. "But I was hoping we'd have found some time to talk."

Damnit, he's being nice.

I sigh. "I'm sorry about throwing my drink in your face." I don't sound sorry.

His smile grows. "You're not sorry."

I roll my eyes. "Obviously. You were being a jerk. You had it coming."

"See, how on earth could I be done with you? You're just too much fun to be around. I never know what's gonna happen."

He steps closer. The look on his face turns predatory.

I step back.

He steps closer.

I step back.

"Keep running, little Banshee. I'll always find a way to hunt you down."

I'm trying to remember why I was mad at him, but his stupid closeness is throwing me off. Time to pay it back.

I shift closer, placing my hand on his chest.

His hand comes up to cover mine, and I almost lose myself in the warmth. But then I remember the smug look on his face a moment ago.

Biting my lip, I look up to meet his eyes, hoping I look seductive.

He leans down, and I reach up to place my lips next to his ear.

"When I first saw you here," I whisper, "I thought Samuel was your lover."

Sebastian rears back with a look of pure disgust on his face.

Priceless.

I don't know how, but I hold my shit together and slip past him, striding back to where Samuel is waiting with a shit-eating grin on his face.

"It's perfect," I tell him with a nod.

"Perfect indeed." He holds his arm out for me to take.

"Come join me in my office. We'll compare calendars and find a time for you to come back after hours."

"Deal."

As we walk back towards the elevator, Samuel calls over his shoulder. "Hurry up, Lover!"

Laughing, I swear I hear Sebastian grumble something about *fucking twin hearing*.

Chapter 32

Meghan

"Katelyn..." I use my best scolding tone.

"What?" she replies, full of false innocence.

"Don't get cute with me, you whore."

"How does one 'get cute' over the phone. Hmm?"

"What is *wrong* with you?! Don't you think a little heads-up would've been the nice, *friendly* thing to do? '... *Oh, hey Meghan,*' " I try to imitate her voice, "*... since we just had an A&E -style intervention with you last week about keeping secrets, I figured I should probably mention that Sebastian's twin-fucking-brother* is my connection at the museum!" My imitation wears off as my voice raises to a yell.

There's a pause. "Okay, but tell me you don't love Samuel."

I let my head fall gently against my kitchen counter in defeat. "Of course I love him. That man is pure happiness."

"And would you have gone if I'd told you who he was?"

"It's probably 50/50," I admit.

"And aren't you glad you went?"

"Ugh, yes *mom*."

"See? No harm, no foul. It's not like I set you up with Sebastian."

My chuckle is muffled, since my face is still pressed against my counter. "Didn't I mention? Sebastian showed up."

Katelyn's shrill sound of joy has me pulling the phone away from my ear and changing the audio to speaker.

"Holy crap, shut up!" she shouts. And I'm pretty sure I can hear her clapping. "You know what this means, right?"

"Like, yeah!" - I go full Valley Girl. "It means he's going to be like, a total - like - *pain in my ass.*"

"*Now* who's being cute?" I can 100% picture the smug face she's giving me right now. "It means... that he likes you."

"*Likes* me?" I scoff. "What are we, 12?"

"God, you can be such a dense bitch sometimes," Katelyn drops all pretense. "If he didn't like you. If he was all butthurt about you tossing that drink in his face. If his ego was sore about you blowing him off for three months. If he didn't still jerk off to the memory of you two boinking. Then he wouldn't go out of his way to crash your walk-through, *with his brother*, at the museum."

"Huh."

"Yeah, *huh.*"

"And did you seriously just say *boinking*?"

She ignores me. "Let me ask you this. Was he surprised to see you? Did you stumble into their weekly bro lunch or something?"

"No. Honestly, he didn't look the least bit surprised to see me."

"See?"

"Ugh. Yeah okay. You're probably right." I start to pace my kitchen. "Sebastian was waiting for us up in the event space."

More shrill sounds from Katelyn.

"Alright," I say. "I'm gonna need you to take it down about

a thousand notches. Just because he was there, possibly looking for me, doesn't mean anything spectacular. It's not like it was some declaration of love or anything. He might just be trying to get a replay of the alley scene. And he didn't say anything special to me when I left."

"What do you mean?"

"I mean, there was no "let's get together sometime," or "I'll call you," or anything like that. He was dicking around on his phone in the lobby while Samuel and I were in the office looking at schedules. And when I left, it was just *Goodnight, Banshee*, nothing more."

"Banshee." Katelyn giggles.

"Oh shut it, *Kitten*."

"Well," she sighs. "You never know. Maybe he'll call you. Or maybe he'll just appear again."

Chapter 33

Sebastian

"Shots!" My sister exclaims as she plunks down a trio of tequilas.

"Anna, what the fuck?" My hands raise in a WTF gesture.

"What?" She rolls her eyes at me. "Fine, be a giant pussy. Samuel can have yours."

"Damn right," Samuel says, slamming one of the shots.

"I'm not a pussy, you twat. I'm a professional athlete. I can't just get drunk whenever I feel like it."

She and Samuel turn to each other and mouth *I'm a professional athlete,* making mocking faces.

"Why am I even here with you idiots?" I look at the ceiling.

This place is the definition of a dive bar. That's even it's name, Dive. It's a piece-of-shit tiki bar, but it's not far from my sister's place, so we often find ourselves here. And as semi-regulars ourselves, the other locals tend to leave us alone, no longer starstruck at my appearance.

Thankfully, Anna looks just as much like a LeBlanc as Samuel and I do, with jet black hair and olive skin, so everyone knows we're family. There's nothing creepier than someone asking you if you're dating your sister. The three of us sitting together leaves no doubt that this is a table of relatives.

It's a shame Curtis is busy with his own set of twins tonight. As the oldest, he's always been the most sensible. I could go for some of his level-headedness to even out the upcoming conversation.

"We're here," Samuel smirks and taps the table, "because you want to know when your sexy little Banshee is going to be at the museum again."

"Wait, what?" Anna asks. "Rewind. What did I miss? I thought we were celebrating a work thing."

Samuel smirks. "In a roundabout way." He turns to face her, leaving me the odd man out. "My work definitely got more interesting since I got to witness our brother here swooning all over a girl, in my museum."

"I don't swoon," I grumble. But I don't know why I even bother, since they're both ignoring me.

Listening to my big-mouth twin retell the encounter with his guaranteed exaggeration is going to drive me mad, so I block them out while I scroll through various hockey scores on my phone until he winds down.

"And now he's begging me to tell him when Meghan will be back so he can stalk her some more."

I tune back in. "I don't beg, dickhead."

Samuel keeps his eyes locked with Anna. "Literal begging. Like - knees on the floor, weeping onto my shoes, *begging*."

Drama-queen Anna is eating this shit up.

"Sebastian," she whines, finally looking at me. "I can't believe I've lived to see the day when you have an actual girlfriend."

I toss my hands up. "She's not my fucking girlfriend. I like her. She's hot. I'd like to sleep with her again. End of story."

"Again?" Samuel narrows his eyes.

Fuck. I didn't mean to say that. Not that I was really trying to keep it a secret. We may swing for different teams, but Samuel's my twin and we normally share every graphic detail. Half the time, we're just trying to gross the other out. So I don't really have a reason for not telling him, other than the fact that I've been busy.

I sigh. "Yeah, well, there was this one time..."

"At band camp..." my sister chuckles.

I roll my eyes, but Samuel's staring at me like he's trying to see inside my brain.

Then his eyebrows fly up. "Wait! Please tell me you banged her in an alley."

"What the fuck?"

"What the fuck!"

Anna and I reply the same way, but our tones are very different.

Chapter 34

Meghan

HUMMING ALONG with my Mariah Carey throwback album blaring in my headphones, I jot down some notes on my clipboard. Clipboards may seem like a thing of the past, but sometimes it's easier to sketch out my ideas rather than writing. And they're super handy for writing on the move.

I've been wandering the museum for about an hour, and I'm well into my groove. Samuel said he'd be in his office to catch up on paperwork, but the main spaces are pretty much empty of people. I saw some cleaning staff earlier, but I think they're all wrapped up now.

The dinner and dance will be up in the event space on the top floor. But I'm searching out the best place for the ceremony, and all the must-have photo spots. Katelyn and Jackson are seriously going to have the most killer wedding album ever.

I walk into a dark room that's meant to immerse you in the universe. There are subtle spotlights on each of the planets suspended around the space. And there are little tiny lights embedded in the walls and ceiling, representing the stars.

Honey starts playing, and I bump up the volume another

notch. Something about nostalgic music just gets me in the zone. I jot down a few more notes, and my humming turns into a hum/sing combo. Mariah really has no equal, and no one should ever try to sing along, but I dare you to resist the pull.

Spotting Orion, my favorite constellation, on the far wall, I walk over and pull out my phone to take a selfie in front of it. It'll be dark and artsy and hopefully awesome.

Holding my phone out, I turn slightly to get the framing right. I've snapped a few shots when movement behind my phone catches my eye. The materializing form of a large man startles a scream out of me.

Instinct has me dropping my belongings and stepping back, but I don't make it far before I'm stopped by the wall.

Backlit by the hallway lights, the silhouette nears, sharpening. And it's motherfucking Sebastian!

As I curse the man for scaring the shit out of me, the song switches to *Hero*, nearly killing me with the irony.

The shock of fight-or-flight is too much for my body to deal with, and I sag back against the wall. Crushing my little backpack in the process, I let my knees bend until I've slid all the way down to the floor. My heart is still trying to beat out of my chest, and Mariah belting out *cast your fears aside* is too much. I burst into teary laughter and bury my face in my hands.

What a messed up life I live.

My fingers are still trembling from the adrenaline jolt when large hands gently grip the outside of my thighs. I let out a few more shaky laughs before I raise my head, using my fingertips to quickly wipe away my tears before meeting Sebastian's gaze.

When I do, instead of seeing a smirk, I see a concerned look scrunching his features. He's crouched in front of me, lips moving, and close enough that his knees are nearly touching mine. I let out one more deep breath before pulling my earbuds out, releasing me from the clutches of Mariah's voice.

"I'm so sorry," Sebastian's voice sounds even deeper than usual. "Are you okay?"

"It's okay. I'm fine." I put my hand over his, where it's remained on my thigh, and squeeze. "Really."

As his eyes trace over my face, I'd swear his expression shifts to anger.

What the hell could he be mad at me for?

"I made you cry - " he growls the words.

Ah, he's angry at himself.

I shake my head and smile. "No, big guy. Mariah did that." When he continues to glare at me, I wave him off. "Never mind. You didn't make me cry, but you did scare a decade off my life."

I lean forward to shove him in his chest, but he just catches my hands.

"Come on." He rises, and - keeping his grip on my hands - pulls me up to standing with him. "I'd like a do-over. Ya know, without the screaming and tears." He gives my hands a squeeze. *"Hey, Banshee. Fancy meeting you here."*

He's so damn adorable like this.

I fight hard to keep my grin at bay, and I roll my eyes, pretending the honey badger bopping around in my ribcage isn't making goo-goo sounds at him.

"Oh. *Hi,* Sebastian. How on earth did you find me here? It's almost like someone must have told you where I was."

He leans in and whispers, "I have someone on the inside."

"Ooo, *the inside.* How scandalous. Sounds like you're in the mob or something."

"*Or something.*" He smirks.

Letting go of my hands, Sebastian turns around before bending to pick something up from the floor.

I don't look at his ass.

Not for too long.

"I think you dropped this," Sebastian holds out my phone.

"Ah, yes. I meant to do that. I always toss my phone when I'm done taking stupid selfies."

"Not stupid. Bet those pictures are gonna be cute as hell."

"Yeah, right."

"Well, let's see."

I laugh.

He gestures to the phone now in my hand. "Come on, I wanna see them."

I *am* a little curious to see how they turned out, so I unlock my phone and pull up the photos. "Hmm. Not terrible."

Sebastian steps up behind me so he can look over my shoulder at the screen. The first pic is actually pretty good. The light blue hue of the room gives me an angelic glow. Totally believable. The second pic has the background more aligned. The third, my smile is gone, and I'm looking past the camera. The fourth pic is a little blurry and my mouth open in a scream. I clearly didn't mean to take that one.

"Eesh." I shudder.

"Snipe." Sebastian reaches over my shoulder and snatches my phone.

"Hey!"

He turns his back to me and holds the phone high above his head, well out of my reach.

"What are you doing? Give that back!"

He spins as I circle him, keeping his back to me. "Just a moment," he sing-songs.

He's such a cock.

I grab a hold of one of the belt loops in his jeans, so he can't turn away, and step around so we're chest to chest. Or close to it, with our nearly foot height difference.

"Give it back, you oversized dick."

"That's right, Baby. You know it's oversized."

"Oh my god, that's not..." I reach up and pinch his nipple.

Instead of jumping back, he groans. "Do it again." He's using his husky voice, and I feel the rumble go straight to my core.

I don't know if I want to laugh or moan. But I'm nothing if not obedient, so I do it again. Only a lot harder. And with both hands.

Sebastian drops his arms to encircle me, which is exactly what I was hoping for. I quickly snag my phone from his grip and dart from his reach.

"What were you doing?" I ask, walking backwards, scanning through my phone.

"A little thing called *you'll see*."

"Wow. Super mature."

"Says the girl who just gave me a titty twister."

I snort. "Yeah, at your request."

I look up in time to see him adjusting himself. It should weird me out that he enjoyed that, but I like it.

Sebastian clears his throat, and my eyes snap up to him. I'm not sure which one of us should be embarrassed. Me, for staring at his junk, or him, for getting hard. It's a draw.

I change the topic. "What're you doing here?"

"Bringing you coffee, obviously."

I raise my eyebrows, holding my hands out.

He grins and strides past me towards the entrance of the room. Near the doorway, I see two to-go cups of coffee sitting on the floor.

"Ah, yes, obviously," I nod.

Picking them up, Sebastian gestures towards a bench out in the lighted main hallway.

Looking around, I find my clipboard and other discarded items before following Sebastian. Dropping everything into a pile at the end of the bench, I remove my backpack and store away my earbuds.

Sitting, he hands me one of the cups. "Dark roast with a splash of cream."

"How'd you know?" I take the cup and sit next to him, then remember. "Oh right, our da..."

Shit. Fuck. Damn. I almost said date. Well, more than almost. I said it. Half of it. *Shit.* It wasn't a fucking date.

I feel him shrug next to me. "I'm good at remembering details."

I hum in agreement and busy myself with taking a sip, glad he's ignoring my poor choice of words.

We sit quietly, both pretending to be immersed in our beverages before Sebastian breaks the silence.

"So... was that *the* Mariah Carey you were singing along with?"

I groan. "You heard that? Can't we just erase the last few minutes from memory?"

"Sorry, Banshee. Had I known what I'd walk in on, I'd've been recording. That shit would've made a great personalized ringtone for when you call me."

I backhand his chest. Lightly, so as not to arouse him. "Ass."

He chuckles.

"And how is it you recognize Mariah Carey that easily?" I ask.

"I have a sister, who I think is right around your age. However much you listened to Miss Carey, I guarantee Anna listened to it more."

"That's a lot of Honey."

"Fucking right it is. Can't stand the shit, but I could probably recognize any of her songs after only a few notes."

"Well your sister must have great taste. I bet I'd like her."

He turns his body towards me, so I do the same.

"I'll do everything in my power to keep you two away from each other." He's trying really hard to portray how serious he is.

I smile. "I don't know, I mean I've already become besties with your twin. Which, by the way, I'm a little shocked you left that detail out when we were talking about siblings the day you stalked me at the grocery store."

"Stalked? I thought it was a date." He smirks.

My cheeks heat.

"And I did tell you about Samuel," he continues. "I told you I had two brothers and a sister."

"Yeah, okay, *technically* you told me about him. But I would think that being a twin was kind of a big deal."

He shrugs. "It is. I mean we're close and all, but we're all close with each other. Samuel and I definitely have more shared stories, sharing a womb, then a room for so many years, but we try to not gang up on Anna and Curtis. Unless, of course, they deserve it."

"Yeah," I chuckle. "I heard about your shared room. And how Samuel defiled your bunk beds."

Sebastian's laugh is loud and deep.

God he's hot.

"I can't believe he told you about that."

I grin at the memory. "Honestly, me neither. It was good bonding, but I don't know how we got on the topic."

Sebastian arches a dark brow. "Is that when you told him about us fucking in an alley?"

I open my mouth, but no sound comes out. Just a puff of air.

"That's what I thought," Sebastian says smugly.

"I never told him *who* I had sex with. I could've been talking about some other alley fuck I've had."

Sebastian narrows his eyes. "Make a habit out of it, do you?"

"Make a habit out of stealing girls' panties?" I toss back.

He just smirks.

The thought of him with another girl makes me want to claw his eyes out, so I busy myself by slipping my backpack back on and picking up my clipboard.

"Well, thanks for the coffee."

"You're welcome."

I rise. "I should get back to work."

He stands. "Okay."

Okay. I give him a little smile and nod and start to walk away. On to the next exhibit. Back to reality.

Except Sebastian is following behind me.

"Umm, what are you doing?" I ask, over my shoulder.

"Working."

"Working?"

"Yeah, Jackson asked me to supervise you."

I stop. "Uh, pardon? *You* supervise *me?*"

"Yep." He leans over, trying to read off my clipboard, so I hug it against my chest. "He said, 'Please watch over Meghan. She's crazy and I want to make sure my wedding is tasteful.'"

My jaw drops. "He said that?!"

Sebastian stares at me for a beat. Then the corner of his mouth ticks up. "No."

"What do you mean, *no?*"

"I mean *no*, he didn't say that. I'm just messing with ya. But he did tell me I could involve myself if I wanted to. You know, be around to help make it easier on my brother and his workload."

"Easier on your brother." I give him my are-you-fucking-kidding-me face.

"You know how Jackson is." Sebastian rolls his eyes. "He's all considerate and shit. So he didn't exactly take into consideration the fact that Samuel is having the time of his life working with you."

"And yet, here you are," I gesture to him.

"How could I pass up such a golden opportunity to see the museum after hours?"

I place my fisted hands on my hips. "Pretty sure you could do that any time you want."

"Perhaps. But the company right now is just so pleasant."

"You're unbelievable."

"Say that again." He steps closer. "In your *sex* voice."

I laugh and shake my head.

"So, what's next on the checklist?" Sebastian stands up straight, trying to look professional.

I give him a slow once-over. He's wearing another pair of perfectly fitted jeans, and a black long-sleeved shirt that looks like it might be a size too small with the way it stretches over his chest muscles.

"This is how you dress for a management position?"

"What?" He holds his arms out and looks down at himself before giving me a pointed look.

It's then I realize that our outfits are alarmingly similar. I'm also in a pair of fitted jeans. And a black, cotton, long-sleeved V-neck shirt. The only difference is my blue tennis shoes, matching my blue velvet backpack, to his solid black skater shoes.

He gently tugs on one of the curls framing my face. "I'd say I dressed perfectly for this role. It's almost like we were meant to do this together."

I like that statement a little bit too much. I don't want to read into it. But, he is here. He did come out of his way to show up. Again.

I really should just be an adult and ask him what exactly he wants. Does he want to date? Does he want a fuck buddy? Does he just want to be friends?

And what do I want?

Sex. I want more sex.

And possibly a relationship. And a happily ever after. And to win the fucking lottery.

I grind my teeth to stop myself from screaming out in frustration.

"I thought the wedding was going to be upstairs?" Sebastian's question brings me back to the present.

"It is."

"So, what are you doing down here?"

Deciding to be an adult, I explain to him about the set up, and what I'm looking for. He asks to see my notes, and since he seems genuinely interested, I show him.

I tell him about my photo ideas for the planet room. How we can get the entire group of wedding attendees on the main three-story staircase, and how cool that'll look with the bride and groom at the top.

Katelyn and Jackson decided to not have a wedding party, so that allows for more creativity on my end. Plus, it means I won't get stuck buying some dumbass dress that I'll never wear again. I don't care what color it is, or how cute it is. It'll always be a bridesmaid dress.

We make our way to the human body exhibit and spend way too much time touching everything and examining the thin sliced sections of the human body.

It's fascinating and disgusting and like every other time with Sebastian, I'm loving every second. When I see him around other people - in front of the press, with fans, even with most of his teammates - he's always so serious. So cut off. But - with me - he's funny, and clever, and he laughs at my jokes. He hasn't been outright flirty, but he's always nearby. And he's found plenty of reasons to put his hands on me. Turning me to face something. Halting me with a hand on the shoulder. Guiding me with a hand on my lower back.

His touches have to be deliberate. I'm about ready to start panting, I'm so turned on from all the proximity. But he's acting like he's not even affected. I wonder if he knows what he's doing to me.

"This exhibit is cool, but I think we can both agree that this isn't wedding appropriate... " I say, needing to get us moving. Hoping the walk will help to cool me off.

"Fair enough." Sebastian says as he follows me towards the stairs. "But I can promise you that I'll be sneaking down here for some sweet selfies the night of."

"I hear nothing." But I can already picture myself sneaking off with him.

Leaving the bodies behind, we make our way to the lowest level.

I spread my hands out and spin around. "This. This is where we'll do the ceremony."

Sebastian looks around as his smile grows. "Yeah. There's no better choice."

"Right?" I smile back. I gesture to a spot in front of us. "Katelyn and Jackson can stand right there. It's perfect."

Standing side by side, Sebastian and I look up at the full-size brontosaurus and tyrannosaurus rex skeletons.

He chuckles. "Beauty and the beast."

Chapter 35

Sebastian

WATCHING Banshee sway her ass around the museum for the past hour has left me in a constant state of hardness. I don't know what it is about this girl that just completely zaps my brain, but I can't get my shit together when I'm with her.

I've been trailing Meghan through the dinosaur exhibit like a horny shadow. Getting close to her whenever I can. Reading over her shoulder. Sniffing her hair. You know, normal shit.

If I was an actual adult, and not a man-child, I'd just sit her down and talk to her.

I like Meghan. I like spending time together. And I definitely want to spend more time with my cock buried deep inside of her. And unless I'm reading this entirely wrong, I think she's down for all that too.

But I haven't asked her. Because I'm a giant pussy.

I'm not worried she'll slap me when I tell her I want to fuck her again. But I think there's a good chance she'll smack me when I tell her I don't want a relationship. It's nothing personal, I just don't have the time right now. Or the desire to mess up good sex with a bunch of complicated feelings. And as chill as

Banshee is, she's still a female. In my experience, even when that conversation goes okay, in the end it all crashes and burns.

Fuck buddies. That's what I do.

I think Megs and I would make great buddies. But what if I ask and end up ruining what we do have? I think I'll stick with *ignorance is bliss* for as long as possible.

Banshee's laugh pulls me out of my daydream, and I find her in the next room standing in front of a large display.

Walking up behind her, I see we're in the *Early Man* exhibit.

"What's so funny?"

"This guy," she points to the life-size primitive male in front of her. "He looks just like my college boyfriend."

I look at the figure and feel a wave of discomfort. It takes me a moment to place the feeling, and I'm disgusted when I realize that I'm feeling jealousy. Towards *him*. The fucking plaster-filled prehistoric man. *I really do need to take looking for a therapist more seriously.*

Meghan moves down to a display showing a group of males hunting a wooly mammoth.

She starts to read aloud, "... while their hunting skills sharpened throughout the centuries, language as we know it didn't evolve until a couple hundred thousand years later."

"Interesting," I murmur.

She shrugs. "Figures. Oral skills don't seem to be all that important to the males I've known."

I feel my growl more than I hear it as I press the front of my body against her back. For a split second, she tenses, before she melts into me.

"Banshee." I lean in and press my nose into her hair, taking a deep inhale. "You should've worn a dress."

I have so many mixed emotions right now. I don't want to think about her with other men. But I'm happy they sucked at pleasing her, because I can't stand the thought of her coming on someone else's face. But then I'm also angry that she hasn't been getting the pleasure she deserves. And I'm annoyed at her for being with idiots that didn't know how to appreciate her.

But in the end all I can think about going down on her, and it's sending all of my blood straight to my dick.

I slide my hands around, gripping her hips, and pull her ass tight against my erection.

Meghan tips her head back against my chest as she arches into my grip, grinding her lush curves against my hardness. "Dress?"

"Yeah, Megs. A dress." I drag my teeth across her exposed neck.

"Why?" She groans.

"Because then I could get on my knees, put my head up your skirt, and lick your sweet pussy until you were too weak to stand. I can't have you thinking that my entire gender is worthless."

Never breaking contact, I slide my hand from her hip and cup her sex.

"Fuck, I can feel the heat rolling off you." I kiss the side of her jaw. "Tell me," I increase the pressure against her core, "are you wet for me?"

I move my hand up a few inches, with the intention of slipping it down the front of her jeans. The thought of her wet and ready has me twitching with need, and my restraint is fraying.

My fingertips just pass the band of her pants when she pushes my hand away and spins to face me. I think she's going to shove me. Or punch me. But as is her habit, she takes me by surprise.

Gripping the front of my shirt, she pulls my mouth down to hers for a ferocious kiss.

My body knows how to react, even if my mind hasn't caught up.

My hands tangle in her hair, tipping her head back even more so I can plunge my tongue into her mouth. Her hands are roaming my chest. Nails scraping down my abs. Every touch sends another jolt of need to my cock.

A sharp pinch to my nipples makes me break the kiss, tipping my head back on a moan.

Taking advantage of my position, Banshee reaches up and grabs a fistful of my hair. She must be on her tip-toes, since I can feel her lips feathering over the base of my throat. She tugs a little harder, keeping my head tipped back.

"Lucky boy," she whispers, lips brushing against my pulse. "You don't need a skirt to sample my oral skills."

At the same time she lets go of my hair, I lose the feeling of her body pressed against mine. Not realizing I'd closed my eyes, I open them.

And my heart damn near stops when I see she's dropped to her knees.

"Fuck - " I breathe out the word.

It's a statement. And a prayer.

Not wanting to pressure her, I ball my hands into fists at my sides.

Meghan reaches out and runs her palm down my stiff length over the denim. My gaze pinballing between watching her hands and watching her face.

Her eyes haven't left where my cock is pressing against my jeans.

She looks sexy as fuck. And turned on.

Meghan bites her lip as her second hand comes up to help undo the button.

Slowly lowering my zipper, she glances up at me.

My breathing is already so heavy I can see my chest heaving. I can't look away, and I can't think of anything to do aside from stare.

When the zipper's all the way down, she breaks eye contact.

Banshee's been sitting back on her heels, but she rises, so she's up on her knees. Like this, her height is perfectly aligned with where I want her most.

One hand tugs at the band of my boxer briefs, while the other reaches in and pulls me free.

I remind myself to breathe.

Her grip is gentle, slowly stroking my length, root to tip, with her fingers almost reaching around my thickness. I'm a big guy, and she's a small woman, with small hands.

Her other hand grips the base of my dick, holding me still.

I exhale on a groan.

Wanting to memorize every moment, I look away from the view of her hand on my dick, to see her chest rising and falling in sync with mine. My Banshee is wound up tight.

I watch as she leans forward and gently licks the tip of my dick.

The sound I let out is strangled.

Banshee looks up at me. Lips shiny. A smile tugging on one cheek.

Then she squeezes me, hard, and licks up the full length of the underside of my cock.

"Shiiiit." I clench my fists tighter.

Meghan hovers her lips around the girth of my cock. Darting her tongue out to catch the spot of precum on my tip. But there's no pressure with her lips. No suction.

I'm about to lose my goddamn mind.

When her teeth graze over my tight flesh, I lose the tether completely.

"Baby, if you don't start sucking my co-"

Sleet Banshee

My words are cut off as Banshee takes me into her mouth. As far as she can go. The wet heat of her mouth closing around my length.

"Fuck... Yes..." I reach out and wrap both my hands in her hair.

I have full intention of letting her set the pace, but I need to hold onto something.

Meghan moans against the tug of my hands, and I feel the vibrations all the way up my spine.

Just as I think I won't last long if she keeps this up, she takes me deeper than I imagined she could.

I close my eyes and tighten my grip.

"Holy shit... That's it, Baby... Take it..."

One of her hands comes up to cover mine on the back of her head, and I think she's going to swat my hand away. Instead, she applies pressure.

"Fuck - " I groan. "You want me to take control?"

She hums in agreement and I damn near fucking come.

My phone vibrates in my pocket and I ignore it.

With one hand still holding the base of my cock, she braces the other on my hip. And I start to rock.

"There you go. Relax for me." I tell her, while memorizing the view as I slide back and forth through her lips.

This is the exact scene I fantasized about when I first saw Meghan. Remembering that moment, and feeling the reality of it now, engulfing my cock, gives me an added boost of control. I slowly guide her to go even deeper, then pull all the way back out of her mouth.

"Breathe, Baby."

"Don't call me Baby," she pants, running her nails up the length of my cock in warning.

I smile, and groan, because I'm a sick motherfucker.

My phone vibrates again in my pocket.

She looks up at me. "If you answer that, while I have your cock in my mouth, I'll use my teeth harder than even you'd enjoy." To punctuate her statement, she snaps her teeth and winks at me.

I smirk. "Pretty sure you have better things to do with that mouth than talk."

She laughs, but then she wraps her lips around my cock just how I want her.

I thrust, a little rougher this time.

"Good girl."

She may be on her knees, with my hand in her hair, but she's fully in charge of my body.

My phone vibrates again, but I barely feel it this time.

With Banshee's hot mouth on me, the tip of my cock bumping against the back of her throat, it will take a lot more than a phone call to make me stop.

My brother's voice over the intercom, however, does the trick.

"*I hate to break up the suck-fest, but I thought you'd like to know we have surveillance cameras. Everywhere.*"

Chapter 36

Meghan

CHOKING on a dick is a great way to make a bad situation worse.

The sound of Samuel's disembodied voice causes us both to startle. Sebastian's body jerks forward at the same time I inhale in surprise. His giant cock is already shoved further down my throat than I thought possible, and our combined response pushes him even deeper.

I don't have much of a gag reflex, but having something that size unexpectedly filling my airway causes a bit of a spasm reaction.

Thankfully, Sebastian pulls back just as I reach out to shove him away.

Hunching over I cough and massage my throat, trying to get my muscles to relax. Pretty sure having one of the LeBlanc brothers use a defibrillator on me right now would push me over the edge of embarrassment-induced insanity.

"Shit, Banshee. Are you okay?" Sebastian sounds breathless and worried.

I nod as I look up.

Then I cough on another inhale. "Jesus Christ, Sebastian! Put that away."

He's crouching in front of me, hard dick still sticking out of the top of his pants. The band of his briefs causing it to point straight to the sky.

Sebastian ignores me, leaving his dick to salute the sky, and cups my chin. "Are you okay?"

I roll my eyes, swatting his hand away. "I'm fine. Just suffering the side effects of accidently inhaling your stupid monster cock."

He smirks.

"Laugh it up, Blue Balls." I push up to standing and use my sleeve to wipe off my mouth. "Have fun with your brother. Please don't let that video get put online or anything."

"Wait, you're leaving?"

"Uh, *duh*." I snag my bag and rush up the stairs.

Sebastian's deep laughter echoes in the empty space. "An adventure as always, my little Banshee."

Chapter 37

Meghan

The rain stick of coffee beans announces my arrival in BeanBag.

"Meghan! How's it hanging?"

Really? Starting the morning with a dick innuendo?

I huff. "It's hanging *rigid*, Benny. Hanging really fucking rigid."

Approaching the counter, I see that his eyes are open wide and he's tilting his head to the side. Following his not-so-subtle gesture, I see a group of old ladies with their big red hats sitting at a table not far from the door. *Oops.*

"Benny, if you had any idea, you'd be pleased with my current amount of restraint."

"Copy that," Benny says with a snap of his suspenders.

I take in his attire: skinny jeans, tight flannel buttoned all the way to his throat, and the newest accessory.

"I'll take a large Sweet Vigorous, please - " I swipe my card through the reader. "And while you're packing that espresso, you can explain to me why you have suspenders on. Pretty sure those pants wouldn't fall down if you had them unbuttoned, unzipped, and you were slathered in butter."

"Are they too much?" Benny asks, with a cringe.

"No. Sorry," I sigh. "I'm being a bitch. They're cute. I mean they're hipster-as-hell, but cute."

"Cute?" Benny's cringe deepens.

"What?" I ask.

"Really?" he replies, tone flat.

"Yeah. What's wrong with that? I'm saying I like them."

"Okay so let's say you put on an ensemble..."

I hold my hand up - "*Ensemble?*"

"Shut up, I'm trying to make a point here."

"Okay, okay. I have my *ensemble* on," I run my hands down my sides.

Fairly sure he grumbles something about me being the worst, but he continues. "So, you get up in the morning, put on a new *outfit* that you think is great, and you run into a hot guy who says you look *cute*."

I smirk. "Did you just call me hot?"

"Meghan, you and I both know that you're a bombshell. You're also being a total taint right now."

I laugh. "Good insult. Okay, so I'm feeling like a bombshell and some dude calls me cute... "

"Yeah. Imagine it's someone like Ash. Do you want him to call you *cute*?"

I narrow my eyes. "Now why would you go and use him as an example?"

"Oh gee, I donno - " his voice is dripping with sarcasm. "Maybe because you two were spewing sexual tension at each other like a teenage boy with pre-ejac problems."

I fake a gag. "Oh my god! Can you not?"

"Perhaps, but I'm not wrong."

"Fair enough. But I can tell you one thing. If I was trying to look sexy, I probably wouldn't put on suspenders." I pause as I think about it. "Unless they were attached to a pair of lacy boy shorts, and that's it."

Benny has this glazed-over look, and I'm sure he's trying to picture it.

I reach over the counter to snap one of his suspenders, but he jumps out of the way. "Make my drink."

As I walk to my usual table in the front corner, one of the red hat ladies catches my attention.

"Excuse me darling, what's in a Sweet Vigorous? I like your energy, and I'm wondering if the drink is part of it."

I smile. "It's a triple shot topped with coffee and sweet cream. It doesn't tamp down my attitude, that's for sure."

"Careful, Gladys - " one of the other ladies says. "Pretty sure that drink would send you into AFib."

Gladys smiles. "If it gets me a man like that, I'll risk it."

She motions behind me, and I assume she's gesturing at Benny.

I chuckle. "Hey, we all have our type."

"Deny it all you want Banshee, but you know I'm your type."

Sebastian's deep rumble has me spinning around.

"Sebastian! What the hell are you doing here?"

"We have unfinished business."

My mind flashes to the last time I saw him, dick sticking out of his pants.

I glance around at the coffee shop we're standing in. "You can't possibly..."

He shakes his head and addresses the table of swooning hats. "You see ladies, I try to do the right thing, surprise my girl, and this is the reaction I get. I just can't win."

Then he pouts. He literally pouts. And my pussy nails an Open For Business sign on the front door.

Wait. Rewind. His girl?

"Oh, you poor thing," the old biddy coos, " ... you can come join me for comfort whenever you want."

"Hands off, Gladys!" I snap.

I reach out to grab ahold of Sebastian's sleeve, and that's when I really take him in. He's in black dress pants, shiny black shoes, a white button up with the top two buttons open, and a black dress coat tossed over his arm. When I realize his white shirt is thin enough to see his tattoos I start to salivate.

Holy. Fuck.

"Eyes up here, Banshee," he uses two fingers to gesture to his face.

I'm about to snark back when Benny calls out, louder than normal. "Meghan, your large Sweet Vigorous is ready."

Sebastian's eyebrows shoot up, and the ladies start to cackle.

My nostrils flare on an exhale as I stalk over to the counter.

Benny hands me my oversized mug with a grin, and I point at him - "One more word out of you and I'm going to strangle you with those stupid suspenders. I swear to god."

He mimes zipping his lips and walks away.

Sebastian's busy taking selfies with the Red Hats, so I pretend to focus on setting up my traveling workstation, but I'm really just watching him.

He really does know how to turn on the charm for the public. Not that he's not charming when we're alone, because he is, but when it's just us, he's more casual. More... sincere. The wide smile he has on now looks perfectly natural, but a part of me knows it's fake.

And I like it. I like that I know a different version of him than everyone else. It feels special. Intimate.

The sound of the rain stick draws my eyes to the door, and I'm shocked to see Izzy and Zach walk in.

Since he's only feet away, they spot Sebastian first. But the greeting between them doesn't show surprise. It's clear that they expected to see each other. Which is weird on top of weird. *What is going on with my life?*

Izzy hugs Sebastian, then turns to find me. She nearly skips in my direction with the boys following right behind her. Zach's dressed the same as Sebastian, his brown hair tamed a bit more than normal, and the details start to click in my brain.

I stand and greet Izzy with a hug. Her ice-blue wrap dress and bright blond hair have her looking like a sexy winter queen.

"Hey, Izz."

"Hey Meghan!"

I nod to the guys. "I take it the boys have some sort of team thing they're going to?"

"Yeah, Jackson and Katelyn should be here soon. Their publicity whatnot is just down the street from here. Katelyn and I figured we would find you in your normal spot and decided to make a girls' day of it."

I smile. "You guys do realize it's a weekday, right?"

She rolls her eyes at me. "I don't have any meetings today, and Katelyn just wrapped up a book she was working on last night. And since you're working on *her* wedding, our little coffee date will technically be work related."

She has me there.

"Hey, Meghan," Zach greets me as he steps up, then he turns to Sebastian. "Jackson just pulled up."

I give Zach a little wave before he pulls Izzy aside. Presumably to have some lengthy goodbye even though they practically live together now. They're so in love it's disgusting. And I have to tamp down on the jealousy that suddenly rises up in my chest.

A body I know all too well steps in front of me.

I drag my eyes up, looking at the handsome man standing

before me, and for once I'm not quite sure what to say. Watching Izzy and Zach's easy love has pushed me a little off balance.

I bite my lip. And not in a sexy way, but a nervous way.

The look in Sebastian's eyes builds on my sudden vulnerability. He's not smiling. Not smirking. Just staring.

"I'll talk to you later, Banshee." He leans closer to trace his thumb over my bottom lip, removing it from my tooth's grip. "Enjoy swallowing down that sweet vigorous."

I'm about to huff out a laugh when I feel his lips place a soft kiss on the top of my head.

What? No. He can't do that! That's breaking the rules. It's too much.

Straightening, Sebastian turns and strides toward the door.

My legs tremble and I drop into my chair.

Not wanting to watch him leave, I busy myself straightening my laptop until I hear the door open and close. Dropping my forehead to the tabletop, I let out an exhale.

Two chairs across from me are pulled out and I know that both the girls are here.

"Uh, hey Meghan," Katelyn greets me as she sits.

I raise a hand and wiggle my fingers at her.

Izzy's voice is suddenly filled with concern - "You okay?"

I lift my head, not bothering to hide the strain of emotion on my face.

"What happened? What did he just do?" Katelyn asks.

"He kissed me," I whisper, then point to the top of my head. "Here."

They both coo out sounds of adoration, while I drop my forehead back onto my keyboard.

Chapter 38
Meghan

"Ohmygod this is so adorable!" Katelyn squeals.

"No, not cute. Not Adorable." I jab my pointer finger in the air at each of them. "This is not good, you guys. This is not good at all."

"Aww, our little girl's all grown up and catching feelings," Katelyn says to Izzy.

Izzy's responding grin is so big I want to smack her. But I won't. Because, friends.

"*Catching feelings?* Really?" I reply, not amused.

"Oh, come on, what's so bad about that?" Katelyn asks.

I throw my hands up. "Everything!"

"Ah, of course. *Everything.* How did I not guess that?" Katelyn rolls her eyes.

"Come on, Meg - " Izzy's voice softens, "he's a good guy. And he clearly likes you too. I don't see what the problem is."

"The problem is that I don't want to care about someone more than they care about me." The honest admission catches me off guard. "*Fucking hell.*"

Katelyn reaches over the table and grabs my hand. "Meghan, you don't know that that's what's happening."

"It sure feels like it." It's an uncomfortable feeling, but saying it out loud helps.

"Have you talked to him about it?"

I shake my head. "No. I wouldn't even know where to start." I use my perky girl voice, "Hey Sebastian, I know we've only fooled around a couple of times, over the course of several months, but I'm pretty sure I'm falling for you. What do you think? Do you love me, too?"

"Why are you so afraid of falling in love?" Izzy asks. "If you recall, you pretty much shoved Zach down my throat."

Heat moves across my face at her choice of phrase.

Katelyn cocks her head as she looks at me. Probably wondering why the hell I look embarrassed. I wave it off.

"Go ahead and tell her," I sigh.

Katelyn keeps watching me as she speaks to Izzy. "Okay, so this is the CliffsNotes version. The first, and only, guy that Meghan's ever said the dreaded L-word to was in college. He said it back, along with all the other right things. They talked about marriage and forever and all that crap. Then she found out he was cheating on her pretty much the whole time."

Izzy's hand goes to her mouth. "Oh, no! Are you serious?"

"And then he dropped out, after stealing my laptop and the cash I had in my wallet." I lay the rest out.

"What a creep!" Izzy hisses.

"Pretty much," I agree. "I know it was a long time ago. And I know that he was just a piece-of-shit assbag. And yeah, I know it's not fair to project my baggage onto someone else. But... I don't want to be put in that position again. When you think you're both on the same page, only to find out that they're reading from an entirely different book. Not to mention sticking their bookmark between a bunch of other pages. It really fucking sucks."

Katelyn chuckles, then holds up a hand. "Sorry. You know I love a good book joke."

Izzy gives me a sad smile. "I get it. Really, I do. But why do you seem to think that Sebastian is reading from a different book?"

"Well, for one, he's a known player. Maybe he's not a total slut, but in his entire hockey career I don't think he's been in one actual relationship." I tick off another finger. "Two, the hot-and-cold signals he's given me have been all over the fucking board. Three, and most importantly, he made an actual joke about the idea of me loving him." I sit back in my chair and cross my arms. Feeling like I made a perfect argument.

They don't look convinced.

Katelyn holds up a finger. "One, *that you know of*. And even if he hasn't had a girlfriend in a while, it might just be that he hasn't met the right person. Two, men have mood swings even worse than women do. But since you've reconnected, I think he's been all hot signals. And three, men are idiots. They make jokes to get reactions. They don't think about the negative ramifications. You can't read too much into that one." When I think she's done she holds up another finger. "And four, what the hell had you blushing a minute ago? I have a feeling there's another piece of this puzzle that you haven't told us."

I purse my lips.

"Oh damn!" Katelyn grins. "What happened?"

"I'm not done talking about the *feelings* crap yet," I snark.

She rolls her eyes, but Izzy speaks up. "Can I ask you something?"

"Sure."

"If he sat you down and said he only wanted a casual thing.

Like no strings attached, just sex and whatever, but no labels. What would you say?"

I mull it over. "So, in this scenario he's basically asking me to be his fuck buddy?"

She thinks. "Yeah, I suppose."

"Can I demand that he only fucks me? No other buddies?"

Izzy shrugs. "I guess you could add that to the equation. I've never been a fuck buddy, so I don't know how that works."

"That's totally a thing - " Benny calls out from behind the counter.

We all turn to look at him.

"Benny, what the shit?! Privacy much?" I give him a WTF look.

"Geez, sorry. I wasn't trying to listen, you guys are just loud. And I thought, based off your recent question, you'd be happy to know that you can totally set rules like that with fuck buddies." He holds his hands up and starts to back away.

"Okay, hold up, FDR. You've already butted your way into our conversation, so spill it," I demand.

He smiles and tucks his thumbs under his suspenders. "I usually don't kiss and tell..."

"Benny, so help me god, I will come back there and squeeze that nozzle of small batch organic whipped cream up your nose until it comes out your ears." I punctuate my threat with a slap on the table.

I see him visibly swallow, but he starts talking. "Okay, so I've had a couple FBs." I roll my eyes at his abbreviation. "And the rules, so to speak, have always been different. If there's no conversation, then you treat it like a booty call - no rules, no limits. But there was this one FB that I went with for a while. We were both busy, and both recently out of relationships, so we didn't want to *date*, but we liked each other. We made the agreement that we'd be casual hook up buddies, but no sleeping with other people. If it got to the point where we were interested in other people, then we'd end our arrangement."

"Huh. Okay, thanks for sharing. Now please, stop creepin' on our girl talk."

"Yeah, yeah. You're welcome." He heads to the back room.

"Alright," the girls turn back to face me. "Back to Izzy's question," Katelyn says - "He wants to be FBs. What do you say?"

"FB? Can we not?" I shake my head, but consider the question. "Truthfully, if he agreed that we'd only be with each other during the course of said arrangement, then I'd say yes. I like him. I like spending time with him. And the smart part of me knows that this would be a stupid idea, but the other parts of me just want to have him however I can get him. And just hearing myself say that makes me want to lobotomize myself."

Katelyn lets out a large breath. "Honestly, I'd probably do the same thing."

"Me, too." Izzy says. "You can't help who you like."

I slump in my chair. "This is going to end badly."

"Oh come on, you're super lovable. And if he doesn't think you're absolutely fucking amazing, then he can go right to hell." Izzy pounds her fist down, and I almost laugh at her sugary outburst.

"Plus," Katelyn chimes in, "orgasms release endorphins and make us happy. And we like being happy. So, if nothing else, fuck buddies should be a sure-fire way to build a stockpile of happiness."

I snort. "Well, in that case leaving a guy hard and wanting might be counterproductive."

"Come again?" Katelyn asks.

"He sure didn't." I can't help it, I start to laugh. A lot.

The girls look back and forth between me and each other.

Katelyn leans closer. "Care to share with the class? Or is this you having a nervous breakdown?"

I take a gulp of my Sweet Vigorous, then speak quickly. "I gave him a blowjobinthemuseum and we got caught."

"Uh, what?" Izzy asks.

"Yeah, try that again at human pace." Katelyn leans closer.

I bury my face in my hands. "He found me at the museum last night, and one thing led to another. Long story short, I went down on him in one of the exhibits."

I spread my fingers to peek at the girls. They're both sitting there with their mouths wide open.

I continue, "It's normally not my thing."

"Blow jobs, or blow jobs in public?" Katelyn smirks, clearly over her shock.

"Either, I guess. But he was being all... *him*. And I didn't have a dress on." They both start giggling. "So anyways, I was, you know. And it was actually really fucking hot. Like, I didn't think *giving* could be that freaking sexy. Things were getting pretty heated, and I think he was close, but then we got interrupted."

Their giggles have grown in volume. "Who caught you, a security guard?"

I give it a beat. "His brother."

Chapter 39

Meghan

ONCE THE GIRLS settle down from my blow job story, we get into the details of Katelyn's wedding. Even with the oral detour last night, I still got everything I needed for planning. There are a few things left to square away, but after asking Katelyn a few quick questions, I think I'm set.

We decide to continue our day with some brunch at the little deli next door. The girls stand. As I start packing up my stuff, my phone rings.

"Go on and grab a table, I'll be over in just a minute," I tell them.

The girls leave, and I answer the call. "Hello, this is Meghan."

"Hi! Is this *The* Meghan, like from Meghan's Moments?" a chipper voice sounds from the other end of the line.

"That's me. What can I do for you?"

"You can save me, that's what." She laughs.

I smile. "I'll sure try! What do you need help with?"

"A silent auction. My organization is having its annual fundraiser and the planning was supposed to be done weeks ago, but Gwen left on maternity leave and no one realized she was the one who was supposed to plan this thing. So now we have just over a week and nothing but the venue is set." I can hear her big inhale when she finishes rambling.

"Well then, I'm glad you called. I can definitely help. And I have relationships with all sorts of vendors, so I'm sure we can make this specular within your timeline."

"Oh thank god! You're the best!"

"Wait until I actually do something to thank me." She sounds fun, so I feel comfortable being myself. "How about we start with your name, and when you can meet."

"Ha! Right, okay. Tomorrow'd be perfect. And my name is Annabelle."

After making arrangements to meet Annabelle, I pack up my things and rise to exit.

Walking past the front counter, I stop. "So, what ever happened with you and the girl you were exclusively a FB with?"

"Nothing." Benny lifts one shoulder in a shrug. "I kinda fell for her, she wasn't interested, and we broke it off."

My chest tightens.

Fuck.

Chapter 40

Meghan

DEAR DIARY,

The girls had a fucking field day hearing about my blow job blunder. I'd probably laugh until I puked if someone else went through that. But it wasn't someone else. It was me!

Honestly, I wouldn't mind getting caught by a stranger, because really, who cares. But getting caught by someone who I have to see again - not cool.

At least out of everyone I know, Samuel will probably be the most chill about it. Actually scratch that, he'll be a terror. But that's because he'll think it's hilarious. I can only pray that the cameras were aimed at Sebastian's back. That way the view wouldn't actually show anything. If they did show more...

Nope. Not going there.

Except... Except I'd pay good money to get my hands on that video. Honestly, I'm not really a blow job girl. I mean, I'm all for reciprocation, but it's usually done as a precursor to sex. A little foreplay. A little natural lubing up. But that..? That was going to be a full-on BJ. And it was hot. Like - Really. Fucking. Hot. Like, I went home and jilled off to the memory of sucking him off. I don't know why it was such a turn on. Probably something about having the power. I may have been the one in a submissive position, but I literally had him by the balls. And he was loving it.

I'm disappointed that we got interrupted. And I do feel bad about leaving him in such a worked up state. But I'm also not super bummed that I didn't have to swallow what probably would have been too much jizz. Eesh, gives me the chills just thinking about it. Swallowing in the heat of the moment is one thing but thinking about it after the fact is a touch gaggy.

Ack! Okay, *focus*. We're getting into the final wedding countdown and it's going to be amazing. And keep me busy. Not to mention the new gig I just got. Some chick named Annabelle. She sounded cool on the phone, so hopefully this will be a fun little project.

XoxoX

Chapter 41

Meghan

SEBASTIAN: Goodnight, Banshee. I know what I'll be dreaming about tonight. (Your sweet hot mouth. And killing my twin.)

Waking up to Sebastian's text this morning got me all flustered. I'm almost glad that I was asleep and didn't wake up when he sent it, since I probably would've responded with a request for phone sex. Which may not have been a terrible thing, now that I think about it.

Seriously, that man has my libido on speed dial, and I need to get him out of my mind. At least for the next hour or two.

Taking a deep breath of the chilly spring air, I mentally shake my thoughts clear and push through a pair of heavy glass doors.

Since we're short on time, I chose to meet Annabelle right at the venue. Their event is going to be at The Syndicate, a historic rehabbed hotel that overlooks the Mississippi River in downtown Minneapolis.

It's a gorgeous building with a lot of history. Rumor is there's a secret tunnel under the building that was used to supply the basement speakeasy during prohibition. Which was apparently run by the local organized crime family. And rumor atop the rumor is that the then head honcho of the Mazzanti family killed his brother somewhere in the building, then dumped the body in the river. But that's rumors for you. Probably a bunch of scandalous bullshit.

Having done events here before, I know my way around. There's an art deco feel throughout the hotel. Everything's been redone, but they stuck to the original design, and it's beautiful.

Stepping through the threshold into the infamous ballroom, I take in the details again. The space itself is large without being intimidating. Perfect for a decent-size event or wedding. The ceilings are about 20 feet high, and the wall opposite me is all windows, overlooking the river. The floors are shiny black tiles, with gold inlay, that reflect the light from the three elaborate chandeliers evenly spaced throughout the room. The walls are painted an antique cream and host ornate sconces to complete the lighting. On opposite ends of the room, the walls are covered in geometric metallic panels. They almost look like mirrors, but they refract the glow of the room rather than reflecting the image back and forth a million times.

I grin. This place is amazing.

The sound of heels clicking down the hallway pulls my attention back to the open double doors just as a stunning woman enters the room. She's on her phone and holds up a finger, with an apologetic smile letting me know she'll be a minute. Which gives me a moment to take her in.

Wearing a pair of heeled black ankle boots, she's about my height, and I'm glad I wore flats so I'm not towering over her. I'm also glad I decided to dress up a bit today, in a simple but flattering all-black ensemble. My only dash of color - yellow feather earrings - just so happens to match her bright yellow blouse. If I tried to wear that much sunshine, I'd look like that mobster's corpse after spending a night in the river. But on her - with her olive skin, sleek black bob, and leather leggings - she looks like a model. She's slim and beautiful, and I almost hope she's a bitch so I can hate her.

"Gah, sorry!" Annabelle says as she shoves her phone into her bag. "You must be Meghan, it's so fantastic to meet you!"

"Annabelle, I presume. And the pleasure's all mine."

I shake her hand and am happy to feel that she has a strong grip. Nothing grosser than a limp handshake.

"Thank you so much for coming on such short notice." She's beaming at me, and I swear she gives me a once-over.

"Thanks for meeting me here - " I gesture around the room. "This is one of my favorite spaces in the city; you won't need any decorations."

She laughs. "That's one thing off the list then!"

"It's a start!" I smile. "But don't worry, we'll make this fundraiser the talk of the town."

"Here's hoping," she puts her hands together, as if in prayer.

"I don't think I got the name of your organization yesterday."

Annabelle makes a self-deprecating sound. "Sorry, that's my bad. I was a bit of a headcase when I called you since I'd just found out about all of this. But I work for Snips. We're a non-profit and we work with different organizations throughout the Midwest to spay and neuter cats and dogs. They can be shelter animals or pets of families who just don't have the money." She sighs. "As you can imagine, the green dollar is our biggest need, so this event is huge for us."

"Huh - that's a pretty fantastic mission. I watched enough Price is Right as a kid to know it's important."

Annabelle chuckles. "I had a super-inappropriate crush on Bob Barker as a kid."

I laugh. "I'd love to unpack that, but since we're short on time, how about we just jump right into it?"

"Perfect. I'm all about cutting through the bull and getting shit done."

I smirk. "You and I are going to get along just fine.

For someone who claims to have been caught off guard, Annabelle sure has a handle on the details. We slowly walk around the room as she tells me how many they're expecting. What items are coming in for the auction. What sort of food and bar set up they'd like to have. And lastly, her desire for live music.

"I'm going to be honest with you," I turn to face her fully.

She meets my eyes. "Please."

I smirk. "This is gonna be a piece of cake."

Annabelle waits a moment, maybe thinking I'm joking. "Really?"

"Yeah, really. Like I said on the phone yesterday, I know people. And I mean that in a serious way, not a douchey way."

She laughs. "But the timeline, it's so soon…"

I wave her off. "I have a few favors I can cash in. If you trust me to make the right decisions for you, and give me the authority to make menu selections, things like that, we'll make this happen. I promise your event will go smoothly, your guests will have a great time, and I'll keep you on budget."

Annabelle gives me a deep curtsey. "I defer to you completely. You come highly recommended."

"I was meaning to ask, who was it that recommended me?"

"Oh, it was Sa… umm, I think it was Samantha, in the office. But you didn't work for her, it was someone she knew. But I don't know who… Sorry, that's not helpful!"

"No, that's fine. I just like to know if I should be thanking someone for the recommendation." I tuck my notebook into my bag. "Oh, and as far as the number of expected attendees, did those invites go out a while ago, or do you need help on that end?"

Annabelle shakes her head. "Thank the gods, Gwen sent those out before she left. We should be right on target, otherwise I'd probably be sitting in a puddle of my own tears right about now."

"Good thing, then. Too bad the event is next Friday. I know some of the Sleet players; I probably could've gotten some of them to come and bid on things."

Annabelle smacks a palm to her forehead. "Holy duh! Why didn't I think of that? We should've picked a different night. Too late now."

This girl is funny, and more than a little weird. "Well, you couldn't have known that Gwen would leave the planning unfinished, and that you'd hire me, and that I'd know some of the Sleet guys."

She looks confused for a moment, then rolls her eyes. "Wow, extra duh. I think I'm caffeine deprived."

I smirk. "I know a place that makes a mean latte."

Chapter 42

Meghan

Dear Diary,

It's official, I adore Annabelle. She's a freaking riot. Since she'd hitched a ride to The Syndicate, I gave her a ride back to her office, stopping at BeanBag to load up on caffeine. And I think Benny's heart fell out of his butt when he saw her. She is super sexy, so I get it.

By the time we got to her building we were in complete agreement to go with round foods for the event. Bahahaha! For real, this event is going to be the shit. And what says *Let's Neuter* like meatballs and cake pops. We'll be subtle about it, but the fun people will get it.

I'm really looking forward to this event, and not just for the testicle-shaped foods. I'm excited to spend more time with Annabelle. There's just something about her that makes me feel like I've known her forever. I've decided that it's one of those déjà vu Matrix situations, so I'm not going to overthink it.

Something else I'm not going to overthink: Sebastian. I never did respond to his text from last night. Maybe I'll do that now...

XoxoX

Chapter 43
Meghan

MEGHAN: Goodnight, Sebastian. I hope you enjoyed your dreams last night.
Sebastian: Little Banshee, you have no idea. But it doesn't compare to the real life experience.
Meghan: Real life, hmm? Maybe you need your own little drawer of wonders.
Incoming FaceTime call from Sebastian.
Declined.
Sebastian: WTF, answer my call.
Meghan: I don't think so, buddy.
Sebastian: I want to see what's in that "little drawer".
Meghan: That seems like an in-person thing. The camera won't do it justice.
Sebastian: What's your address?
Meghan: OMG, go to bed! You have a game tomorrow, remember?
Sebastian: Thanks for the reminder, mom.

Meghan: Anytime, sweet-ums.

Sebastian: So... are you coming tomorrow night? To my game.

Meghan: Yes. Now go to sleep.

Sebastian: One last question.

Meghan: What...

Sebastian: Do you sleep naked?

Meghan: GOODNIGHT, SEBASTIAN.

Sebastian: Night, Baby.

Chapter 44

Meghan

"You guys are such idiots. How did I let you talk me into this?"

Miles, my oldest brother, throws one arm around my shoulder and ruffles my hair with the other. "Because you love us."

I swat at his hand - "Get off me, Beast!"

He releases me and steps back, but Max - my next-oldest brother - steps up to my other side. Before he can do the same thing, I elbow him in the ribs.

"Seriously, you guys are the fucking worst!" I say.

"Hey! I'm behaving." This comes from Marvin, the baby of the family. "As promised," he says, pointedly looking at our brothers.

He may be the youngest, but the three of them have pretty much the same stats. They're all six feet tall. They all have medium length, medium brown hair, hazel eyes, and perfect grins. They look just like our dad, while I look just like our mom.

"Thanks, Marv. That's why you're my favorite."

Miles and Max scoff.

"That's also why he's buying," Max says.

"Yeah, I don't think so. I'm only paying for Meg. You jackasses can buy your own beer." Marvin pushes me ahead of him in line.

As much as I pretend to be annoyed, I'm actually really excited that they're at the Sleet game with me.

Being fans, they come whenever they can. But ever since Katelyn met Jackson they've been bugging me to get tickets. They all have jobs and could buy their own damn tickets. I think it's the idea of being a guest of the team that has them so jacked.

They stopped bugging me about coming to a game after my little confession about *the* Ash LeBlanc a few weeks ago. I think they were hung up between being starstruck that I'd hooked up with one of their favorite players, and disgusted that one of their favorite players slept with their sister. Not to mention, wary of dealing with my emotions.

We haven't talked about it since, but my guess is that sweet baby Marv will be the one to crack and ask me about it sometime tonight.

Collecting our beers and brats, we file down the stairway to our seats. I'm not sure if it was Katelyn or Izzy who scored these amazing tickets, but we're in the second row, near the Sleet home goal. The teams switch sides each period, so it will suck for the second period when Sebastian is guarding at the far end of the ice. But I'll get to drool over him for two thirds of the game. Not bad.

"Holy Hell," Max says as he drops into a seat.

I didn't tell them where we'd be sitting.

Marv's on my right, at the end of our row, and closest to the goal. Since he played goalie, he seems the most excited about our seat placement. Max is on my other side, and Miles is next to him.

The girls show up just after we sit down. Steph is sitting with her mom tonight, since Mary's friend cancelled, so it's just Izzy and Katelyn. Since Katelyn knows my brothers, she sits next to Miles. I give a quick round of introductions to Izzy. My brothers all know she's taken, so they keep their greetings appropriate.

I'm bringing my beer up to my lips when Max lets out a loud whistle, making me jump.

"The fuck? You almost made me spill!" I glare at him.

"Almost doesn't count," he replies, and I roll my eyes. That's one of our dad's favorite sayings.

Max stands and whistles again.

I tug on his jeans. "Sit down, you moron."

He gestures, like maybe I didn't see the players skating onto the ice. "What? I'm just cheering on our boys."

"Cheer during the game like a normal human. Not the freaking warm up." I tug on his jeans again.

"Keep tugging, Megs, and we'll end up on ESPN for flashing the arena." He lets out another loud whistle.

"Dude - " Miles says, from Max's other side. "Are you going commando?"

"Ahh, what?!" I yank my hand back.

Max shrugs as he finally drops back down into his seat. "Laundry day came and went."

"You're such a slob." I shudder.

"Takes one to know one. I remember what your room used to look like."

I sigh. "Shut up and go back to whistling."

Max says something to Miles, but I don't catch it. I'm too distracted by the appearance of the #1 jersey on the ice.

Sebastian.

I watch him skate around for a minute before he drops down to do some stretches. I know it's what all goalies do to warm up, but it's hard to watch while I'm sitting with my brothers.

Sebastian's knees are spread on the ice, weight supported by his hands, hips moving front to back, side to side. I want to jump the boards and splay myself out beneath him. In our few times together, I've never gotten under him. And I really want to change that.

My thighs clench of their own volition.

Marvin nudges my elbow.

I blink at him. "Huh?"

"I asked, uh, if you've seen Ash. Since, you know, that um, talk we had?"

I stifle a laugh at his discomfort, but I note that the other brothers have gone quiet.

They really were nice to me about the whole thing, so I figure I owe them an answer.

"Umm, yeah. A few times."

Then, unbidden, my mind flashes to the museum and I blush.

A round of groans goes up around me.

"Come on, Megs," Max whines. "We didn't need fucking details."

I throw my hands up, keeping my eyes forward. "I didn't say anything!"

Max reaches behind me to shove Marv's shoulder. "How does it feel to be wearing our sister's boyfriend's jersey?" he jokes.

I cross my arms. "He's not my boyfriend."

I glance over and see Marv frowning down at the giant 1 on the front of his jersey. I can't help it, this time I laugh.

Marvin makes a face at me, then his eyebrows shoot up.

"Wait, does that mean we can go down to the locker room? Meet some of the guys?" He gives me the most hopeful look. "Maybe you can introduce me to Sebastian."

"Yeah," Max says. "If you're not dating Sebastian, then maybe Marv has a shot."

"Like you're one to talk, Mrs. Wilder," Marv leans over me to snap at Max, who is sporting a Jackson Wilder jersey.

I ignore their jabs. "If you want to go downstairs, you'll have to ask those two." I toss a thumb in Katelyn and Izzy's direction.

Katelyn leans forward, grinning. "Consider it done!"

Of *course* she's listening to us.

The boys nearly fall out of their seats telling her how amazing she is. They really are just overgrown children.

Taking a gulp of my beer, I sit back and get ready to enjoy the game.

Chapter 45

Sebastian

Who the fuck is Banshee sitting with?

When I texted her last night asking if she was coming to my game, I thought it was pretty fucking clear that I wanted her here for *me*. But then she shows up with a whole group of guys? What the hell?

And it's not like I wouldn't see them. Even if she wasn't seated a few dozen feet from my net, her goddamn hair calls to me like a siren. I could find her anywhere in this arena.

The mental image of her sitting there surrounded by guys that she clearly knows well makes me clench my teeth all over again. I swear to god, if she tries to friend-zone me, after giving me half a blow job, I'm going to lose my shit. And whichever one of those assholes thinks that they can steal her from me will find themselves bloody in a fucking dumpster.

I heave out a breath. We've finished warming up and are back in the locker room. I need to get my headspace right for this game. We're playing California. They've had a tough week of losses, so it should be an easy win, but I can't get sloppy out there. The goalie isn't allowed those luxuries.

"You ready, Ash?" Zach pounds his glove against my back.

I nod my head once. "Yeah. I got this."

"You're pissed." It's not a question.

I'm good at keeping emotions off my face, but anger is just one of those feelings that claws in deep.

"She's sitting with a bunch of fucking guys."

Zach doesn't have to ask. He knows who I'm talking about.

"Use it." He steps forward and tugs on my jersey until our helmets clink together. "She's sitting there watching you. Thinking about you. If some jackass with beer breath and skinny arms thinks he has something on Ash LeBlanc, then he's got a lot to learn. Take that anger and turn it into power."

I nod.

Zach shoves me. "Now let's go out there and fuck some shit up."

Finally a grin breaks through. "Hell yeah!"

With that, the music changes and we rush down the ramp and onto the ice.

Chapter 46

Sebastian

N<small>EVER GET COCKY</small>. You'd think I'd have learned my lesson by now.

These California douchebags are bringing the heat tonight. Whatever kinks they had earlier this week, they've smoothed them out.

Luckily, my guys are matching their speed and intensity. It's been nothing but high-stress, fast-paced skating, and non-stop attempts on goal.

I keep hearing Coach yell at me. I like to move. To play outside the goal, going to the puck. Coach knows this is how I play, and that I'm good, but he claims I'm responsible for most of his grey hair. I can't help it, I play aggressive.

We went the entire game tied 0 – 0. Now there's twelve seconds left on the clock in overtime.

We have the puck down at the other end of the ice, but unless they sink a shot in the next few seconds, we're going into a shootout.

From my position, it's hard to tell exactly what's going down. But when the buzzer goes off, I know we didn't score.

We're out of time.
We're headed into a shootout.
Oh, joy.

Chapter 47

Sebastian

"Alright boys, here's what we're doing. Luke, you're shooting first. Jackson, you'll go third." Coach pauses a moment, clearly deliberating his next choice. "And Zach, I want you second."

Zach's grin is a little manic. "Whatever you say, Coach."

Coach points a finger at him, "Keep that crazy look on your face." My teammates chuckle. "You've got a reputation, and you're still new enough that their goalie won't know your style. Go in hard and fast; throw him off. And you two, just do your thing."

The three shooters nod.

"Ash." Coach tips his chin at me. "Keep it up."

I roll out my neck. "You got it."

Times up.

Here we go.

Skating over to my net, I look up to where Banshee's sitting.

Scratch that, *standing*. Soaking in the energy surrounding me, I see that the entire arena is on their feet.

Meghan looks so nervous, and - surprisingly - it makes me feel calmer. I'll let her stress for the both of us.

We lock eyes, and I take one deep inhale.

The next six shots will determine the game, and I'm in control of three of them.

I got this.

As the home team, Coach has decided that we'll start.

Luke is up first.

The ref blows the whistle, and Luke's off. He swings out wide, showing off his stick skills as he makes his way to the front of the net.

He waits until the last second to take the shot. The sound of his stick reverberates around the quiet arena. The puck flies, and the goalie catches it.

0 – 0.

Another deep breath.

Cali boy number one is at center ice. Whistle blows. He's moving my way.

My eyes stay focused on the puck. He can do whatever he wants with his body; that puck is all I care about. He fakes a backhand, but I don't fall for it. I read his swing as he aims low and to the right.

I kick out my leg and feel the impact against my pads.

Puck deflected.

0 – 0.

Zach's turn.

The whistle blows, and Zach goes from a standstill to a sprint. He's a fast motherfucker. I can imagine the intimidating look on his face, and I fight a smile at the thought. Zach skates straight, causing the goalie to back up into his net.

Zach takes the shot.

The goalie dives for it.

He misses the catch, but knocks the puck off course.

0 – 0.

I exhale.

Cali boy number two is up. Whistle blows. My focus narrows.

This guy is taking the same approach as Zach. Fast and straight. But I've played against Zach. A lot. And I know how to handle this.

He's closing in.

I hold my ground; I won't back up.

He slaps his stick against the puck, aiming high.

I catch it.

0 – 0.

Jackson's turn.

This is our last chance.

The ref blows the whistle. Jackson starts at center ice and keeps his speed steady. He's cool. Collected. Coach couldn't have picked three more different players. Jackson's stick skills are some of the best I've seen. He switches directions a few times, the goalie mirroring his movements.

At the last second, Jackson shifts his stance. His stick blurs, and the puck streaks between the goalie's skates.

Goal!

1 – 0.

Last shooter.

I relax my jaw and breathe.

Cali boy number three is staring me down from center ice. He needs to make this to continue the shoot out. But I need to stop this to win. So, fuck him.

This is my game.

My ice.

My girl watching.

Whistle blows. Player three snags the puck and comes at

me slower than the rest did. The pressure is on and he's taking his time. That's okay. I'm not going anywhere.

He's twenty feet away. Fifteen. Ten. Five. He pulls the puck across his body, moves the stick forward to shoot.

I slide to my left, dropping to my knees to block.

It was a fake.

He pulls the puck back across. Shoots for the right corner.

Still sliding to my left, I stretch out to the right.

My stick hits the ice a split second before the puck can pass the line.

Deflected.

No goal.

Sleet win.

The volume in the arena is deafening. Everyone's screaming, clapping, jumping. It's a good fucking feeling.

My teammates pour onto the ice. Circling me. Crushing me in a ridiculous group hug.

It's hard to hear their words over the noise, but I know they're jacked. I'm jacked too. Jacked that it's over.

Breaking free, I look over to where Meghan is. Knowing she'll be cheering for me.

Her arms are up over her head, but she's taller than she was. My eyes trace down her body to where a pair of arms are wrapped around her waist, lifting her in the air.

My relief turns to rage.

This changes.

Tonight.

Chapter 48

Sebastian

"Come on, man. Let's go find your girl, so you can finally ask her out."

Zach's words make me pause. We're showered, dressed, and about ready to exit the locker room.

"Ask her out?"

He lifts a brow at me. "Uh, yeah. Ask her the fuck out already. You keep getting your panties in a twist over her. That'd probably stop if you just manned up and put a claim on her."

I open my mouth but I have no ready response to that.

"Seriously, what is there to think about?" he asks me.

"Ask her out? Like to be my girlfriend?"

He rolls his eyes. "You could have her check a box - yes or no. Maybe get permission from her dad to go steady. Or ya know, just Ask. Her. Out."

"I don't date."

"You don't date." The look Zach's giving me tells me that he thinks I'm a moron.

Yeah, the argument sounds as dumb as it feels.

I reach up and rub my temples. "I'm not looking for a relationship. Not right now."

"Okay. But you don't want her dating other people? Swiping left or right? Fucking other guys?"

"Dude." I drop my hands and glare at him.

"Just trying to get this straight. You like her. You want to see her, talk to her, bang her. But you don't want to ask her out. Don't want to have *a relationship*. But you also don't want her going out with other people."

I hold his gaze. "Exactly."

Zach laughs. "Allow me to grab some popcorn for this one."

"Shut the fuck up," I push him to get going.

Moving to the door, we step into the hallway.

A lot of the guys have left already. I was taking my sweet time to let my irritation fade. But it was all for nothing, because the first thing I see is Jackson talking with the guy that had lifted Meghan into the air. This must be the one that's interested in her. The other two are probably his friends.

I don't have a game plan, but my feet are walking towards him before my brain can catch up.

I'm two strides away when he spots me. His face was already animated talking to Jackson, but when he locks eyes with me, his mouth opens into a wide smile.

"Holy shit! Ash! Man, it's an honor to meet you. I'm a huge fan!" He steps forward with his hand out.

Looking down, I see that he's wearing *my* fucking jersey. The nerve of this guy.

He doesn't even seem to notice that I'm ignoring his attempt to shake my hand. "Seriously, tonight's game... Holy balls, dude. You had a complete shut out!" He reaches back to get the attention of his friends. "Guys!"

Sleet Banshee

The other two step closer, but psycho number one is still talking. "That was probably the best, most stressful shootout I've ever seen. I mean, I knew you could do it, but still. What a rush."

This guy can't take a goddamn hint. I haven't said a word. I'm glaring at him. And he's still babbling like a toddler with a new favorite toy.

Red hair catches my attention and I glance up to see Meghan walking up next to me.

Time to put everyone in line.

I reach out, hook an arm around her waist and pull her into me. Her hands press against my chest. I know I'm being a little rough, but I'm doing this to make a point.

Meghan lets out a short squeak of surprise, and I catch a glimpse of her smile before I'm pressing my lips to hers.

I squeeze her waist and feel her fingers twist into the fabric of my shirt.

Perfect.

When I pull away, Banshee blinks her eyes open. She looks stunned.

Keeping my arm around her, I turn back to psycho number one. "Who the fuck are you?"

All three of the guys look a little uncomfortable over my display, but I don't sense jealousy.

Meghan snaps out of her daze. "You idiots didn't introduce yourselves? You just walked up and started drooling all over Sebastian and didn't think to tell him who you were?"

She starts by pointing to my main nemesis. "This is Marvin. That's Max. And that's Miles, the oldest. Though not the smartest. That'd be me." Meg tips her head up to give me a wink.

"Huh?" Those names. They sound familiar.

She reads the look on my face and rolls her eyes. "Men. It's like you're there, but you're never actually listening. Sebastian, my I present to you," she sweeps her arm out, gesturing to the guys, "my brothers."

Brothers?

Whoops.

Chapter 49

Meghan

EVERYONE IS silent for a moment before Sebastian says, "Oh."

It's hard to read his tone off that single syllable, but he sounds surprised. Taken off guard. And then I feel his body relax against mine. I hadn't realized how coiled he was, but since he's still holding me tight to his side I can feel the softening of his muscles.

Then it clicks. The tension. The faceoff with my brothers. The scowl. The grabbing and the kissing.

A bark of laughter escapes my lips. He looks down at me and I'm sure he can see the humor in my eyes.

I smirk. "Oh my god, you thought…"

Sebastian's grip on my waist releases and in a flash his arm is wrapped around my shoulders, his large hand covering my mouth.

"Brothers, of course. Nice to meet you guys." He reaches his free hand out to Marv. "Which one of you played goalie?"

My traitor brothers don't even care that Sebastian is physically silencing me. They all shake hands and start telling stories about putting Marv in goal before he knew how to skate.

Marv laughs. "These assholes didn't even take the time to teach me. I had to play in my tennis shoes that first winter."

I cannot believe that Sebastian thought I was on a date with my brother. Gross.

And I cannot believe that they're all acting like I'm not even here anymore.

Screw that. Parting my lips, I stick my tongue out and lick Sebastian's hand.

He has no reaction. None.

I do it again.

And feel his bicep flex against the back of my neck. That's it.

Guess I need to escalate.

Opening my mouth a little farther, I bite the underside of his finger. Hard.

He grunts and yanks his hand away from my face, shaking it out. "Fuck, Banshee. That hurt."

I pat his chest. "Suck it up, big guy."

"Banshee?" Miles asks.

I step towards him, pointing a finger as I talk. "No. None of you get to call me that." I glare at them all. "Don't even *think* it."

"Aww, why not? It's perfect for you, you little psychopath." Max says pouting.

Sebastian chuckles behind me. "Yeah, Baby, why not?"

I whirl on him. "And you! Don't call me *Baby*."

Sebastian looks right over my head to my brothers. "Has she always been like this?"

"Difficult?"

"Crazy?"

"Annoying?"

I shut my eyes and shake my head. Goddess grant me the strength to survive this encounter.

Katelyn pops her head into our group. "Hey, do you guys want to come over to our place for a little bit?"

An image of my brothers and Sebastian ganging up and trading stories flashes before my eyes. But before I can decline, my brothers are all agreeing.

Oh, bother.

"Great! Meghan has our address. We're heading out now, so we'll see you there in a bit!" She waves and takes off.

Sebastian's hand grips the back of my neck. "Text your brothers the address. You're riding with me."

"Okay."

I pull my phone out and send the location in a group text to all three of them. "There's a parking lot under the building, and the apartment is on the top floor."

The guys nod, but Miles steps up, looking at Sebastian. "I trust you'll get there the same time as us. No lengthy detours."

"Miles! Can you not?" I feel my cheeks heating.

Miles looks at me. "You might be old now, but you're still our sister. And Ash might be an amazing hockey player, but we don't know him."

His unspoken words are clear to me. They only know what I've told him. When I cried over him.

Sebastian nods. "We'll be right behind you. Promise."

Chapter 50

Meghan

Our walk to the player's parking lot has been silent, and I can't quite tell if it's comfortable or awkward. I'd lean towards the latter, but Sebastian's been holding my hand the whole time, so...

I decide to be fine with the quiet and take in my surroundings, since I've never been down this way. I'm sure this is just a normal everyday hallway, but it feels like I'm in some super-secret spy bunker.

When we reach a metal door at the end of the hall, Sebastian lets go of my hand. Holding the door open, he lets me step through first.

"So, your brothers seem fun," he remarks, placing a hand on my back to guide me.

I shake my head. "Fun's one way to put it. Obnoxious is another."

"Miles though..." He pauses. "I don't think he likes me."

I make a noncommittal humming sound and chew on my lip.

Sebastian stops us next to an all-black Jeep Wrangler. He's

parked in the back corner of the subterranean lot, and - over here, on the far side of the Jeep - we're shrouded in shadows.

Using the hand on my back, he turns me to face him. "Banshee?"

I opt for playing dumb. "Oh, no, I'm sure he likes you."

He steps closer, resting his hands on the passenger door, caging me in. "I don't like it when you lie to me."

I bat my eyes and smile. "Why, does it make you want to punish me?"

Sebastian presses his hips against mine, allowing me to feel his reaction to my question. "Baby, I always want to spank you. No matter how bratty you're being."

His growly voice rolls through my body and out my toes. I don't even have a choice, I lean into his body. My hands reach out to press against Sebastian's chest. The muscles bunched beneath my fingers.

He leans his face closer, and I hope he's about to kiss me, but he speaks instead. "I'd love to take you home right now and teach you a lesson."

"Yes, please - " I beg.

"But I promised your brother that I'd bring you straight to Jackson's."

Well, bringing up my overprotective older brother is one way to kill the mood. "Fucking Miles. He just needs some time to get over it."

"Get over what, exactly?"

Not wanting to look him in the eye, I keep my gaze locked on my hands as they continue to press against Sebastian's warm chest. "I may have gotten drunk with my brothers after a family dinner a while back. And I may have been a little upset at the time."

"Upset with me?" he asks.

I shrug.

"Banshee - " he grips my chin and makes me look up at him.

Those damn dark eyes. They make me want to confess everything.

I sigh. "In hindsight, no. But at the time, yes. So... they may not have gotten the best first impression of you."

"Well that clears it up," he deadpans.

With his grip still in place, I look away. "I didn't want to face my role in the fight that night. It was easier to blame you than it was to face my own guilt."

"Meghan, none of what happened was your fault," Sebastian says before placing a kiss on my forehead.

I want to melt into the sweet gesture, but instead I shake my head. "You don't get it. Girls *need* to stick together. We're safer in numbers. I was supposed to be with her, but instead I was with you."

To my surprise, Sebastian pulls me into a hug.

His lips are pressed into my hair, but I can still understand him. "It wasn't your fault. Even if we hadn't been out back, having the best sex of my life, you can't tell me that anything would have turned out differently. I'm sorry your friend got hurt. I'm sorry my friend got in trouble. But I'm not sorry that you weren't anywhere near that. I know the world is a dangerous place for women. I have a sister, and the worry I have for her nearly strangles me at times." He squeezes me tighter. "And now I have your crazy, sexy ass to worry about. If fucking you in alleys will keep you away from violence, then I'll do it every chance I get."

His words undo me.

My arms wrap around his body and I'm holding on for dear life. Every time I try to distance myself from him, he shows me another layer of his personality. And this layer, this *I protect what's mine* emotion seeping off him? It's addicting.

Feeling his sincerity, I try to comfort him. "You don't need to worry about me. I'm careful."

With my ear pressed against his chest, I hear his rumbling laugh at the source.

"There's a reason I call you Banshee, Megs. You live in your own world and do your own thing." He gives me a squeeze. "If I think about it too hard, I'll give myself a fucking ulcer."

He's not wrong.

Sebastian sighs, and a sliver of unease trails down my spine.

"I like you." The words themselves are positive, but his tone is heavy.

I swallow, waiting for the *but*.

"But I need to focus on my career. I'm not in a place where I can have a serious relationship. I want to see you, spend time together, but I need you to know where I'm at. I don't want to lead you on, make you think this is something else. Something that it's not."

I squeeze my eyes shut and nod. Now the hug feels less like a gesture of affection and more like something to hide behind. But I'm grateful for it, since it means I don't have to look into his eyes while he tells me he wants me, just not like *that*.

As is the pattern with Sebastian, he goes from hot to cold in an instant. A moment ago, he was proclaiming that I'm on the list of women he worries about. Which almost felt like the speech you'd give someone before you told them you loved them. It had made my own worry about our future unravel, knitting itself into a blanket of hope. But his words right now, they've disintegrated any delusion I'd started to build.

I knew this was coming. This is the fuck buddy conversation I was preparing myself for. It just doesn't sound the way I'd imagined. His tone is apologetic. Like he knows that this isn't what I want. Like he's ready for me to push him away and tell him to fuck off. Like he really does mean everything he's saying. And for some reason that hurts my heart even more.

I already know my answer. I'd decided long before tonight. I'll take Sebastian however I can get him. I just need to find a way to remember that this isn't real. That it's temporary. That I can't let him in too deep.

I can do that.

Probably.

He must take my silence as a bad sign. "It's not personal. It's just that I wouldn't be able to commit the time it takes to have a girlfriend. And that's not fair to anyone. Mostly it's not fair to you..." He lets out another deep breath. "I'm not trying to be an asshole. I just want to be upfront, so nobody gets hurt."

I force out a laugh and hope it doesn't sound as fake as it feels. "Sebastian, please don't give me the *it's not you it's me* speech. You're the man, of course it's you." I push him back so I can face him. I don't really want to look at him right now, but I need him to believe me. "I'm not looking for a husband, so you can quit freaking out. Okay? I'm more than happy to keep this casual. But thank you for being so forthcoming."

I was expecting to see relief on his face, but his clenched jaw makes him look almost mad.

No time like the present to lay out my one rule. "I do have a stipulation."

"Stipulation?"

"Yeah, big guy. A rule. An agreement for our arrangement."

He drops his chin. "I know what stipulation means."

"Good." I pat his shoulder. "My only request is that so long as you're fucking me, you're not fucking anyone else." His eyes widen, and I'm not sure if it's from shock over my bluntness, or my request itself. "This isn't me trying to turn this into a relationship, this is me not wanting to catch the clap from some stupid hoe."

It's not the whole truth, but the end result is the same.

"I can agree to that. Hoes aren't really my thing anyway." He smirks.

The uncomfortable tension between us snaps, morphing into something more primal.

One heartbeat he's standing in front of me, and by the next, his body is slamming into mine.

Sebastian grips my hips, and - in a show of libido-fueled strength - he lifts me off the ground. My legs instinctually wrap around his waist, my feet barely touching behind his back.

When his lips find mine, my brain forgets all about the internal conversation we just had about guarding my feelings. And when his tongue breaches into my mouth, I forget my own name.

My eyes are closed, letting the darkness heighten the feel of his body against mine. My fingers are clawing him, trying to pull him even closer.

Our kiss becomes so frantic, our teeth clank together. It makes me want to grin, but I refuse to break contact. This feels like a first kiss, but also like we've done it a million times before.

His mouth is warm and demanding, and so fucking delicious.

There are two layers of denim between us, but my core is lined up perfectly with his rock hard cock. I undulate against him, and the friction is nearly enough to get me off.

His flip from calm to animal was like the strike of a match. And I caught fire. I'm so wet, so hot, so *ready*.

Sebastian's hands are on my ass, squeezing and holding me tightly against him. I moan and wriggle around, trying to get pressure right where I need it.

He bites my lower lip, making me clench my thighs around him.

I'm dangerously close, and a moan pours out of my throat.

I arch my back, reaching for release and Sebastian breaks the kiss...

He loosens his grip, causing me to drop my legs and sets me down.

"There," he says, stepping back. "Now we're even."

Then he turns and walks around to the driver's side door.

Stunned.

I am mother fucking stunned. And horny-as-fuck.

I hear his door open and shut, and I angrily rip the passenger door open, slamming it behind me after I climb in. "New stipulation. No more of that bullshit. Orgasms or bust."

Sebastian laughs as he backs out of the parking spot.

Chapter 51

Meghan

SITTING HERE with my arms crossed, I continue to give Sebastian the silent treatment.

I'm so turned on it hurts. My poor vagina is throbbing, and I'm getting very cranky.

I glance over and see that he still has a stupidly-smug smile on his face. He's pretending to ignore my silence by turning up the radio.

Then the world's best idea hits me like a vibrator to the face, and my scowl slowly turns to a smile. Sebastian's busy driving, but I'm not. And his windows are tinted. And it's dark out. And I have more than enough time before we get where we're going.

Uncrossing my arms, I reach down and unbutton my jeans.

The movement immediately catches Sebastian's attention.

"What are you doing?" he asks, glancing between me and the road ahead of him.

I pull down my zipper. "Some jackass left me all hot and bothered. And since I'm sitting here with nothing else to do…"

I slide my hand under the band of my underwear. "You just worry about keeping your focus on the road."

I've never done anything like this before, but having Sebastian next to me, unable to stop me, makes this even hotter.

I close my eyes and slide my hand lower.

When my fingers connect with my clit, I groan.

"Fuck." Sebastian's growl spurs me on.

My jeans are tight but there's just enough room for me to get the friction I need. I lean back in the seat, spreading my legs.

Eyes still closed, I don't hold back my moans as my fingers work a familiar pattern.

Sebastian's breathing is getting heavy, spurring me on.

Wanting to give him more of a show, because I'm courteous, I slide my free hand up under my shirt.

The Jeep lurches to a stop, and I open my eyes to see we're at a red light.

I slowly roll my head to the side until my gaze meets Sebastian's. The lust in his eyes is just about enough to finish me off.

"I'm close," I whisper.

"Come, Baby. Let me watch."

That does it. With our eyes locked, my mouth drops open and my body shudders. The orgasm rolls through my body.

"Holy fuck," Sebastian growls.

I'm still trembling when he reaches over and grabs my wrist.

Before I can ask him what he's doing, he pulls my hand out of my jeans and brings my fingers to his mouth.

"Holy fuck," I pant, as I watch him lick my fingers clean.

He grins around my fingers. "Delicious."

And just like that, I'm turned on all over again.

The car behind us honks.

The light is green.

Chapter 52

Meghan

Dear Diary,

Brothers are the worst. If it weren't for them, I could be spending the night in Sebastian's bed. But no... Miles insisted on driving me home tonight.

I'm not happy about the sleeping arrangements, but I guess we did have a fun night. Thankfully the three stooges were able to act chill hanging out with the trio of Sleet players. I'm glad Zach and Izzy showed up. The boys occupied their time talking hockey, and us girls were able to chill over a bottle of wine.

It's a little weird to have Sebastian befriending my brothers, since by his own request this is just a casual thing.

Casual. Casual. Casual.

The fact that I won't get to see him for a while should make it easier to keep on the casual track. He's leaving for a series of out-of-town games and won't be in town again until the night I'm working the Snips auction.

It's probably better that I don't know when I'll get to see him next, but seriously, what does a girl have to do to actually get laid around here?

XoxoX

Chapter 53

Meghan

SEBASTIAN: **I hate your brothers.**

Meghan: **You're the one that agreed to the whole "we'll be right behind you" thing.**

Sebastian: **I regret everything.**

Meghan: **Sweet dreams, big guy.**

Sebastian: **Wet dreams, Banshee.**

Chapter 54

Meghan

MEGHAN: Ugh, it's like you're famous or something. My stupid sports newsfeed is filled with highlights from your shutout last night.

Sebastian: Get used to it, sweet cheeks. I'm kind of a big deal.

Meghan: I'm rolling my eyes real hard over here.

❄

Sebastian: Fucking Canada. It's cold as balls up here.

Meghan: That's such a strange saying, don't you think? The last set of balls I had in my hands were pretty warm.

Sebastian: I'm on a bus filled with big stinky men. Don't talk about having your hands on my balls. I can't afford a boner right now.

Meghan: Who said I was talking about your balls?

Sebastian: Keep it up, Banshee. You just earned yourself a spanking.

❄

Meghan: Bravo on another win tonight.

Sebastian: Thanks. It was close, but we got the W.

Meghan. The W is the best.

Sebastian: So, is the V.

Meghan: Wow, nice one.

Sebastian: Yeah, I'm pretty funny.

Meghan: Whenever someone has to tell you they're funny, it usually means the opposite.

Sebastian: I'm super smart, too.

Meghan: *gasps* I'm so impressed.

Sebastian: I'm also incredibly strong.

Meghan: And I'm turning my phone off.

❄

Sebastian: Seriously, this back and forth between hot and cold climates is going to kill me.

Meghan: What's that I hear, are you complaining about being in Florida?

Sebastian: Yeah, yeah, I'm an ungrateful bitch. But this 70 degree temp swing is going to make me sick.

Meghan: Sick I can help with. Just don't get bit by an alligator.

Sebastian: Why would you even put that out into the universe?!?

Meghan: Don't tell me that you're superstitious...

Sebastian: I'm an athlete, of course I'm superstitious!

Meghan: Is that a thing?

Sebastian: Definitely. Don't be jinxing me like that.

Meghan: My bad. Alligator joke retracted.

Sebastian: *wipes sweat from brow*

Meghan: *whispers to self about this ridiculous man*

Sebastian: Back to your earlier comment about handling the sick. Does that mean you'll make me some homemade soup? I still need to try that cooking of yours.

Meghan: If you come home ill, then I promise I'll make you some soup.

Sebastian: I'm feeling pretty *cough* bad already. You should probably get started.

Meghan: Oh sure, I'll drop everything and make you food right now.

❋

Meghan: Saw you made it out of the sunshine state with all your limbs intact.

Sebastian: Too exhausted to type. Calling you instead.

❋

Sebastian: Good riddance, Texas.

Meghan: What are you griping about? You won!

Sebastian: Yeah, but it was even hotter than fucking Florida.

Meghan: Well it's nice and cold here at home. You guys land late tonight, right?

Sebastian: That we do. Will you be at my game tomorrow night?

Meghan: I wish I could. I have an auction for work that I have to attend. It was kind of a last minute thing, so I need to be there to make sure it all goes well.

Sebastian: An auction?

Meghan: Yeah, it's for a big fundraiser for this local spay/neuter organization. My contact there is really cool so it should be fun.

Sebastian: Interesting. Last minute you say?

Meghan: Yeah, Annabelle called me just about a week ago asking if I could help. Luckily, I'm amazing and got her hooked up with the best of everything.

Sebastian: Lucky indeed.

Chapter 55

Meghan

"Girl, I can not believe you pulled this off." Annabelle makes jazz hands as she shuffle-runs towards me in her stilettos. "I mean, I knew you could pull it off, but this..." she gestures to the Syndicate ballroom around us. "You've outdone yourself."

I grab the skirt of my dress and give her a curtsey. "Twas my pleasure, m' lady."

"Honestly, how can I pay you back?"

I laugh. "I did send you my bill, so you'll be literally paying me."

She shakes her head. "No. Not good enough. Everything here is pretty much wrapped up. Give me a few minutes to stroke a few more egos, then let's go get drunk."

I don't answer right away. She's a client, and I don't really know her.

Annabelle tugs on my arm. "Please, please, pretty please?"

I cave. "Okay, okay. Let's get drunk!"

Tonight's event was seamless. The food was tasty and not overtly testicle-like. The string quartet played beautifully.

Everything in the auction sold, and the donation box is overflowing. So a celebratory drink is well-earned.

I take up a post against the back wall while I wait for Annabelle. Checking the score on my phone, I see that the Sleet won, so I text Sebastian a quick congratulations. It's the only home game this week, and then they're back on the road tomorrow until next weekend. Just in time for the wedding.

Considering I haven't seen Sebastian since the "brother game" it would've been nice to see him tonight. *See him. Sleep with him. Whatever.* But other than asking if I'd be at his game, he didn't say anything about meeting up after. And after his little speech about not having time for a girlfriend, I didn't want to pester him about hanging out at the very first availability he had. He's the one with the tough schedule, and the no-girlfriend rule; he can reach out to me.

"Okay, I'm good to go!" Annabelle rubs her hands together as if anticipating something great. "And I just asked, the hotel's fine if we leave our cars parked here overnight."

"Nice planning," I grin. "There's lots of cool bars around, but have you ever been to the one in the basement here?"

"Here? Like in the hotel?"

"Yeah."

Annabelle just shakes her head.

"Come on. You're gonna love it."

Before leaving the room, I push Annabelle towards the coat check.

"Oh, right. I suppose these guys will be gone before we're done," Annabelle says, as we wait for our jackets.

"True, but we'll want them anyway."

She cocks her head. "I thought you said the bar was in the basement."

"It is," I confirm. "But we need to walk outside for a bit to get there."

"Ooo, I'm intrigued."

Coats in hand, we exit the ballroom and work our way deeper into the hotel. The building's old, and several additions have been added over the years, so there are lots of strange hallways and passages that are easy to get lost in.

After several minutes of what seems to be mindless wandering, Annabelle's intrigue turns to skepticism. "Are you sure this bar is real?"

I can't really blame her for asking, but being hard to find is kinda the whole point of a secret bar.

"Trust me, it's here. I knew that last turn was wrong when I took it." I wave off her concern as we turn a corner, and I see what I'm looking for. "Ah, here it is."

Annabelle follows my lead and pulls her coat on before I push open an exterior door.

Stepping out, we let the door slam shut behind us.

"Uh, this is feeling very stabby." Annabelle murmurs.

Admittedly, at first glance it does look a tad sketchy. We went from a luxurious warm interior to a no man's land behind the hotel.

The wind's cold, and it's pretty dark back here, but there's a lone old-timey streetlamp standing sentry in the lawn, lighting the small cobblestone walkway before us.

I smile at Annabelle. "I promise to intervene between you and any potential muggers."

"How very reassuring," she jokes before gripping my hand.

Over the wind, I can make out the sound of moving water. The Mississippi River is just a few dozen yards downhill.

We follow the path around another corner of the odd shaped building and are met with another flickering streetlamp. It's light illuminates a worn wooden door, tucked into the lowest part of the back wall.

"Well, I'll be fucked," Annabelle whispers to herself.

Sleet Banshee

Stopping in front of the door, I knock a quick *tap tap-tap* against the wood.

"This is so fucking cool!" Annabelle bounces next to me, like a kid about to meet Santa.

The door creaks open in front of us and I put a palm on Annabelle's back to move her forward. We silently walk past the large suit-clad doorman and down a narrow brick hallway. As we advance, sound starts to fill the space.

Taking the final turn at the end of the hall, we step into a dimly lit 1920's speakeasy.

The entire far wall is lined with a worn wooden bar. Behind which, all the bartenders are wearing white shirts, snug black button up vests, and black arm bands. Most of the barstools are full, but there are low wooden tables filling up the room, a third of which are empty. One of the walls is stacked with whiskey barrels, and there's a piano in the corner, currently being played by a woman in a tasseled black dress.

Unlike some modern remakes, this room is nearly original. It's dark. The ceilings are low. The furniture is simple. It's not glamorous, but it is amazing.

I look over to see Annabelle's mouth hanging open, and I flick her chin.

Chapter 56

Meghan

"Okay." Annabelle plunks our third round of sidecars onto the table. "Enough about work and blah blah boring shit. I want to get to the good stuff."

Annabelle's starting to slur a little bit, and I'm just drunk enough to find it hilarious.

"To the good stuff!" I giggle while holding my drink up.

We clink glasses and take a sip.

Annabelle sets her drink down and leans over the table like she's gonna tell me a secret. "Let's talk about boys."

"Boys?" I snort.

"Okay, men. Whatever."

I groan and take another drink.

Annabelle smirks. "The mention of men causes you to drink. Interesting."

"Yeah, well, men are annoying. And complicated. And hot." I groan again. "Seriously, if you saw this guy, you'd throw your thong at him fast enough to break the sound barrier."

Annabelle makes a choked sound before taking a large pull

off her drink to match my own. "That's quite the description. Now, tell me everything."

"There's not much to tell - " I lift a shoulder. "I mean, we've kind of had a thing for - I donno - a couple months, I guess. Well, not really *a thing*. It's been a complicated road. But we have an agreement now."

Annabelle gives me a very unimpressed look. "You're the worst storyteller ever. Back this train up and start from the beginning."

"Hmm. Okay, fine." My alcohol drenched brain tries to rewind the memories. "It started at the Santa House. I was just trying to get Izzy and Zach together. I wasn't looking for a hookup for myself. But I wasn't upset when we ended up making out in the corn maze, because Sebastian is hot as fuck."

Oops! I didn't mean to say his name. Crap... I don't know if he wanted to keep us a secret. That might be part of the agreement. Whatever, it's too late now. And I only said his first name.

"Santa? Corn maze? This sounds made up."

I wave her off. "It was a haunted house thing."

Her eyebrows go up. "Like for Halloween? This started in October?"

"Well, that's when we first met. Since then we've had a few encounters."

"*Encounters...*" Annabelle winks.

"They weren't all wink-wink nudge-nudge encounters. During one of them he was a dick. Then the next one he gave me the dick." I laugh at my own joke.

"Oh my god, you did not just say that?!" Annabelle takes another drink. "I hope it was worth the wait."

"Sooooo worth it. So fucking good. Like, crazy good. It was spur of the moment and I don't know if that makes it better, but it did make it super hot."

"So, you guys have just been fooling around since then? I notice you haven't called Sebastian your boyfriend."

I tip my hand back and forth, signaling sorta. "Yeah he's not my boyfriend. And that was the only time we've had sex."

"What?" Her eyes bug out a little. "Only once over months? How is that possible?"

"It's a long story."

"And..."

"The night we hooked up..." I sigh. "One of my friends ended up getting hurt."

"Oh, no!" Her hand flies to her chest.

"It's okay. She's fine now. But I sorta freaked out. Well, maybe more than *sorta*. I blamed myself for leaving my friend, and him for distracting me. So like a mature adult I cut him out of my life for a few months."

"Okay. But you're back together now?"

"Not exactly. He's not looking for a relationship." I try to keep the annoyance out of my voice. "So, we're just friends-with-benefits, I guess."

Annabelle rolls her eyes. "Men can be such dense idiots sometimes."

I tip my glass towards her and take another pull. "Can't argue there."

"But you like him?"

I nod. "I do. And I'm starting to think I'm the idiot in this equation."

"How so?"

"Because I like him a lot. Like..." I take a large swallow of liquid courage, "bordering on love. And that can only end one way. In a fucking disaster."

"No. That's bullshit!" Annabelle slams a fist down on the table, causing our glasses to shake.

I start to giggle again. I really need to stop drinking, I'm not a giggler.

Annabelle points at me. "I don't believe that for a second. He's just scared of falling in love and letting it distract him. I don't know where he gets these dumbass notions from, but don't give up on him."

"How do you know that?" I ask, afraid to hope.

She shrugs. "I know the type. He's into you just as badly. I guarantee it."

"I doubt it." I slump in my seat.

"How often do you guys talk, or text, whatever."

"Um, probably like every day."

She smirks. "What sort of uninterested man would message you every day? And you said you haven't hooked up other than that once, so I'm guessing these aren't just texts for a booty call."

"No. He's been out of town."

"He's out of town." She jabs her finger into the table top. "He could be doing whatever, or whoever, he wants, but instead he's texting you."

Even through my haze of drunkenness, just the thought of him with someone else causes me to clench my fists. "We agreed that there would be no one else."

Annabelle's eyebrows shoot up. "Seriously?"

"Yeah. So?"

"So... You're exclusively sleeping with each other. You're talking every day." She gives me a *you're dumb* look. "You, my dear, are dating this guy."

She's making sense. "But..."

"No." She puts up a hand, swaying slightly. "No, buts. This guy is just too scared to admit what he wants. He'll get there." She gestures to my purse. "Pull out your phone. I bet he's texted since we got here."

He probably has, since I messaged him earlier about winning his game.

Pulling out my phone I see a new text.

Sebastian: Thanks. How'd the testicle party go?

I smirk.

"I was right, wasn't I?" Annabelle asks.

"You're right that he texted me, but it's not like it was a sexy text."

"That's kinda my point. Are you gonna text back?"

I bite my lip. Then, carefully, I type out a text.

Meghan: It was spectesticular.

His response is immediate.

Sebastian: Cute. You back home?

Meghan: Nope.

Sebastian: Nope? The fundraiser can't still be going this late.

I glance at the time and see that it's nearly midnight. I'm surprised he's still up.

Meghan: It wrapped up a while ago. I'm at a bar with my new friend.

The bouncing dots start then stop. But before I can type something else, my phone starts to ring. It's Sebastian.

I look up at Annabelle and whisper. "He's calling me!"

She whispers back. "Why are we whispering?"

"I don't know!" I whisper again, a fit of giggles taking over.

"Answer it!" Annabelle waves her hands around like she's afraid I'll miss the call.

I try to calm my giggles as I bring the phone to my ear. "Hey there, big guy."

I put a hand over my mouth as Annabelle starts laughing. *Holy shit, I sound super drunk.*

There's a pause on the other end of the call. "Hi Megs. Are you drunk?"

"Psssh, no."

"Meghan." He sounds all stern. I kinda like it.

"Well, I mean, we've been drinking. And..."

"And what, Baby?"

I grin. "And, I'm pretty drunk."

"Hmmm."

Fucking hell. The vibrations of his deep voice go straight through the phone and right into my panties.

"And don't call me Baby." I already sound breathless, and he's hardly said anything.

I hear his soft chuckle through the phone. "Where are you?"

"At the bar. I told you."

"Which bar, Meg?"

"Oh, um, I'm not sure if it has a name. But it's super cool. Annabelle's never been here before so I wanted to show her. She really likes it. Right, Annabelle?" My eyes had been on the table, but I look up as I ask her.

Her eyes are wide, and she has a goofy grin on her face, but she nods in response.

"Yeah, see. She likes it." I say, as if Sebastian could see her nodding.

"Can I talk to Annabelle?" Sebastian asks.

"Um, sure, okay." My drunk brain doesn't find the request weird.

I hold the phone out to her. "He wants to talk to you."

She leans away. "What? Why?"

"Oh, umm..." I bring the phone back to my ear. "Annabelle wants to know why you want to talk to her."

"I want to ask her what she thinks about the bar."

"Oh." I hold the phone back out. "He wants to ask you about the bar."

She slowly reaches out and takes the phone. "Hello, Meghan's not-boyfriend."

I crack up. *Oh my god, Sebastian's going to kill me.*

At least she doesn't know his last name. Oh, shit. I hope he doesn't say anything about his game tonight. Not that he would to a random stranger.

Watching Annabelle nod into the phone, it hits me just how tired I am. I try to focus on what she's saying but I only catch a few words here and there.

I lose track but I think a few minutes pass before she holds the phone back out for me. "Here you go."

"Thanks." I take it and set it down on the table.

She tries to smother a laugh, pointing at the phone. "He's still there."

"Oh, whoops!" I pick it back up. "Hey!"

"Hey."

Miraculously I remember the point of his talk with Annabelle. "I was right, wasn't I? She likes the bar."

"Of course you were right."

"Ha! I knew it."

"Clever girl. How about you? How are you feeling?"

"I'm good. A little sleepy. It's been a long day. But I bet you're even more tired because of..." I pause and glance up to see Annabelle inspecting her nails, but I still turn to the side and drop my voice to a whisper. "Because of the game. I hope you didn't say anything about that to Annabelle. I didn't tell her you were a hockey player."

"No, it didn't come up. But why wouldn't you tell her?" he asks.

I nervously bite my lip. "Just I figured that maybe you wanted it to be a secret."

"That I play hockey?"

I keep my voice quiet. "No, I mean us. I figured you didn't want anyone to know about me. And I really like Annabelle, but I don't know if she's a gossip or anything like that. So, I didn't tell her your last name. I didn't even mean to tell her your first name but it just kinda happened. But I promise I didn't tell her more. I told her you don't want a girlfriend, but if she knew who you were and accidentally said something, then you might get mad. Or it could cause you problems. And then you'd have to do one of those PR things where you say you're not dating me. And that would be pretty... not great." Saying it all out loud like that makes me feel more than a little bit awful. "So, you know, I just figured..." I trail off.

"Meghan. That's not... " I hear him exhale. "Where are you? I'll come give you a ride home."

"No, don't do that. You need to go to bed. I'm good. And I won't tell her about the hockey. I promise."

Sebastian curses. "Babe, I don't give a shit about that. Tell whoever you want *about the hockey*. I just need you to get home safe."

"Oh, okay." Shit, I think he's mad. "You don't need to worry about us. We'll split a ride."

"No. Just, hold on a second. Okay?"

"Okay."

I can still hear him breathing, but he's not talking.

Looking over, I'm happy to see that Annabelle is scrolling through her phone. I didn't mean to ignore her for so long.

"Meg, you there?" Sebastian asks.

"Yep, I'm here."

"Okay, Samuel's on his way to get you."

"Samuel? Like your brother?"

"Yeah. That okay with you?"

"Sure. Did you, uh, clear up the camera thing?"

I haven't seen Samuel since the whole blow job debacle. Now I'm glad that I'm drunk, I'll pretend it never happened and blame my memory loss on alcohol.

"It's all taken care of. I've got the only copy."

"Good. Wait, what do you mean you have the only copy?"

"You might be surprised at the quality of those museum cameras," I can hear his grin through the phone.

"Oh." I feel my body temperature rising, the heat helping to wash away the icky feeling from a few minutes ago. "Is it good?"

"Oh, it's good. In fact, once you let me know you're home safe, I'm going to watch it. Again."

My pulse picks up at the desire in his tone. "And what will you do while you watch it?"

"I bet you can guess."

I cup my hand over my mouth and the phone. "Can I come over and watch you watching it?"

Sebastian chuckles. "I promise we can make that happen. Just not tonight."

"Crap, that's right. I'm sorry, I forgot how late it is. You should be in bed."

"That's not the reason, my devilish Banshee. Trust me, I want nothing more than to fuck your brains out right now." *Oh yes, please.* "But I'm not going to do it while you're drunk. Or at least not while you're drunk and I'm sober."

Well... crap to that.

"But we've had sex before, so it's not like you should feel like you're taking advantage of me. That wouldn't be it at all."

"Maybe not, but it's still..."

"What if I asked you to?"

"Banshee," he says my name as a warning.

"What if I begged you to?" My thighs clench.

"Fucking hell. You are going to be the death of me," his groan sounds like a mix of annoyance and lust.

I smile. "You're a good guy, big guy."

Sebastian huffs out a laugh. "Yeah, well being good doesn't always feel good."

"Hey, at least *you* have that video."

"True."

There's a moment of silence and my drunk brain decides to just blurt out what it's thinking. "I miss you."

Shit. Balls. WTF.

"Is that right?" Sebastian asks, sounding teasing, not mad.

"I mean, just a little. Like a teeny-tiny bit."

"Is that right?"

"Just because you're so hot. No other reason."

"He's here!" Annabelle's voice cuts off my ramble.

"Who?" I ask, looking around.

"Samuel." She stands and starts to put her coat on. "He just texted that he's out front."

"How did he find us?"

"I sent him the address while you were on the phone."

"Wait, you know Samuel?" My drunk brain can't keep any of this straight.

"Oh, yeah. I've known him for ages."

Sebastian laughing in my ear pulls my attention back to him, distracting me from my line of questioning. "Ages indeed."

"Talk about a small world." I say. "Okay, we need to go."

"Text me the second you get home. And make sure Samuel brings you home first." Sebastian tells me.

"Okay."

"And go right there. Don't let him talk you into hitting up another bar."

I roll my eyes. "Don't worry, mom." I joke, and Annabelle

nearly tips over with laughter. "I gotta go. I promise I'll text you."

"Be safe. Bye, Baby."

I hang up the call and drop my phone into my purse.

"Like I said." Annabelle says as she grabs my arm to walk out. "He has it B-A-D for you."

Chapter 57

Meghan

Dear Diary,

I am never drinking another sidecar ever. Like *never* ever. It took me half the day to even get my ass out of bed. Thank god I ate the rest of my leftover coffee cake before I passed out last night. I still feel like shit, but at least I never got sick.

Based on the text I got from Annabelle this morning, it sounds like she feels just as crappy.

I need to send a plate of muffins or something to Samuel for the ride home.

The details of everything that happened after round two are pretty blurry. I remember talking to Sebastian. Not sure exactly what I said, but I remember feeling like an idiot. After that I remember Samuel greeting me with a hug. I remember him laughing his ass off at how drunk we were, ragging on us both. I remember them being super friendly.

I forgot to ask how they know each other. And shit, I wonder if that means Annabelle knows Sebastian, too? But she talked to him on the phone so she would've said something if she knew him. Right?

S. J. Tilly

Ah, Sebastian. What a conundrum he is.
But today is for hangovers, not heavy thinking.
XoxoX

Chapter 58

Meghan

"I can't believe this is our last Sunday brunch before you get married!" I say dramatically.

Katelyn laughs. "Getting married isn't going to stop me from brunching with you. Of course, from now on you'll have to greet me as Mrs. Wilder whenever I come over."

"Oh, okay," I roll my eyes.

With my French toast casserole baking in the oven, we take our coffee mugs over to the couch. I tease Katelyn about tying the knot, but there's a part of me that's worried that everything will change. I'm not sure how, since they've been together for over a year, and living together for months, but it just feels like it will be different.

But maybe that's just me being jealous.

Katelyn sighs. "It is a little crazy. Friday night, I'll become a Mrs."

"I'm not asking this to be a dick. I just believe there should be at least one person who asks you this question before you get married. So as your best friend, tell me, are you one hundred percent sure you want to marry Jackson?"

Katelyn smiles. "Thank you. I love you."

I smile back. "I love you, too."

"And I'm sure. I've never been more sure of a decision in my life. I've been in love with him for so long. I think it started that first night I met him, when I fell asleep against his side watching his favorite movie. He was so sweet and funny and nice and I didn't even know who he was. Then he made me those flashcards. Remember that?"

I laugh. "Yeah, he made those because of the whole *Mother Mary* incident."

Katelyn grins. "And now she'll be Mary-in-law."

I hold my warm coffee cup against my chest like a security blanket. "So when did you know? Like *really know* that he was the one?"

"It wasn't really any one moment, but a combination of the little things. I think I started falling hard when he kissed me at that hockey game. And not because he did it in front of so many people. It was the possession in his eyes. He was so fierce, and it made me feel so incredibly wanted. Then on our first real date, when he took me ice skating and my brother called. Jackson took the phone away from me, to go talk to him. It should've been rude, but it showed me he was interested in more than just a fling. If he wasn't in as deep as I was, he wouldn't have made such an effort with my family. It was such a simple thing, but it meant a lot. And the sex." She drops her head against the back of the couch. "The sex was so much... more. I'd had good sex before, but the feelings I had for him amplified everything. All of that, and every other little moment, made me fall in love with him. I think I denied it to myself for a while. Worried that it might be unrequited."

"When did you accept it as real? Your feelings for him."

"Honestly?"

I nod.

She closes her eyes. "When I went to Jackson's apartment, and I found his bitch ex Lacy standing there in her slutty robe."

"Seriously?" That's not the answer I was expecting.

"Yep. That's when I realized just how completely in love I was. Because thinking that I had lost him, truly lost him, was worse than anything I'd ever felt before. I thought I knew what heartbreak felt like, but I had no idea. It felt like my heart was being pried from my chest. And I knew that if I didn't love him, then it wouldn't hurt so bad."

"Well, fuck. That answer was more intense than I was expecting." I stare at the coffee in my mug, watching the steam curl off the surface.

I'm not sure how long I've been sitting like this, but Katelyn's hand on my knee brings me out of my daze.

She raises a brow at me. "You're looking awfully hard at your coffee. What are you searching for?"

"Maybe once you get married, you'll stop being so perceptive." I scoff.

She smiles. "Doubt it. Now tell me what's going on in that brain of yours. I'm going to take a wild guess and say it has something to do with Sebastian."

I narrow my eyes. "You're so annoying."

"I know. Now spill it."

I wave her off. "We can talk about that later. Like next week. I'm sure you want to go over wedding details."

"Oh hell no. You're not deflecting this. And you've already squared away even the tiniest of details for my wedding. I know Friday will be perfect. But what I really want to know is how my bestie is doing."

I chew on my lip for a moment, and decide to tell her.

I tell her how we text each other every day. I tell her how we talk on the phone a couple times each week. I tell her about our goofy conversations. I tell her how I think about him all the time. About the other night with Annabelle, and all of the theories she had. I tell her about Sebastian calling, finding us a ride, then insisting I tell him when I got home. I tell her how we talked for over an hour last night after he got to his hotel room.

Then I tell her how terrified I am. That I'm almost certain I'm already deeply, madly, truly in love with Sebastian. That I don't know what to do about it. That I'll keep falling harder in love with him while I hope that he's either been lying about not wanting a relationship, or that he'll change his mind. And how entirely stupid that makes me feel. The idiot girl who's hoping that a boy will change just for her. *How fucking cliché.*

Then I tell her that I can't do it. I can't just let myself keep on this path. I need to protect my heart and my sanity. I can't give up entirely, not yet, but if I'm going to wait for him to want more, then I'm going to wait from a distance.

Chapter 59

Sebastian

"Dude, you look fancy," Zach says as he smacks me on the back.

"Yeah? You look like a waiter."

Zach laughs. "I see you still have your panties in a twist."

I clench my jaw. He's fucking right, I have been in a mood. But that ends tonight.

"Have you seen her yet?" Zach asks.

I ignore him. I know he's talking about Meghan. He's been hassling me about her all week. When I didn't see her last weekend, the one night over the past two weeks I was home, he asked if I fucked it up already. I punched him on the shoulder and told him he was dumb. But now, I'm not so sure. I might be the dumb one.

Everything was good between Banshee and me. I mean, yeah, I've been on the road pretty much non-stop, but that's not my fault. I knew she was going to be busy the night of our one home game. But I was a little annoyed when I found out she was at a bar drinking afterward, rather than at my house, fucking. But after about two seconds I realized I never actually told her I wanted to see her. I never asked. So that was my bad.

But it was also my sister's fucking bad. What the hell was she thinking? To say I chewed her out the next day would be an understatement. As always, she had an excuse for everything. She was curious to know more about the girl that Samuel claimed I was swooning over and then she was suddenly in need of an event planner so who better to ask than Meghan. And gee, could I blame her for the coincidence?

The answer's yes. Yes, I can blame her.

Because now I'm in a tough ass position. I need to tell Meghan that Annabelle is really Anna, my sneaky little shit of sister. If I don't tell her, and she finds out another way, I'm sure it will mean hell for me.

I'd have gladly blown Anna's cover right then and there, but they were both too drunk for me to attempt to unravel that over the phone. I called Meghan the next night with the full intention of telling her, but we ended up deep in conversation and I forgot all about it. Then I swore to myself that the next time I talked to her, I would tell her.

But there hasn't been a next time. I haven't talked to her since last Saturday. She's replied to my texts, but she's been different. Brief. And I swear she's been screening my calls. I don't know if she's just been busy with wedding stuff, or if she's been avoiding me. But I'm finding out tonight. And I'm putting an end to it.

Zach pushes a glass into my hands.

It's something brown on the rocks. Good enough.

I take a drink. "Thanks."

"Anything to get you to loosen up." He clinks his glass against mine. "Here's to drinking, eating, and sleeping with beautiful women. And most importantly, to our day off tomorrow."

Sleet Banshee

I take another sip. I'll drink to that.

"Speaking of beautiful women, where's yours?" I ask.

Zach shrugs. "I'm assuming she's in a back room somewhere doing whatever the hell women do to get ready for a wedding. I love her. I really do. But I can only listen to so much wedding talk before my mind goes to sleep." He gestures to the giant dinosaur skeletons around us. "When we arrived, she told me to come down here. And that she'll find me before the ceremony."

There are several rows of black chairs facing the dino duo, with an aisle down the middle. I remember Meghan saying something about 100 or so guests, and the number of chairs looks to be about that. Lining the aisle are tall, heavy-looking vases filled with some sort of wild grass. I'm not a florist, so I have no idea what it is, but it's natural and bold while still being classy.

Centered in front of everything is a small area that's been lined on three sides with the same tall grass. With the right camera angles it'll look like they are standing in a field with the dinosaurs. It's brilliant. It's Banshee.

"When we get married," Zach's words pull my attention back to him, "I'll let Izzy do whatever the hell she wants, but I'm gonna insist on a pre-ceremony bar. This is genius." He takes a sip from his glass.

The little bar down here really is a nice touch, but that's not the part of his statement that I care about. "You're planning to marry Izzy?"

He looks at me like I'm dense. "Of course. She's fucking perfect. That woman is it for me."

I guess I should've known that. He's been head over heels for her since day one.

My face pulls into a frown without my permission. Why does that make me feel so... off?

Zach steps closer. "Don't worry man, you'll find someone who makes you feel that way. I didn't mean to push you before. It's okay if Meghan's not it for you. You'll find the right one eventually."

I take a large swallow of my drink. Then another.

I'm not worried that Meghan isn't the one for me. I know that she is. I think I've known since the grocery store. When I got home that day, I couldn't stop thinking about her. I couldn't stop thinking about how much fun I'd had with her. How I wanted to go shopping with her again. *Grocery shopping.* The best date I've ever had involved buying grapes and ended with a brief kiss in a parking lot. Ridiculous, but true.

So no, I'm not worried about Meghan being my One. I'm worried that I'll fuck it up, or that I already have. And regardless of my hesitations, I need to let Banshee know how I feel. Maybe I'm not ready to make proclamations of forever, but at the very least I need to ask her to be my girlfriend. I made a mistake when I told her I didn't want a relationship. It was a lie then and it's a lie now. It's time for me to set things straight.

I open my mouth to reply to Zach, but movement on the stairs catches my attention.

It's Meghan.

My Banshee.

My sassy little firecracker.

She's coming down the main staircase, one hand on the railing, one hand gripping the skirt of her dress, with her eyes focused on the steps in front of her.

She looks like a fairytale. Like a dark mermaid. Like everything I've ever wanted. And everything I'll ever need.

I remind myself to breathe.

Her hair is tamed into perfect curls, with the top half pulled away from her face. Her eyes look darker than normal, and I want to see them up close.

I take my time slowly soaking her in, burning this image into my memory.

Her sexy curves are draped in a soft material. The top connects behind her neck, leaving her shoulders bare. There's no exposed cleavage, but somehow that's even more enticing because I know what's there. The black fabric clings to her before flaring out at her waist. At her thighs, the material slowly morphs from black to red, so by the time the hem of the dress brushes the floor, the fabric is a deep maroon. A color that perfectly matches my tailored button up shirt. A shirt that's surrounded with an impeccable black suit.

A smile pulls at the edge of my mouth. She's been pushing me away all week, but somehow, we look as though we planned this.

My mind flashes to a fantasy so crisp, I'd swear it was a memory. Banshee discussing fabrics with my clothier to find the perfect selection. Her asking for my input then ignoring me entirely, doing whatever the hell she wants anyways. Her keeping her dress zipped up in a bag in our closet and telling me not to peek. I peek. Of course, I do. And I run my fingers over the material, imagining what it will look like on her. I tell myself to act surprised when she puts it on for me. But I won't have to act. The sight of her in it will stagger me. It will be so much more than I'd pictured. And she'll have to smack my hands away to keep me from taking her right then and there.

I take another large pull from my glass.

"Never mind," Zach's chuckle brings me back to the present. "Clearly I had it right the first time."

Chapter 60

Sebastian

I LOOK AWAY for one moment, to tell Zach to shut the fuck up, and she's disappeared.

How does a goddess vanish into such a small crowd?

Ignoring Zach, I take a step toward the stairs. She's gotta be hidden behind someone. Most of the team is here, so there's a lot of large bodies. My Banshee might have a big presence, but she's tiny in comparison to me and the rest of the guys.

"Mr. LeBlanc. Mr. Hunt." A hand clamps down on my shoulder.

"Hey, Coach." I'm tempted to brush him off, but Zach and I turn to face him.

"Coach," Zach greets.

"My, my. Don't you boys clean up nice."

"Ash here says I look like a waiter," Zach pouts.

Coach lets out a bark of laughter. "He's not entirely wrong, son."

Zach scoffs. "Izzy picked this out. You better not let her hear you say that."

Sleet Banshee

Sometimes I forget that his girlfriend is the coach's daughter.

Coach nods. "Copy that. How about you, Ash? You bring a date with you tonight?"

I sigh. "I think you two have been spending too much time together. Zach's gonna turn you into a meddling old biddy if you're not careful."

Zach chuckles, then answers Coach's question for me. "He's here with Meghan. Or at least, he's hoping to be."

"Our Meghan?" Coach asks. "How interesting."

Now they're both looking at me. Of course Coach knows Meghan, she's good friends with Izzy. Not sure how I could've overlooked that bit of information.

Coach gives me a slow once-over, and I can tell he's looking at me from a father's perspective. "I can see it. You two could actually be a good match. She's a bit of a firecracker." I smirk, having just thought the same thing. "But you're a bit of an ass, so you need someone like that to keep you in line."

"Hey!" I say, indignant.

"Dude." Zach laughs at me. "Coach has you fucking nailed."

I roll my eyes. "Alright, you two can stay over here gossiping. I'm going to go find... someone."

Zach throws up air quotes as he repeats, "*Someone.*"

I flip him the bird, and go on a Banshee hunt.

Chapter 61

Meghan

THIS MIGHT BE a new low for me. I'm chugging a glass of champagne, hiding behind a bank of elevators, at my best friend's wedding.

But, gah! Sebastian looks like sex on legs. He looks like the Devil. But like a sexual Devil that will tie you up and do orgasmic things to you until you beg for him to put you out of your misery. So, like, a good Devil.

I take another long pull from my glass.

And, on top of him looking sexy as fuck, it looks like we freaking coordinated our outfits together. We couldn't look more like a couple if we tried!

I figured he'd show up in the standard black suit, white shirt. But noooo, Sebastian had to swap the classic white out for a deep red that perfectly matches my dress.

I don't know if he noticed our matchy-matchyness, but I know he noticed me. He was staring at me so hard while I was walking down those stairs, the dinosaurs could have come to life and he wouldn't have noticed. He was so zoned in that I don't think he even noticed me watching him.

I know we'll end up talking tonight, but I need to get a few more servings of bubbly in me, and get through this ceremony, before that happens.

Taking another sip, I feel a presence join me behind the elevators.

Knowing who it is before I even look, I brace myself as I slowly turn my head. Finding myself staring into Sebastian's eyes, I admit no amount of bracing would've made a difference.

He's so goddamn good looking.

Sebastian steps closer, not breaking eye contact.

With every foot that disappears between us, my heart rate increases.

And he hasn't said anything. At all.

My self-consciousness growing, I glance away and smooth my free hand over my dress. I've never been this dressed up around Sebastian before. I need him to say something, anything, about how I look.

A large hand cups my cheek, and my eyes slowly rise back up to meet his.

He's closer now. Mere inches between us.

His other hand comes up, and now he's cupping both sides of my face. The heat from his palms seeps into my blood, raising my body temperature.

Slowly, he leans in, stopping with his lips a breath away from mine. "You look beautiful."

I swallow.

"Thank you," my words are a barely audible whisper.

"I'm going to kiss you."

Instead of responding, I lean into him.

Our lips connect and it's... heart-wrenching.

This is nothing like the frantic or frenzied kisses of our past. This is slow and sweet. It's a greeting. A promise.

I've been trying to pull back, to put distance between us,

but I can't. I can't fight these feelings I have for him. And I don't know where that'll leave me.

When he presses his mouth more firmly to mine, I part my lips on a sigh. I lean into the kiss. I can think later.

Sebastian's hand slides around to the back of my neck, as he teases his tongue across my open lips. It's innocent, but so dirty that I'm clenching my thighs. I'm pretty sure I moan.

Sebastian breaks the kiss, but - instead of pulling away - he rests his forehead against mine. "Hi."

"Hi." My kissed lips pull into a smile.

"You okay?"

I give a tiny nod. "Yeah."

His thumbs are rubbing small circles at the base of my neck. "Good. Because it almost seemed like you were avoiding me."

I make a small humming sound. "That's preposterous," I mumble. "Why would I do that?"

"Hmm. Why indeed."

His thumbs are fuzzing out my brain, and all I want to do is kiss him again.

A throat clears behind Sebastian.

"Sorry to interrupt you lovebirds, but we're being told to sit down." Zach chuckles.

Sebastian rises to his full height but keeps his eyes on mine. Whatever he's searching for, he must find it, because he nods. Stepping back, he places a hand at the small of my back to guide me towards the ceremony.

I can't believe I lost track of time. I should've been the one to let people know it was time to sit down.

I look up to Sebastian as we walk towards the rows of chairs. "I need to sit in the front, so I can adjust Katelyn's dress if she needs it."

"Okay."

Sleet Banshee

This is where we'll part ways for a bit. I know he'll want to sit in the back.

But he keeps walking with me. All the way to the front.

"Which side?" he asks.

"Oh, um, they aren't really doing *sides*, but I'll go over here - " I gesture to our left.

"Alright, but let me take the chair at the end. That way my big head won't block anyone's view."

"Oookay?" I can't help the questioning tone.

He wants to sit with me? At a wedding? In the front row?

We take our seats, and Sebastian rests his arm across the back of my chair. This is so boyfriend-like that I'm about to lose my mind. I want to run off to find Izzy and Katelyn so I can ask them what this means.

As if she heard my mental plea, Izzy steps into the row right behind us, with Zach at her side. They look gorgeous together. He's in a classic black-and-white getup, with a blue silk pocket square. The color is a few shades darker than Izzy's periwinkle silk gown. She looks like a princess, and he looks like her prince.

I twist in my seat, my back to Sebastian so I can face Izzy.

"Hey!" she says cheerfully, and I can see the moment she takes in Sebastian next to me, and how he's sitting.

Her eyebrows go up, and I widen my eyes in a *I have no idea what the fuck is happening* look. I don't even care if Zach can see my expression.

Probably having the same thought as Sebastian, Zach shuffles past Izzy to take the end seat.

"I was worried I lost you," Izzy says to me as she takes her seat.

"Don't worry, Sugar," Zach mirrors Sebastian by draping his arm behind Izzy. "I found them making out in the coat room."

"We were not in a coat room!" I blurt, before clamping my lips shut.

Zach grins as Izzy gapes at me.

Sebastian leans forward to talk into my ear, but he's loud enough for them to easily hear. "Just ignore him, Baby. He's an idiot."

I spin back around in my seat and tug on Sebastian's lapels until he's close enough for me to whisper in his ear. "How many times do I have to tell you? *Don't* call me *Baby*."

"At least once more." He surprises me with a quick kiss on the lips.

Izzy's giggles float around us.

I narrow my eyes as I watch Sebastian, but he seems calm as can be, leaning back, stretching his feet out in front of him. As if kissing me in public, in front of all our friends, is a normal thing.

My brain's about to throw in the white flag, when the overhead lights dim. It's almost time.

The rest of the seats are quickly filled. Katelyn's parents and brother join our row, and I give Alex a little wave. He smiles back, then seems to stutter-step when he realizes who is seated next to me. I pretend not to notice. Being best friends with his sister for decades means he treats me just like a sister, and I don't need the third degree right now.

I smile when I see Jackson walk his mother down the aisle to her seat in the other front row. She gives him a huge hug before she sits, and I can see tears already tracking down her face. Jackson smiles at her, and he looks so happy. And handsome in his dark grey suit. He's wearing a white shirt, with no tie, under his jacket. It's simple and perfect and I know it'll look great next to Katelyn's dress.

Katelyn's aunt is officiating the ceremony and has slipped into position. With Jackson joining her, we're ready.

The spotlights highlighting the two large dinosaur skeletons in front of us, morph until the light glowing down is purple. The other spotlights throughout the room vary between purple and white light. The mood is a perfect blend of romantic and sexy. And the photos are going to be killer.

Soft instrumental music begins to play over the speakers, and that's the cue. We all rise, and turn as one, to see Katelyn walking down the staircase with her father at her side.

My breath catches.

She looks like a fairy. Like a dream. Like a bride.

Her dress is made up of various shades of blush in flowy tulle panels. The color is perfect with her dark brown hair, which is in a loose braid with just the right amount of escaping curls. With her hair pulled back you can see the beautiful little cap sleeves that lead to a plunging neckline. The top half of the dress is embroidered with small white flowers, and they're sparkling like diamonds under the spotlights.

Tears fill my eyes. She's perfect. This is perfect. And I could not be happier for her.

I remind myself to breathe as she makes the walk down the aisle. When Katelyn's dad kisses her on the cheek, before handing her off to Jackson, I lose the battle against my tears. A few escape and I quickly wipe them away with my fingertips.

I've been so preoccupied with Katelyn's entrance that I haven't even looked at Jackson. The love and tears in his eyes cause more of mine to spill over. Damnit. I should have picked a dress with pockets. I need a tissue.

Sebastian catches my wrist as I reach up to wipe away another tear.

I almost jump.

I've been so involved in watching Katelyn, I forgot he was even here with me. Before I have a chance to be embarrassed about crying at a wedding that's only just started, Sebastian places a tissue against my palm.

I stare down at it, like he just gave me a stolen jewel.

With his hand still holding my wrist, he uses his other hand to close my fingers around the gift.

When the officiant tells us to be seated, Sebastian wraps his arm around my shoulders instead of just putting it on the back of my chair.

Leaning into Sebastian's solid body, I dab at my tears and watch my best friend marry her Happily Ever After.

The ceremony's half over before I even remember to look at the train of her dress. Thankfully, it's a short train that naturally laid out perfectly. On a relieved exhale, I melt further into Sebastian's side. This man is a mess of mixed signals, but - for the duration of tonight - I'm giving in to temptation.

Chapter 62

Meghan

"I NEED to wear dresses more often. You can eat as much as you want without fear of a tight waistband," I tell Izzy as we polish off a pair of cupcakes.

"I know, right? Why do you think I live in wrap dresses? They can literally be adjusted mid-event." Izzy winks.

Jackson only had one request for the wedding reception. He didn't want anyone to have to wait for food. Like, *at all*. So I gave the guests options.

After the ceremony, the newly married couple take some time for photos throughout the museum, while the guests congregate on the top floor. As soon as we get off the elevator, there are waiters walking around with trays of champagne and the signature cocktail for tonight - the Kitten Cuddler. It's a real thing. As soon as I found it, I knew they needed it. And - obviously - there's a full open bar, so there's no reason for anyone to stay sober if they don't want to.

To accommodate Jackson's request, there are also waiters walking around with trays of finger food. All night. The menu will change each hour, so there's always something new and tasty at hand. But that part is really just for snacking. When the bride and groom finish their pictures, the buffet opens. I had figured with the money Jackson was dropping on tonight, he'd want table service meals, but they both agreed they preferred a laid-back atmosphere. So a bursting-at-the-seams buffet is what they got. From sushi to mini pizzas to tacos, this setup has everything. Not to be outdone by the savory stuff, there's also a full dessert table that's been open-and-ready from the get-go. Since I had my first cupcake before dinner, I don't feel that bad about the second one I just had. I may have had a tart, too. And maybe a truffle.

Izzy licks the frosting off her fingers. "I can't believe they still have cake."

I laugh. "When Jackson found out that I knew the owner of RitaCakes, he insisted. Not like having extra cake is ever a bad thing. Speaking of which, they'll probably be cutting that soon."

As soon as I say it, I see the happy couple head over to the cake table with the photographer.

"Ugggh, Rita's is the absolute best! I need to dance this cupcake off a bit so I have room for more," Izzy tugs my arm towards the dance floor.

"Can't argue there."

Tonight is the first time I'm using this particular band, and they're amazing. They have a full DJ table, a singer, a guitar player and a saxophone player. Sounds weird on paper, sounds fabulous in person. And clearly the guests agree, since the dance floor is hopping. Now that dinner's over, the lights have dimmed, and the volume has turned up. It's officially a party from now until midnight when they kick everyone out.

Finding a spot in the middle of the crowd, Izzy lets go of my hand and starts to twirl. The band puts their own remix on popular songs, making them even more danceable.

Sleet Banshee

Soaking in the mood around me, I drop my reservations, put my hands in the air, and dance like a loon.

Chapter 63

Meghan

"I'll be right back!" I mouth to Izzy.

I'm not sure if she read my lips, but she's veering into Dirty Dancing territory with Zach, so I'm sure she doesn't care that I'm leaving.

I just need a moment to sit down, or at the very least ditch these shoes. Even the most comfortable heels turn into torture devices after so many hours. My dress is long enough; I think I'll just go barefoot and hope no one notices.

I've made it a few feet past the edge of the dance floor when a body appears in front of me. I don't need to look up to know it's Sebastian.

The tension has been brewing between us all night. It started as a sizzle with that kiss downstairs. Then, with all the light touches and glances throughout dinner, it's turned into a five-alarm fire. Pretty sure a strong breeze could bring me to orgasm by now.

He holds out a hand. "May I have this dance?"

Even though my feet hurt, I don't hesitate. I place my hand in his as I lift my gaze. "Since you asked so nicely."

Sleet Banshee

He smiles, and it's not snarky or smug. It's just... sweet.

The song changes to *Candyman* by Christina Aguilera and a roar of laughter fills the room. This has become Jackson and Katelyn's theme song, whether they like it or not.

I expect Sebastian to pull me back towards the dance floor, but he doesn't. Instead, he pulls me to his chest, keeping his grip on my hand, wrapping the other arm around my back. And I die a little. Pretty sure my little honey badger is squeezing my heart so hard it's killing me.

With my pain-inducing shoes still on, I'm almost tall enough to lay my head against his shoulder. I settle for pressing my cheek against his chest and gripping the back of his shirt with my free hand.

Ignoring the heavy beat, we gently sway together for the remainder of the song. When a new song starts, Sebastian lets go of my hand, moving his to my lower back. He pulls me in until our bodies are flush, and I feel him nuzzle into my hair.

"You smell good," he murmurs.

I smile. "Sebastian LeBlanc, are you drunk?"

I hear him take another deep inhale of my hair. "Nah."

"Nah?"

"Not that drunk. Just happy to have you."

Gah! My poor heart swells in my chest.

He rubs his nose against my hair again.

"Let's go," he says, pulling back.

I look up at him. "Go?"

His eyes are so piercing, and I can't tell if he's actually drunk or just super horny. Maybe both.

"I need to kiss you." He says this so seriously I can't help but laugh, but it doesn't deter him. "Come on, I know a place."

"You *know* a place?" I ask.

He doesn't answer, he just tugs me along, weaving between tables, heading towards the back of the room.

All this walking reminds me how much I hate my shoes right now.

"Hold on," I tell him.

I drop his hand and kick off my shoes.

I'm crouching down to pick them up when Sebastian spins around, probably to see what stopped me. From my spot on the floor, I look up into his eyes, and they're smoldering. I'm not sure I've ever used that word before, but it's the only way to describe how he looks. And I'm positive he's thinking about the last time I was on my knees in this museum. Because that's what I'm thinking about.

I quickly grab my shoes and take his hand again. As we near the back, I toss my heels toward the corner. If someone wants to steal my sweaty shoes, they're welcome to them.

With three walls of windows, this back wall is the only way in and out of the room. There's a hallway hosting the bathrooms, a kitchen, the elevator, a stairwell, and a handful of other doors. Sebastian walks us halfway down the hall, then - with a finger to his lips - he gently presses open the door on his left.

I bite my lip and follow him in. I'm not sure why we're being quiet, but it's fun, so I play along. Keeping a hand on the door, he lets it shut slowly.

Turning in a circle, I see we're in some sort of storeroom. There are stacks of chairs, some tables leaning against the front wall, and a few rows of shelving filled with cleaning products and other supplies.

Just as Sebastian and I turn to each other, we hear a noise. It sounded like a giggle.

I bring both of my hands up to cover my mouth. I don't want whoever's in here to know that we caught them. We glance at each and slowly make our way over to the end of the aisle. It's a non-verbal agreement that we want to see who else is in here trying to get lucky. Whoever it is, they aren't concerned about being quiet and they clearly haven't heard us enter.

As we reach the corner, I hear another round of giggles followed by. "Oh, Don!"

Don? Who do I know named Don?

I feel Sebastian slow next to me.

I crouch down and peek my head around the corner. And thank fuck I have my hands over my mouth. I'm not sure who I expected to see, but I sure as hell wasn't prepared to see Coach, aka *Don*, feeling up Mother Mary.

I don't want to see this, but I can't seem to look away. It's like a train wreck... an old person, motorboating train wreck.

Sebastian's arms wrap around me, lifting me from my crouched position. Bearing my weight, he walks backwards towards the door. With every step he takes I have to fight harder against my own giggles, as Mary's grow in volume.

Sebastian sets me down and eases the door open. Hurrying, I make it one foot out the door before I lose the battle.

Laughter bubbles out, and I run towards the stairs. I don't think they heard us, but I absolutely don't want to be identified as the person who caught Coach and Jackson's mom getting it on in the supply closet.

We start our retreat down the stairs at the same time, but Sebastian's long legs and athleticism gets him to the landing between levels first. He's turned to face me, and I let myself crash right into his body. With or without alcohol, I know he can handle it. And he does.

In one swift move, Sebastian stops my forward momentum and captures my mouth with his. Before I can even decide what part of him to touch with my hands, we hear voices on the stairs above us.

Seemingly of the same mind, we break the kiss and start

running down the stairs again. We keep going past the third floor, continuing on to the second. Guests are encouraged to stay at the reception, but nothing is actually on lock down.

When we reach the landing, Sebastian takes my hand and slows our pace.

He doesn't say anything to me, and I don't break the silence. I let him lead me through the exhibits, enjoying the feel of my small hand in his big one.

Without pausing, Sebastian walks under an archway of clouds and into the weather exhibit.

The room is dark, but there's just enough light coming in from the hallway to see the outline of the interactive stations scattered around the room.

Sebastian walks us to the center of the room, then slowly turns to face me. It's too dark to see his expression, but I'm sure it matches my own.

I want him. I'm ready.

He puts his hands on my shoulders but instead of pulling me in, he pushes me back. He walks me backwards until my butt hits a ledge. He must have planned for this, because he moves his hands to my waist, and lifts me. I'm not used to being picked up so easily, and I'm not too proud to admit that I love it.

My skirt is flowy, so when he sets me down on the tabletop I'm able to spread my legs wide enough for him to step between my thighs. Sebastian takes my face in his palms, just like he did earlier. But this kiss, it's nothing like the slow one we shared downstairs. This is the kiss of a starving man.

Not waiting for me to catch up, his thumb pulls my chin down, opening my mouth. The moment I comply, his tongue tangles with mine.

It doesn't matter that it's dark. Our mouths know each other, they know how to move together. When to suck, when to bite, when to caress.

Sleet Banshee

My palms run up his chest, and I'm glad he removed his suit jacket at dinner. The fabric of his shirt is smooth under my touch, and I feel the power of his muscles rippling beneath my fingers.

When my fingers reach his nipples, I pinch them both.

Sebastian groans into my mouth, then mirrors my move by cupping both my breasts. His squeeze matches my pinching, and we both moan.

That's my tipping point. I've been letting him lead tonight, but I want more. *I need more.* I need all of him.

I drag my nails down his torso until I reach his belt. Too impatient to bother with undoing it, I go straight for the zipper. I tug it down and reach my hand in the opening. He's rock hard but the cotton of his boxer briefs is keeping me from his silky skin.

With a growl of frustration, I realize my error with skipping his belt and button. He's too big, I can't pull him out like this. With his mouth still devouring mine, I feel his lips pull into a smile.

Sebastian's hands leave my chest and get to work on his pants. He's quicker than I could've been and - in a matter of seconds his pants are undone, and his cock is released. My greedy little fingers wrap around his length, and I sigh.

I've missed him. I've missed his body. I wish I could see more. My eyes are starting to adjust, but we're both still shrouded in darkness.

Sebastian grabs one of my wrists and pulls my hand off him. I'm about to protest, when he presses a condom into my hand. It's already out of the wrapper and ready for me to roll onto his cock.

Even though we've had sex before, the act of putting a condom on him feels incredibly intimate. I take my time sliding it on, squeezing him as I do.

Once the condom is in place, Sebastian steps back and bends down to grab the hem of my dress. Straightening, he brings the skirt with him, sliding it up my thighs. My breath is already coming out in rapid pants.

Leaning back, I put my hands behind me for balance. My palm comes down on a large flat button, and the room springs to life with a silent blizzard.

We both pause in surprise. I know it's a projection, but the snowflakes fluttering around us look so lifelike that I expect to feel cold. It's so surreal. And beautiful. Thankfully, the narration stays quiet.

The snowstorm isn't bright, but when I bring my attention back to the man in front of me, I'm able to see all the details between us. Sebastian is standing between my legs, with his hands buried in my dress bunched at my waist, and his sheathed cock straining out of his pants. It's lewd, and out of place, and the sexiest thing I've ever seen.

My eyes travel up to his face, and I find him watching me.

Our eyes stay locked, and his lips pull up into a devilish smirk.

With my dress out of the way, Sebastian steps forward. His hands grip my hips and he drags me until I'm sitting on the edge of the table. I grab his face and bring it back to mine. I'm not done kissing his delicious mouth. Our lips meet as the snow continues to swirl around us.

His hands leave my hips, but I can hardly focus on what's happening with his lips hypnotizing me.

My fingers work their way into his hair and scrape against his scalp. With his chest against mine, the rumble of his approval rolls straight through me.

One of his hands moves between my legs, his fingers hooking around the edge of my panties and pulling them to the side. The cool air ghosts across my pussy, sending a shiver up my spine. The color in the room changes and my eyes flick open to see that the snow around us has turned to sleet.

I start to smile, but Sebastian plunges inside me, bottoming out in one harsh thrust, shattering all my thoughts.

It's so good. So intense. And he's so fucking big, I cry out.

Predicting my reaction, he catches my scream with another kiss. But he doesn't stop.

He pulls nearly all the way out, making me arch towards him, then without warning he slams back in. There's no time to adjust to his size. There's no slowing down. There's only a frenzied need.

A tug on my hair, and my eyes open. I'd been squeezing them shut, clenching my entire body against the intensity.

With my eyes on his, he buries his cock as deep as it'll go once again, then holds still.

Without a word, he watches me. I force myself to take a slow exhale and relax. The moment I do, he starts to move again. Slowly at first, but not for long.

The sound of our heavy breathing and the sight of the rainstorm now surrounding us makes this feel like a dream. I'm in the middle of an outdoor exhibitionist fantasy I didn't know I had.

The sting of his entry has turned into an ache of need. Up 'till now, we've done little more than kiss tonight, but it feels like we've been engaging in foreplay for hours and I'm officially ready to fall apart.

Sebastian reaches down and hooks one of my knees over his arm. It rests in the crook of his elbow and the new angle is incredible. I've never come just from sex before, without the addition of a hand or a toy, but I feel like that is about to change.

I grab his shoulders and pull him to me. I can't get enough of his kisses tonight, and I'm so fucking close.

My body starts to tense, and he feels it. He keeps his pace steady but his grip on my hair tightens. I moan and he pulls me closer to bite my lip.

The stimulation is too much. My orgasm doesn't build. It fucking explodes. And for the second time, Sebastian swallows my screams.

He doesn't slow and let me come down easily. He pounds into me harder and kisses me deeper until he follows me over the edge.

It's his turn to be loud. I try to capture his sounds, but my brain is only half functioning, and my body is still twitching.

Sebastian finally stills, but his lips never leave mine. With his cock still inside me, he holds my face and continues to kiss me. My pulse is still wild, and the tenderness of the kiss pulls at every one of my heart strings.

As our kiss slows, I can tell the brightness in the room has changed again.

Pulling back, I look around to see a rainbow arching across the ceiling.

Sebastian's looking around the room too, and his smile is something I want to remember forever. He looks as happy as I feel.

Today has felt like something new. Like maybe he wants more. But I can't let myself run away with wishful thinking. This is going to hurt bad enough when it ends, as it is.

Cutting off my spiraling thoughts, Sebastian pulls me in for one more quick kiss, before slowly pulling out and away.

I am sore and sated, and I miss him already.

Chapter 64

Meghan

As we reach the top of the stairs, I realize we haven't said any actual words to each other since we left the reception. And I'm not sure if that's impressive, or weird, given what we just did.

The projection turned off just as we were leaving the exhibit, and we made a quick stop at the restrooms before coming back up here. I feel a little bad about sullying the weather room with sex, but I was sitting on my skirt of the whole time, so it's not like anything got... dirty. But still, I might keep this little rendezvous to myself.

With that thought, we exit the stairwell hand in hand, and halt. Samuel's standing a few feet in front of us. Arms crossed. With a disapproving look on his face.

We have a silent standoff for a beat before Samuel speaks.

"We. Have. Cameras!" He claps with every word, to emphasize his point.

I feel the blood rush to my face. Of-fucking-course the cameras would be on! Why did I forget about that?

"Right," Sebastian says, and I figure he's going to apologize. "Can you get me a copy of that one, too?"

My head whips to the side to look at him, and I let go of his hand so I can smack his chest.

"Oh my god, are you serious?" I whisper-shout at him.

He grins. "Completely." Then he captures my chin in one big hand and kisses me hard. "Grab us some cake. I'll be right there."

This guy.

I toss my hands up and walk away. Avoiding eye contact with Samuel.

It doesn't take me long to hunt down Izzy and Zach. They're seated at an empty table in the back. I detour and grab two little plates of cake before joining them. And not because Sebastian told me to — because I want cake. Only a monster would leave a wedding without eating cake.

I drop into the seat across from Izzy, nod a greeting, then dig into my dessert. Suddenly, I'm famished.

"That for me?" Izzy asks, gesturing at the other plate.

I consider her question for a moment. I can't believe Sebastian's reaction to getting caught on camera, *again*. But on the other hand, he did earn that cake.

Oh man, did he earn it.

"Sorry, Izz, it's spoken for," Sebastian's deep voice rumbles behind me before he pulls out the chair next to mine.

Izzy narrows her eyes and looks back and forth between us. "Where have you two been?"

I shovel another bite into my mouth, so I don't have to answer.

Sebastian grips the edge of my chair and pulls me closer to him. "Talking."

I nearly choke. Talking is literally the only thing we *weren't* doing. I can't look at him. I know if I do, my cheeks will burn up until their color matches his shirt.

Sleet Banshee

Izzy's still glaring at Sebastian, but Zach is grinning like he knows exactly what we were doing.

I just keep stuffing my face, so I don't have to participate in this conversation. The guys start talking about next week's game, and I tune them out.

"Daddy!" Izzy exclaims. "There you are. I was looking all over for you."

This time I do choke.

Sebastian pats my back and leans in like he's saying something into my ear. But really, he's just trying to cover his own laughter.

"You okay there, Meghan?" Coach asks.

I force myself to nod.

Izzy hands me a glass of water. I'm not sure if it was even hers, but I don't care, I drink it.

Izzy's shooting me sideways glances as she talks to her dad. I'm normally not this awkward, so she's got to be wondering what's wrong with me. But there is no way in hell that I'm going to tell her what I saw.

I'll tell Katelyn. She can deal with it.

Chapter 65

Meghan

"I can't believe you're a married woman now! I'm so happy for you!" I squeeze Katelyn in a hug until she starts to struggle.

"Okay, okay. Get off me, you nutball!" She laughs.

I keep my grip on her shoulders as I step back. "Now, I don't want you to be afraid, but tonight Jackson is gonna want to put his penis inside of you."

"Oh my god!" Katelyn shrieks.

"I said *don't* be afraid. It's a totally normal thing that husbands and wives do."

She shoves me away. "What's your excuse then?"

"What do you mean?" I ask.

"If you're not married, why were you fucking Sebastian in the weather room earlier?"

My mouth drops open, and it takes me a beat to recover. "What... How..."

She smiles. "Samuel told me."

"What?! You don't even know him?"

"We've bonded today. And just a few minutes ago, I asked if all the guests behaved themselves in his museum." I grimace at her choice of wording. "Imagine my surprise when he says everyone was just perfect, except for my bestie and his brother, defiling one of the exhibits downstairs."

"Such a fucking gossip," I grumble, then shrug. "Well, if the supply room hadn't been occupied, we wouldn't have needed to go downstairs."

Katelyn tilts her head. "Wait, what? Was there another couple getting it on during my wedding reception?"

I grin. "Yep."

"Who?"

"Coach." I wait a beat. "And Jackson's mom."

Katelyn's jaw drops open.

I walk backwards, giving her a double hand wave. "Congrats again! I love you! Have a good night!"

"Meghan! Don't you dare walk away after dropping that bomb."

Laughing, I spin around and speed walk towards Sebastian. He's talking to Zach and Izzy but I don't bother with words. I just grab his sleeve and start to pull him away. He comes along willingly, calling out goodbyes over his shoulder.

"Just can't wait to get me alone again, huh?" Sebastian asks.

"Sure, uh huh." I keep our pace as we snag our things and head to the elevator.

Most of the guests have left, so we don't have to wait in line. When the doors close behind us, I see Sebastian pull up a ride app on his phone. During my cake binge, he asked me to go home with him. And I agreed.

Something definitely seems different about him. The public displays of affection. The way he kissed me in greeting.

Ultimately, I think we need to have another talk. And it's either going to go the way I want it to, or it's going to be the stake in the heart of our arrangement.

But we're both still a little tipsy, and we should probably be sober for that discussion. More sex though, I'm okay with that. I told myself I'd enjoy tonight, and accepting Sebastian's invitation home is just a continuation of the night. We can talk in the morning.

A car is waiting for us when we get outside and we both slip into the backseat.

Sebastian holds my hand during the drive. His thumb is rubbing little circles on the back of my hand, lulling me into a blissful stupor. We stay silent, listening to the music playing quietly in the car.

Looking out the window, I realize we've made it to the suburbs. I must've really zoned out, because we're probably a 30-minute drive from the museum. I watch the scenery as we exit the highway and work our way through a residential neighborhood. The lots are getting wider, the houses getting larger as we go.

"It's the next one on your left," Sebastian tells the driver.

We pull into the driveway of a gorgeous, two-story home with a wraparound porch, stunning architectural detail, and a three-car garage. I'm still sitting, staring, when Sebastian opens my door from the outside. I was too busy gawking to notice him exiting the car.

He holds his hand out for me. "Come on, Banshee."

I do my best not to totally lose it as we walk up to the front door. Why didn't I think about this? He's a professional hockey player. He makes millions of dollars every year. He has a ton of money. Like a freaking *ton* of money. Somewhere in my brain I knew this, but I hadn't really thought about what that meant.

And yet, I'd guess this house probably costs less than $2 million. It's beautiful, and large, but not over the top. It's tucked away in a quiet little neighborhood and not something you could ever call a bachelor pad. If I'd thought about where

Sebastian lived, I'd have pictured a penthouse like Jackson's. Not... *this*.

Opening the front door, he ushers me inside. There are a few lamps on, but it's mostly dark. I gladly kick my shoes off for the second time, but - before I have time to look around - Sebastian puts his hand on my lower back, guiding me past the kitchen and towards the stairs.

I'm still a little bit in shock, but luckily we've both been quiet since leaving the museum, so my stunned reaction isn't noticeable. I don't want to make a big deal out of his house, it's just so different from what I expected.

The insecure part of my brain starts to spin. How well do I really know him if I'm this shocked by his choice of home? And how can we meld our lives together when we live so differently?

And yes, I know I just left Katelyn and Jackson's wedding, so clearly it can work. But that's different. Somehow. Fuck, I don't know what to think!

At the top of the stairs, we continue down the hall to the last door on the left where Sebastian stops me just inside the threshold.

A soft glow emanates from a bedside lamp allowing me to take in the details. Even if the house is a surprise, this room feels like Sebastian. The walls are a dark grey, and there's a king-size bed in the center of the room with an iron four-poster frame. The bed frame is probably seven feet tall, but the ceilings are high, so it doesn't feel too dominating. Above the bed, there's a lattice of black metal connecting each bedpost creating a sexy, masculine version of a canopy bed. The rest of the furniture is made from light toned wood with matching black iron hardware.

Hardwood floors run through the whole house, but I feel a super-soft rug beneath my feet. I wiggle my toes in it as I look at the walls. It's a little hard to see in the low light, but he has some large pieces of art that seem to match the graffiti style of his tattoos. And that flare of recognition calms me. It's something I can grab on to and understand. Something that makes this place feel real. Familiar.

Sebastian's been patiently standing behind me, letting me look, but he's done waiting.

Brushing my hair over one shoulder, he finds the clasp holding up my halter top and undoes it. I let the straps fall forward as he slowly trails his fingers over my newly exposed skin. This dress has built-in support, so there's no uncomfortable strapless bra to deal with. Sebastian's fingers skim down my spine to the zipper at the center of my back, taking his time dragging it down. As the zipper lowers, so does my dress. And when he lets go, the fabric falls away, pooling at my feet.

I'm left standing here in nothing but my thong as Sebastian runs his fingers up my sides. Goosebumps break out over my entire body when his lips meet my bare back, and I clench my fists. I need something to hold on to. And I want it to be him.

I finally break the silence with his name. "Sebastian."

He hums and trails a line of kisses across my shoulders.

"Please," I whisper.

"What do you need, Baby - " he asks as he steps closer, putting his front flush with my back. "Tell me."

The feeling of his fully clothed body pressed against my bare skin flares every nerve ending.

"You," I arch into him. "I need you."

His teeth drag over my pulse point. "Good answer."

Gripping the band and tugging them down, Sebastian pulls my panties off. I carefully step out of them, then turn to face him.

He keeps a few feet of space between us as he looks at me. I'm entirely naked now, making me feel vulnerable and exposed. And I'd normally feel self-conscious in this situation, but the way Sebastian is looking at me... I feel sexier than I've ever felt before.

I've seen photos of some of the girls he's dated, and they don't look like me. I'm not a twig, and I'm not perfectly smooth, and I'm not for everyone. But right now? Right now I feel like I was made for him. And I want to return that feeling.

Reaching out, I undo Sebastian's shirt buttons, watching each inch of skin as I expose it. When the last button is undone, I tug the shirt free of his pants and push it off his shoulders. It falls to the floor, and I get my first look at a shirtless Sebastian. It's hard to believe that I've never seen him this way. That we've never seen *each other* this way. But I've imagined it, and he's just as glorious as I knew he would be. His tattoos go all the way up his arms, and I want to trace them with my tongue. But I don't. I have more clothes to remove.

My fingers drop to his belt, and I force myself to proceed slowly. There's no rush. We have all night.

Leaving the belt in his pant loops, I undo his button and zipper and let the weight of the belt pull his pants to the floor. Sebastian is standing before me now, in nothing but his tight black boxer briefs, and they are doing nothing to hide his... size.

I catch myself licking my lips as I glance up. His eyes are on mine, and he looks like he's using every ounce of his self-control to stand still.

I keep my eyes glued to his as I hook my fingers in the waistband of his briefs and pull them down. I hold his gaze until I'm on my knees and he's as naked as I am.

I reach out to take him in my hand when he steps back.

"On the bed."

It's not a question. It's a demand.

Doing as I'm told, I rise to standing and climb onto the

mattress. There's no real graceful way to do this, so I sorta slide myself back until I'm laying in the middle of his soft comforter.

Sebastian stands at the foot of the bed, watching.

The look in his eyes is making me feel brave.

Fuck it.

I let my knees drop open.

I think he growls a curse, but I can't hear the words over the blood rushing through my veins.

Sebastian crawls up the bed towards me but stops before he reaches me.

Scratch that. He can reach me just fine.

With a hand on either thigh, Sebastian holds me open. And I have half a second to realize what he's about to do, before his mouth is on my pussy. He doesn't start small. Not a little kiss, or a little lick, he starts straight up devouring me.

My head falls back into the mattress and I cry out.

This is the first time we've been together where we don't have to worry about being loud. And that's a good thing, because what he's doing to me right now is divine and I can't hold in my moans. I don't even try.

A second, a minute, a year passes... I don't know. But when his fingers get involved, I lose all control. I grip the blankets beneath me as my orgasm unravels my sanity. I think I'm chanting his name. I think I'm thanking the gods. I think I'm begging for mercy.

A kiss on my cheek has me prying my eyes open.

Sebastian is looming over me, looking at me like I'm the answer to all life's questions.

"You okay, Baby?"

"Yes," I push the word out between heavy breaths.

He kisses my other cheek. "I'm clean. Are you on the pill?"

It takes me a moment to understand what he's asking. I

release the death grip I still have on the blankets and bring my hands up to his face.

I nod towards my arm, "I have the implant."

I expect him to smile, but his gaze just gets more fierce.

Then he's closing the distance between us, pressing his lips to mine. As they meet, I can taste myself on him. But instead of being repulsed, it sends a jolt down my body and I feel myself getting even wetter.

When he deepens the kiss, I feel the tip of his cock press against my opening. He continues to kiss, his mouth caressing mine, as he slides in, one inch at a time.

This is the first time that he's gone slow. It's worse. It's better. It feels like he's even bigger than he was before. His fast thrusts were a shock, but this slow invasion is torture. I feel every millimeter and my body pulses against the stretch.

I try to arch my hips, to get more of him, but he bites my lip. "Stay still, Baby. Just stay still and take it."

I think I sob. But I hold still. And he keeps going, keeps pushing, and I can't believe how deep he is. His tongue slips into my mouth, mimicking the motion of his cock. It's dirty and hot-as-fuck and I clench around him.

Finally, he bottoms out. Pulling away from the kiss, he buries his face in my neck, releasing a loud groan that vibrates across my skin.

My arms wrap tightly around his shoulders and my legs do their best to wrap around his waist. We stay like this, still, hearts beating against each other. Then he starts to move.

Just like before, I lose track of time. I'm clinging on for dear life, and he's slowly thrusting in and out.

With an adjustment of his hips, he hits a spot even deeper than before.

"Sebastian… " I moan. "You feel so good."

"Fuck, Baby. It's you."

His thrusts continue and I feel a hand sneak between our bodies. His thumb circles my clit and I nearly lose consciousness.

Sebastian's voice is rough as he keeps his pace. "I need you to come again. I need to feel you come on my bare cock."

Words elude me. I moan and writhe.

"That's it, Baby. You can do it. Come for me. Let me feel it."

His words ricochet through my body as I shatter and convulse beneath him.

Sebastian keeps his thrusts slow but I can feel his body tensing. He's close.

"I'm ready, Sebastian. Come inside me."

His thrusts get jerky.

"Fuck." He's losing control. "Fuck. Baby, I love you."

One more deep thrust, and he stills.

With a deep groan, he crests over the edge, and the heat of his release swamps me.

Chapter 66

Meghan

I FEEL the mattress dip as Sebastian climbs into bed beside me.

We took our time untangling our bodies after we finished. The sex. The sex where Sebastian said *HE FUCKING LOVED ME!*

I'm trying really hard not to lose my mind. But I'm not being very successful. When we finally climbed off the bed, I quickly commandeered the master bathroom to clean up. The dim lighting helped me to avoid eye contact as I shuffled away from the bed.

He didn't say anything else after that, and neither did I. Maybe he thinks I didn't hear him. Maybe it was just one of those things you say during a passionate round of lovemaking. Maybe he regrets it. Maybe he means it. *Oh my god I have no idea what to think!*

So, I did what any adult would do. I peeked out to make sure the bedroom was still empty, then hurried to the bed and pretended to be asleep before Sebastian returned from the bathroom down the hall.

I'd found a pair of sleep pants and a t-shirt hanging off a

towel rack while I was freaking out in the bathroom, so I tugged them before my sprint to the bed. It's not actual armor, but I feel a little less vulnerable with the layer of clothing. Now here I lay, curled up on my side, back to the door, my eyes shut, holding still.

He seems to be buying it, since I can feel him moving pillows around but he hasn't said anything to me. Squeezing my eyes shut tighter, I pray to The Sandman to sprinkle Sebastian with his dust so he'll just lie down and go the hell to sleep.

In my rushed effort to look comfy, the blanket got tangled up so my bare feet are exposed to the cool air. I want to adjust them, but I don't dare.

Sebastian moves again, and it feels like he's right behind me. I'm prepared for him to become my big spoon, but instead he reaches over and gently tugs on the blanket until it covers my cold feet.

Just when I think my heart can't take any more, he kisses the back of head and murmurs something that sounds a lot like *sweet dreams, Baby.*

I'm officially losing it, but my whore of a honey badger just pulled up a chair to her writing desk and is readying her quill to sign wedding invites.

I continue to hold still and do my best to keep my breathing steady. I wait for him to drape an arm over me, but he rolls away. I can still feel his warmth. Maybe the psycho is a back sleeper; at this point, nothing should surprise me anymore.

I'm not sure how long it's been, but I'm positive that Sebastian's asleep. He hasn't moved, and he's snoring softly.

I channel my inner Catwoman and slip out of the bed as smoothly as possible. I watch Sebastian for a moment to make sure I didn't wake him. He's flat on his back, with his arms crossed over his chest. The small amount of moonlight coming through the gap in the curtains gives him a macabre appearance. He looks like a sexy olive-skinned vampire. And I don't dare wake him.

Carefully, I tiptoe all the way to the stairs. Pausing at the bottom of the steps, I glance to the kitchen. Part of me is tempted to search for some booze, but I know that's the last thing I need right now. I need to attempt to think clearly.

Instead, I pad into the living room and start to pace. There's still one lamp on in the corner, and it sets the perfect mood for how I feel right now.

I want to call the girls. I need someone to talk me off the ledge. But a glance at the clock tells me it's 2:00 am. It's Katelyn's wedding night, and - even if I got Izzy on the phone - all she'd do is swoon.

I don't even know why I'm so stressed right now. Sebastian falling in love with me is at the top of my wish list. Written in bold. And underlined. But maybe that's it. It's the thing I want most in the world. And I want him to have meant it. I want it so bad that it's making me crazy. Because what if he didn't? What if it was a slip of the tongue? A turn of phrase? Something he says to all the girls?

I can't just pretend I didn't hear him. I can't live like that. I know myself well enough to know that. I'll end up asking him about it. And if I ask him, and he apologies, or back peddles, or does whatever people do to take back an *I love you,* I think I might crumble.

My heart can't take any more ups and downs. I pretended to be okay with casual, but that was the biggest steaming pile of lies I've ever sold in my life. I don't want to be casual. I want to be serious. Because I feel serious. I feel seriously in love with Sebastian. And if he doesn't feel at least a little of what I feel, then I'll need... a therapist. I'm going to need a fucking therapist.

I reach the bookshelf on the far end of the room and start to turn, to pace the other way, when a framed photo catches my eye.

Picking it up, I bring it closer to the lamp.

It's a heavy silver frame holding a photo of four people. In the middle are Sebastian and Samuel. The twins. They're smiling, and have their arms slung around each other. Next to Samuel is a slightly shorter man, who shares the same coloring as the brothers. This must be Curtis, the older LeBlanc boy. My eyes trail over to the woman next to Sebastian, and my brain feels like it's glitching as I blink at the picture.

A beautiful woman, with sleek dark hair, cut into a bob, is grinning at the camera. A woman that I know. A woman I've gotten drunk with. A woman I discussed my man troubles with. A woman named Annabelle, who conveniently never told me her last name. Sebastian's little sister, Anna LeBlanc.

My mouth suddenly feels dry.

I set the frame on the side table and back away.

What the fuck?

Seriously. What. In. The. Actual. Fuck.

Annabelle is Sebastian's sister? Does he know that we met?

I want to slap myself. *Duh, of fucking course he knows!* He called me when I was at the bar with Annabelle. *Anna. Her name is Anna.* Fuck! He asked to talk to my friend, and I didn't think anything of it. If he didn't know before, he sure as fuck knew then. And he didn't say anything. Not a fucking word.

Did Sebastian tell Anna to use me for her event? I mean, the event was real, I was there. But did she fire her planner just to use me, or was it really an emergency and she - for whatever reason - didn't want to tell me who she was?

But why?

I remember my conversation with her. How I told her all about this guy I was falling for. How I felt about him and how I thought he felt about me.

My shoulders slump and I shake my head.

Samuel.

Samuel came and picked us up that night. And he didn't say anything either. Not a word. And what's worse is that he made a point to pretend that he and Anna were just friends. He made a point to keep it a secret. Just like Sebastian.

Sebastian.

My throat constricts.

I know I was drunk that night, but I remember our conversation. I remember thinking that he sounded concerned. That he sounded like he wanted to see me. But then he sent his brother to pick *us* up and he must have told Samuel to keep his mouth shut. To keep the secret.

But to what end? Was it all one big trick? Some fucked up game?

What I feel when I'm with Sebastian doesn't feel like a game. But... then why?

The harder I think about it, the more it makes my head hurt. And my heart hurt.

All I know for certain is that I need to get the hell out of here. Whatever this is, I don't have the headspace to deal with it right now. I'm already in too deep with Sebastian. The thought of him being a liar is too much. And I don't know where to go from here. Other than home.

Chapter 67

Sebastian

I blink my eyes open, and memories from last night swirl through me. I'm not fully awake yet, but my cock sure is.

My lips pull into a small smile. Banshee is going to be the fucking death of me. Every time we fuck seems better than the last, and that's a theory I'm ready to test right now.

Only I roll onto my side and find an empty expanse of bed. I roll the other way, also empty. I glance around the room. The bathroom door's open, so she's not in there, and the clock says it's after 7:00. I sit up enough to look at the floor. Her dress and my clothes from last night are still in a pile, so I flop back down onto the bed. She's probably in the kitchen making coffee or baking something amazing.

It's my day off, and all I want to do is bury my dick in Banshee and then fall back asleep. But the thought of finally tasting one of her baked creations gets me climbing out of bed.

At the top of the stairs, I pause. The house is quiet. Too quiet. And I don't smell coffee or anything else that might signal breakfast.

I start to get a bad feeling as I descend the stairs.

Empty. I don't need to search to know that the house is empty.

When did she leave? And what did she wear home, my pajamas?

I scrub my hands over my face. Why the fuck would she just up and leave? I thought we had an amazing time last night.

Then it hits me.

She heard me. She pretended not to, but she heard me when I confessed that I love her.

Goddamnit.

I didn't mean to say it. It just came out. But that doesn't make it untrue.

I wanted to talk to her about it after, get it all out in the open, but she was already asleep when I came to bed.

Double goddamnit.

I'm an idiot. She wasn't asleep. That little faker. She was avoiding me and waiting to bail.

But that doesn't make sense. I know her. I know her moods and her looks. I know she feels something for me. Maybe it's not love, not yet, but I can't believe that hearing me say it would send her running.

So, what now? How do I address this?

The morning sun breaks through the clouds and a beam of light reflects off something on one of the end tables, catching my attention. I walk over to see what it is, and stop dead in my tracks.

Fuck.

Fucking Fuck!

She knows.

This is bad. This is worse than saying I love you. Sure, that was a little *off brand* for me, but this...

This is a really fucking bad.

"Fuck!" I shout it out loud, hoping it will make me feel better. It doesn't.

I sprint up the stairs to my phone.

I need to talk to her. I need to clear this up. She blew me off for three months over some misplaced guilt after that bar fight. I can't imagine the sort of ice-out she'll give me over this level of deception.

I dial her number.

"Come on, Banshee, pick up." It rings several times, then goes to voicemail. "Banshee. Call me. Please." I hang up.

I stand in place, staring at my bed. That was the wrong thing to say. I need to explain myself. She's not going to just call me.

I call her again. It rings once before it goes to voicemail. Fuck, she's already screening my calls.

"Meghan. Baby. I know this probably looks bad. I get that. But please talk to me. My stupid sister reached out to you all on her own." I heave out a breath. "Yes, I figured it out that night when you guys were drinking, but that wasn't the time to tell you. I know... I fucking know I should've told you at some point since then. I know that. I'm so sorry. I chewed her out the next day, not that it even mattered. She wouldn't shut up about how awesome you were. But that's not the point, she shouldn't have..."

The voicemail beeps and ends, cutting me off.

"Damnit."

I dial again. Not surprised when she sends me right to voicemail again.

"Hey, okay, I'll talk faster. My sister's a moron for what she did, but I'm worse for not telling you. I should have. I planned to. Today actually. But you're not here. Please let me explain. Just don't cut me out of your life again. That's not... That's not what I want. That's not what I want for *us*." I pause for half a second and decide to go for it. "And as far as what I said last night, I don't regret it. You're mine, Baby. You got that? Mine. You can run and force me to chase, or you can just let me catch you. Your choice. But I will get you. Because you're my Banshee."

Chapter 68

Meghan

Dear Diary,
 What. The. Fuck. Should. I. Do.
 Seriously, I'm losing my mind over here. I've baked about a dozen coffee cakes in the past 24 hours, and I've run out of people to give them to. I've started putting them into gallon bags so I can hand them out to strangers on the street.
 I don't know why I thought I could handle this problem on my own; clearly I didn't learn my lesson from the last time. I guess I'm just sick of being the drama queen of the group. I mean, I don't mind it when it's fun drama, but this... this is bullshit drama. I feel like I'm in a sitcom. Or a cheesy romcom, only instead of Kate Hudson the audience is stuck with me - the heavier, psychotic version of a Disney princess.
 I just want to call him. And forgive him. And tell him that I love him, too. And pretend that it's not super weird, and a little bit creepy, that his sister sorta stalked me.
 Ahhh! What should I do?!
 Okay, in the morning I'm calling Katelyn for an emergency advice session. It'll be Monday, her wedding weekend will be

over, so she can drop the goo-goo eyes long enough to help me deal with my shit.

Plus, I have about six more coffee cakes to finish baking tonight.

XoxoX

Chapter 69

Meghan

"ARE you sure I should be doing this?" I ask Katelyn as we find our seats.

"Trust me?"

"I do," I grumble.

And I really do. That's why I called her. Of course, by the time I called her Monday morning to tell her my dilemma, it was about 48 hours before the Sleet's first playoff game.

When Katelyn asked if she could include Jackson in the conversation, I agreed. *What's a little more humiliation.* As Sebastian's friend and team captain, he suggested I wait until after the game to talk to him. Since I didn't know the whole story about Anna, I couldn't say for certain what would happen to *us* once the conversation was over. According to Jackson, it's better for Sebastian (and the team) for him to play filled with even the smallest amount of hope rather than a broken heart.

I've listened to Sebastian's voicemails so many times I could recite them verbatim. He sounded sincere, and I want to believe him. I'm not sure how this chapter of our story will end, but I am ready to talk to him.

We're sitting a few rows farther back than we'd usually be, but our seats are near center ice, so we have a good view. I'm sandwiched between Katelyn and Izzy, which is perfect since I could use the extra comfort right now.

Sitting quietly, I methodically pick half the salt off my giant pretzel while the girls chat. They both have significant others playing tonight, so I'm sure they're nervous, too. They're just doing a better job of hiding it.

I'm ready to crawl out of my skin when the teams finally come out to warm up.

Even without all his goalie pads on, Sebastian would be easy to spot. It's like my girlie bits stuck a tracker on him. I feel like I could pick him out of a stampede.

I watch him skate around a bit before he drops down into his stretches. The hip rolls he's currently doing affect me more than ever after this past weekend. I finally got under him, and it's all I dream about now. I want his hands on me. I want to feel his big strong body against mine again.

I bite my lip to keep from drooling, and that's when he looks straight at me.

At first, I wonder if I'm imagining the eye contact, but the longer he holds my gaze, the more sure I become. I don't know if I should smile or wave or just keep staring, but Sebastian doesn't smile either. He just stares.

My chest feels tight.

He doesn't look happy to see me. Maybe he's confused about me being here. Maybe he doesn't want to smile and look like an idiot if I don't return the gesture. Or maybe he's not happy to see me here. Maybe I've caused him enough stress, and he's done with me now. He hasn't tried to contact me since those voicemails when he first found me gone. I thought he was giving me space, but maybe there's another reason for his continued silence.

I unclench my fist, talking myself up to give him a small wave, when Zach skates up to Sebastian, blocking my view.

There's a continued flurry of movement, then the team is off the ice for their final locker room meeting before the game.

My shoulders slump. I should've called him sooner. I don't even care anymore about what Anna did. About the fact they kept it a secret. I just want Sebastian. And I wish he knew.

Chapter 70

Meghan

M<small>Y PRETZEL IS</small> a ripped-up pile of carbs at my feet, and I know I need to clean it up, but I'm so stressed out right now that I can't keep my fingers still. I've shredded my pretzel, my napkin, the paper plate the pretzel came on, and the thread hanging from the bottom of my Sleet hoodie - and the game isn't even over yet!

"Come on, boys!" Izzy shouts next to me.

It's the start of the third period, and we are up 3 – 2. I know every game can't be a shutout, but I much prefer those. I just hate seeing pucks get past Sebastian. And not because it means the other team scored. I hate it because I know he beats himself up over every single one.

"Shit. Shit. Shit," Katelyn chants.

Both teams are rushing down the ice towards Sebastian in one big clump of bodies and sticks. I can't even tell who has the puck.

Without meaning to, I'm on my feet and biting my fingernails in worry.

The group of players is right in front of the goal. Someone

knocks the puck out to the side and the men disperse enough for me to get a view of Sebastian.

The other team gets control of the puck again, and they descend back towards the net. I don't know how Sebastian can look so calm when I'm over here about to pee my pants.

The movement is hard to track. The puck is passed from one player to another. Knocked out of play by Jackson, then suddenly the other team snags it. The players all shift, unwittingly creating an opening, and the puck rockets towards the goal.

I squeal, wanting to shout out a warning, but Sebastian sees it.

In a lightning-fast move, he stretches out to his right, straining across the distance. His hand darts out and deflects the puck.

The crowd goes crazy, the sound is deafening, but Sebastian's still off balance.

He's hunched, still stretched out across the goal, and it looks like he's in pain.

It happens in a fraction of a second. The lean. The save. And then the player from the other team, crashing into him.

The player's shoulder connects with the underside of Sebastian's jaw, wrenching his helmet off.

Sebastian's body turned with the impact so instead of falling straight back, he twists, and he goes down sideways. I watch in horror as his unprotected head connects with the goal post.

He crumples to the ice.

And I scream.

He's not moving.

I vaguely register Jackson dropping to his knees next to Sebastian, and Zach punching the guy who ran into him.

He's not moving.

Sleet Banshee

The crowd is going crazy with cheers and boos and I can't hear any of it over the ringing in my ears.

He's not moving.

I think there's a fight happening. I try to take it in, but I can't pull my eyes off Sebastian.

He's not moving.

A medic is kneeling down next to him. Leaning close.

He's not moving.

The medic waves for help.

His arm moves.

And I choke on a sob.

"He's okay. Meg, he's okay." Izzy grips my arm, squeezing to get my attention.

I force my lungs to unconstrict, pulling in a shaky breath.

"See? He's getting up," Katelyn says, using her mitten to brush away the tears that I didn't even know were rolling down my cheeks.

I watch the medic help Sebastian into a sitting position. He's swaying with the motion. He's moving, but he doesn't look good.

Katelyn and Izzy keep a hold on me as we all watch. Sebastian's teammates have formed a circle around him, making it harder to see what's happening.

"Come on, Sebastian. You're okay. You're okay." I whisper to myself, as if I can will him better with a few muttered words.

Two players grab Sebastian under his arms and hoist him to his feet. They put Sebastian's arms over their shoulders and skate him off the ice. Watching his back retreat doesn't make me feel any better. His head's hanging low and his feet look like they're hardly touching the ice.

The crowd is clapping, glad to see their goalie up and moving, but I can't clap. My hands are still shaking.

"Here, let's sit back down." Izzy's hand is still on my arm.

"Yeah, let's sit," Katelyn says, guiding me back into my seat.

When my butt hits the hard plastic, my shock starts to subside, allowing worry to overflow me.

I try to stand, "I need to see him."

Izzy puts a hand on my thigh. "We'll go after the game."

"No." I shake my head. "I need to see him now."

"Honey, they won't let you back there. They won't even let me back there. The staff doctors will help him. We'll see him after the game. I promise." She squeezes my leg. "My dad will help us."

"But..." I want to argue, but I know there's no point. I tug on the thread of my sweatshirt, and it finally breaks. "Fuck."

Chapter 71

Meghan

"WHAT DO you mean he's not here!" I practically yell from my spot behind Izzy.

"He was brought to the hospital," the team doc tells Izzy, who - unlike me - is acting like a normal person.

"Why?! What's wrong?! Is he going to be okay?!" I push myself into their conversation.

The guy sighs and looks at me. "Look, I can tell you're upset, and I'm sorry. But I can't tell you any more. Confidentiality and all that." He holds his hands up and steps back. "Sorry."

Izzy grabs my arm before I can tackle him and force him to answer my questions. "They always take the players to the same place."

"Where?" When she doesn't immediately answer I try to calm my tone. "Where, Izzy?"

She sighs. "Amore Medical Center."

"Thank you."

"Zach and I can drive you over when he comes out."

I shake my head. "I'm going now."

"Meghan..."

"Sorry." I start backing away. "I can't wait."

Izzy calls after me but I'm already rushing down the hall.

Chapter 72

Meghan

"Miss, I'm sorry, but I can't tell you that."

I drop my forehead against the reception desk. "Shit."

The receptionist reaches up to pat my hand. "I'm sorry, Dear. You can call him, or one of his family members, and they can tell you. I just can't disclose patient information to non-family. And that includes room numbers."

I slowly raise my head. Family?

"Okay, thank you," I nod before stepping away.

I pull out my phone and stare at the LeBlanc entries in my contacts. I'm sure Sebastian won't have his phone on him, so that leaves me with Samuel or Anna.

I updated her contact info after finding out the truth. I'm still a bit pissed at her, but not so much that I wouldn't ask her for help. The real question is which sibling is more likely to be here and able to tell me where they are.

Always bet on the twin.

I select Samuel's number and press the phone hard against my ear.

It rings a few times before he picks up.

"Hello?" he answers quietly.

I'm so relieved he answered, I have to close my eyes. "Samuel. It's Meghan. Are you here? At the hospital, I mean."

"Yeah, doll. I'm here. Are you?"

"I'm downstairs. They won't tell me where Sebastian is - " I'm trying really hard to not sound as frantic as I feel. "Will you tell me where you are?"

"We're up on the third floor, but I..."

Afraid of what else he might say, I cut him off - "Thanks."

Hanging up, I shove my phone in my pocket and dart toward the elevator.

An elderly couple steps in behind me, so when the doors open on the third floor it takes all the patience left in my body to keep from shoving them out of the way.

As soon as I start down the hall, I realize my mistake. This place is huge. I should've let Samuel finish what he was going to say. I was just worried he'd say "but Sebastian doesn't want to see you - " hence me hanging up. It's harder to turn someone down face-to-face.

Luckily, I paired my hoodie with some flat-soled boots, so I start to jog the halls looking for signs of Sebastian.

After the second nurse glares at me, I slow my pace to a quick walk. It's probably for the best, since I was starting to get winded. Note to self: start doing more cardio. But also, how fucking big is this hospital? I swear I've made a dozen turns already. I should find a map, or just suck it up and call Samuel back.

I'm worried I'll have to do just that, when I turn yet another corner and spot a familiar, beautiful, black-haired woman. Annabelle. *Anna*.

My steps slow as I approach, suddenly unsure how to proceed.

There's no casual way to do this. The setting is intimate,

since it's not a typical waiting room. It's more of an alcove off the hall with a small cluster of couches and chairs.

Anna's facing me, but looking down, so she doesn't spot me. Sitting next to her is a woman that looks just like an older version of Anna. It must be Sebastian's mom.

My steps slow even more. Is this how I want to meet the mother of the man I love? I'm sure I look like a hot mess. And not a cute hot mess, but like a crazed crying woman -kind of hot mess. The kind of mess you might warn your son to stay away from.

My steps still completely when I'm just a few yards away.

There are a few more people seated in the small area. One's a silver fox of a man that I'm positive is Sebastian's dad. *Damn. Good to know he'll still be hot when he gets old.* I'm not sure if the other people are also family members, or if they're here for someone else, but I don't see Samuel. *Shit.*

"Meghan?" Anna's voice snaps my gaze back to her.

She stands and starts walking towards me.

But I'm so unsure of myself right now. I'm fighting against worry for Sebastian's health and worry over his reaction to me being here. Panic about meeting his parents. Hesitation about seeing Anna.

It's too much, so I'm left standing here, completely frozen, looking like a dolt.

Anna looks just about as hesitant as I feel, but she's braver than I am, because she doesn't stop until she's a few feet from me.

I feel like I'm going to barf, but I raise my hand for a stupid little wave. Belatedly realizing it's the wave I was going to give Sebastian before the game.

She gives me a weak smile. "Hey. What are you doing here?"

I shift my weight on my feet. "Umm, I wanted to see Sebastian."

That's obvious, right?

"Oh, right. Of course." She pauses. "Did he, uh, call you?"

My hopes of seeing him plummet as I shake my head.

"Umm, I'm sorry but... he doesn't want to see anyone," Anna tells me with obvious discomfort.

I bite my lips to keep from crying. I'm not sure why I'm on the verge of tears already. It feels like I'm no longer in control of my reactions.

Anna steps closer. "I'm sorry, if it were up to me I'd let you in. But he's pissed and he's only letting Samuel in his room."

I glance over her shoulder and see that their mom is watching us.

"Is he okay?" I whisper. "If... If you can tell me."

"Yeah. The doctors said he'll be fine," she nods. "He just needs a little time."

I swallow against the wave of relief mixing with my unease.

Anna raises her hand like she's going to rest it on my shoulder, then seems to think better of it. "Look, I'm really sorry, about everything. I've been meaning to talk to you, but just wasn't sure where to start. I just need you to know that Sebastian didn't have anything to do with me calling you for that auction. I really did need help with the planning, and when Samuel told me about you - " she lifts a shoulder. "I had to see you for myself. I never expected to like you as much as I did. *As I do.* That next day, Sebastian called and yelled at me for like an hour. He was so mad... " Her voice cracks. "I wasn't thinking about the trouble it might cause between the two of you. It wasn't my intention to mess everything up. I'm so sorry."

Her story makes sense. And I feel myself feeling bad for her, which just messes with my emotions even more.

"And then he called me again this weekend, yelling some more, because you found out." She touches my arm now. "I'm so sorry. I didn't mean to ruin things between you two. I didn't... He's so... I'm sorry. I didn't mean to."

Ruin things? Does Sebastian want it to be over between us? I need to talk to him.

Try as I might, my voice still comes out shaky. "Do you think he'll allow visitors soon?"

Anna hesitates before shaking her head. "He told Samuel not to let anyone in. I'd do it but... He doesn't need any extra stress right now. Not on top of everything else."

The look she gives me is full of pity, and it spears me straight through the heart.

That's it then.

I step back. "I get it."

And I do. I'm a part of that stress, and he doesn't need that. He doesn't need *me*.

"Meg, it's not..."

"No, it's okay - " I take another step back. "Don't tell him that I came here. Or you can. I don't know... " I shake my head. "I'm sorry. I shouldn't have come."

I don't know what I'm apologizing for. Fuck. I don't know anything anymore.

Spinning around, I hurry toward the closest hallway that will take me out of sight.

I bite down on my lip, hard, in an attempt to keep my tears at bay. They've started to track down my cheeks anyways, but I can't reach up to wipe them off. I've made enough of a scene already, I don't need Sebastian's whole family to see me cry as I tuck tail and run away.

How could I be so stupid? I've pushed Sebastian away at every opportunity. I brushed him off for months over something that wasn't his fault. I've been rude and snappy during every one of our meetings. I pretended not to hear him say *I love you*. I snuck away in the middle of the night rather than let him explain about his sister. I didn't call him back after he left me message after message apologizing. God, I'm such a bitch. Of course, he wouldn't want to see me. Of course, he's done with me. I'd be done with me, too.

The rational part of me knew that this would eventually happen. I knew we lived in different worlds. I knew I wasn't the type of girl he usually went for. Hell, he straight up told me he didn't want a girlfriend.

That last thought hits with force. *He didn't want a girlfriend, and I showed up at the hospital like a worried wife, calling his brother, talking to his sister, making eye contact with his mom.*

I feel sick.

Stopping in the middle of a hallway intersection, I realize that I'm completely lost.

A man with a small child walks past me, pressing themselves against the wall to give me a wide berth. My traitorous eyes are still springing tears, and I feel like I'm standing in a hall of fun house mirrors, my humiliation building in layers, one on top of another, forever and ever.

Spotting an empty restroom, I hurry inside and lock the door behind me. I just need a moment. A single moment.

Catching sight of my reflection in the mirror I let out a laugh that sounds like a whine.

I look awful. Straight up terrible. My eyes are bloodshot, my mascara is running down my face, and my hair looks like it belongs in a fairytale, on the villain.

Then I think about Sebastian. I think about every time I've ever seen him. And every time, he's looked amazing. No matter the situation.

Then I try to picture him standing next to me. And the

worst part is that I can see it. I shouldn't be able to. I shouldn't be able to feel how right we are together. But that's just it. Even with all the shit we've been through, I can still see it. *See us.*

It's Sebastian that can't.

With my back still to the door, I slide down until my butt hits the floor and drop my head into my hands. Sitting on a hospital bathroom floor would normally disgust me, but I can't bring myself to care.

Chapter 73

Sebastian

"Who was that?" I ask when Samuel hangs up his phone.

"Oh - no one," Samuel says, his tone tight.

I slowly turn my head against the scratchy hospital pillow to look at him. "No one?"

"Later, okay." He points at me. "You're supposed to be still and calm and resting and shit."

I snort, then wince.

Fucking concussions. Fucking groin pulls. Fucking doctors. Fucking MRIs and poking and prodding.

I close my eyes and do my best to pretend I'm somewhere else. Thank fuck we still pulled out a win tonight, or I'd be in even more of a shit mood than I am right now. I'm still pissed at Samuel for apparently encouraging Anna in her Meghan schemes, but he's my twin. And if there's anyone I can trust to enforce my wishes, it's him. I know he won't stop Coach when he shows up, but Samuel can keep everyone else away. Because my shit mood, mixed with pain and discomfort, is making me a terrible bitch of a person. And I don't want to interact with anyone when I'm like this.

Sleet Banshee

Except for Banshee. She might be the only person who could make me smile right now. Literally nothing would make me happier than seeing her walk through my door.

I was shocked-as-hell when I saw her at the game tonight. I'd hoped she'd be there, but I didn't think that hope had a snowball's chance in Hell of coming true. But like always, she surprised me. And like always, my eyes were drawn straight to her. It's like our souls are magnetically charged to find each other. Sometimes we get turned around, and we repel in opposite directions, but when we get set right again - nothing can keep us apart.

I wanted to climb the boards and go to her. I needed to know what she was thinking. What her being at my game meant. But since I couldn't do that, I had to just embrace the relief I felt at seeing her. I could worry about the rest later. I had a game to play.

But now it's later, and the game is over. So on top of all this physical shit I'm dealing with, I'm back to worrying about Meg. About us. About our future.

The door opens, letting in a shaft of light from the hallway. Even though it's night, the shades are drawn, and the lights are off with the exception of a dim lamp in the far corner. My head is already killing me, and I know that bright lights will make it so much worse, so I wait until I hear the door shut before I open my eyes.

Expecting one of the nurses, I'm surprised to find Mom standing at the foot of my bed.

She looks at my brother, "Samuel, go get me some coffee."

Samuel glances between Mom and me, but doesn't move.

"Mom," I say, "if you're here to tell me that I'm dying, Samuel can stay."

Mom huffs out a breath, then narrows her eyes on me. "Who's the redhead?"

"What?!"

Without thinking, I start to jolt up into a sitting position, and pain radiates from my head and groin.

I groan and curse, laying still and shutting my eyes against the throbbing.

"Language..." my mom admonishes, no leeway given for my injuries.

"Are you talking about Meghan?" Samuel asks.

"Oh good," she snarks, "I see both your brother and sister know who this girl is, but your poor mother hasn't even heard of her."

I crack my eyes open. Mom's hands are fisted on her hips, and she looks more angry than hurt.

"What are you talking about?" I grit out the question. "Is Meghan here?"

"She was."

"Was? What do you mean *was*?" my volume rises, sending a bolt of electricity through my brain.

Samuel puts a hand on my arm. "Bro, calm down. Causing yourself more pain is not going to help anyone."

I take a slow breath. "Mom, what happened?"

She watches me for a moment before replying. "Well, a few moments ago, this stunning little red-haired woman appeared in the hallway, over where you've sent us all to wait." Mom's clearly still bitter about me wanting only Samuel in my room. "I saw that the girl was wearing a Sleet shirt, but I didn't think anything of it. Then Anna spotted her and called out to her by name. The girl was clearly upset, and I was able to deduce that she was here for you. Obviously, I wanted to introduce myself, but the conversation between Anna and this *Meghan* looked tense enough that I stayed where I was."

"What do you mean she looked upset?" I keep my voice level.

My mom sighs like I'm an idiot for not knowing what happened. "I mean the poor thing had puffy eyes, tear tracks down her face, and she was biting her lip hard enough that I'm surprised it didn't draw blood. The dear looked about two heartbeats away from a nervous breakdown."

My throat feels tight. I'm relieved that she came to me. That she wanted to see me. But I hate that I caused her to worry. And I dread where this story is going.

I force a swallow before I speak again. "Where is she now?"

"Anna told her that you didn't want to see anyone, so she left."

"Banshee," I whisper, feeling a noose tighten around my heart.

The room is silent for a moment before Mom continues. "I don't know what's going on, since no one talks to me, but I'll tell you what I saw. I saw a beautiful young woman who looked absolutely devastated. That look, the look of worry on her face, you only have that look for someone you love. That sweet girl loves you. And if you love her too, and since you have a matching look on your face I'm guessing you do, then you need to fix this. Whatever you did, fix it. Love counts for a lot, but it also takes care and cultivation. You can't treat her like one of your usual *ladies*." Her glare tells me just how disappointed she is, even though she has no idea what happened. Then she pats my foot and shocks the shit out me by saying, "Don't fuck this up."

Samuel and I just stare at her. Never in my life have I heard Mom use the F word.

Mom nods once before pulling the door open and stepping out.

A moment before the door closes behind her, Samuel shouts out - "*Language!*"

I wince, then chuckle, then wince again.

Squeezing my eyes shut, I feel a tear trail down my cheek. I'm not sure if it's from the pain in my head, or the pain in my chest.

I've put my Banshee through so much in the short time that we've known each other. I don't know what she's thinking right now, but I'm sure it's nothing good. She doesn't deserve all this heartache. And I don't deserve her. But I don't care. Nothing will stop me from getting what I want. And I want a filthy-mouthed redhead.

Chapter 74

Meghan

Dear Diary,

My neighbors are starting to screen my visits. I know they're home, but they still won't open their doors. So what if I brought them coffee cakes just a few days ago. This is a new recipe. And it's good. But *nooooo* apparently there is such a thing as too much free food. So now I have a dozen dulce de leche coffee cakes filling up the entirety of my kitchen counter space and nowhere to bring them.

It's been 24 hours since I ran out of the hospital in a cloud of tears and embarrassment, and - if I can't keep baking - I don't know what I'll do with myself. I need my prep space back, and one person can only eat so much. Trust me, I've tested the limits already.

The girls offered to come over and hang out, but I turned them down. I used Izzy enough already for information on Sebastian, and Katelyn should be with her new hubby. Plus, I don't need an audience for my shame eating.

Sebastian was released from the hospital this morning. He suffered a Grade 3 concussion, basically the worst kind, along with a groin pull. I had to internet-doctor that one. I hear "groin" and I think dick, but this is apparently more of an inner thigh thing. I think. Based on my not-at-all qualified research, if he rests enough, and the team keeps winning, there's a chance he could play again in a few weeks. I'm sure he's super pissed about missing playoff games, on top of being in pain.

I haven't called him yet. I'm not sure if he knows that I came to the hospital last night. I still don't know what to think about Anna telling me to leave.

Okay, so maybe she didn't say it like that, but she did say I couldn't see Sebastian. Was that an overarching policy for everyone? Did he specifically say he didn't want to see me? When she said he was upset, was he upset at me? At her? At both? And what did she mean by "sorry I ruined everything"?!

See! This is why I keep baking. If I don't occupy my mind, I'll go crazy. And I don't know how I'll cope if this shitty feeling continues on much longer.

Fuck, there's the door. Must be the Thai food I ordered. What? I can't cook when my kitchen is covered in coffee cake.

XoxoX

Chapter 75

Meghan

I SLAM the lid on my laptop and hurry to the door. Katelyn thinks my diary is a physical book, like some Lisa Frank notebook with a picture of a multi-colored tiger on the cover and a lock a four-year-old could pick. Nope. It's all digital and saved in a folder on my desktop labeled Tax Docs. She'll never find it.

"One second!" I yell as I grab the wad of cash out of my purse for the takeout.

This place is old school and won't let you pay over the phone. But it's authentic and delicious, and I always order more food than I can eat in one sitting.

I open my mouth to thank the delivery driver as I yank open my door, but words don't come out.

It's not the delivery guy. It's Sebastian.

Sebastian is here. Like, right here in front of me.

He's wearing black sweatpants, a black zip-up with the hood up, and sunglasses. Somehow he looks amazing, and like shit, at the same time. But to me, he's never looked better.

My heart constricts. He's here. Sebastian came here. To me.

"Megs - " Sebastian's voice sounds raw.

His body language is full of worry and nervousness. But all I can think is *he's here.*

Foregoing words, I step into him and wrap my arms around his body. I've missed him so much. I don't even care about all that other crap right now, I'm just so happy to see him.

The second my chest hits his, I feel his muscles relax. And less than a heartbeat later, his arms encircle me, holding me tightly against his body.

I honestly had no idea what he was feeling about us. But having him show up here, at my apartment, tells me enough. Having him in my arms, with his scent filling my nose, I feel a thousand pounds of stress leave my body.

His lips press against the top of my head. "Hi, Baby."

"Don't call me Baby," I whisper.

With Sebastian's small huff of laughter, I feel the rest of the tension leave his body.

I kiss his chest, since that's where my face is pressed. "Hi, Big Guy."

I breathe him in. I still can't believe he's at my apartment.

Oh, god, my apartment!

Sebastian kisses the top of my head again. "Think we can move this inside?"

I tighten my grip on his torso. "Oh, umm..."

His lips are still pressed into my hair and I can feel him smile. "Something wrong, Banshee?"

"No. I've just been baking."

"Good. I'll finally get to try some."

"Like, a lot of baking."

"Double-good."

I release him and step back. "Okay, just don't judge me."

The door across the hall from mine opens, and my neighbor steps out.

Seeing me, he pauses.

Not wanting to be rude I wave, "Hi, Roger."

"Hey. Look, sorry, I just can't take any more from you."

I try not to pull a face. That sounded really bad. I know he's talking about coffee cake, but Sebastian doesn't.

Sebastian slowly turns to face Roger, pulling his sunglasses off as he does. I assume this is so he can glare at my foolish neighbor.

Roger's a normal-size guy, but standing in front of Sebastian makes him look like the little weenie that he is. And from the expression on his face, Roger is feeling like a little weenie.

"We haven't met," Sebastian says, his voice sounding even deeper than usual. "I'm Ash. Meghan's boyfriend."

If there was a record playing, it would have just scratched to a halt.

Uh, excuse me? Did he just introduce himself as my boyfriend?!

The honey badger in my chest is bouncing around in glee. I also noticed he introduced himself as Ash. The name recognized by the public. Sebastian is going out of his way to make an impression, and watching Roger's jaw drop open tells me it worked.

"Holy shit! Ash, like Ash Leblanc? Holy shit!" Roger runs a hand through his hair. "Dude, you're amazing. Your save in that last game. Oh man, I'm glad to see you up and moving. That hit was wicked."

"Felt wicked," is Sebastian's only response.

"Seriously. Just wow." Roger looks past Sebastian to me. "I had no idea."

I shrug. *Yeah, me neither, Roger.*

He continues, blushing now. "So, um, if you wanted me to take some more of that coffee cake, I'd be happy to."

I roll my eyes, sure, *now* he's willing to take more.

But Sebastian answers before I can - "Yeah, I don't think so Robert."

"Oh, right. No problem!" Roger doesn't even bother to correct Sebastian on his name.

I bite back a laugh, certain Sebastian messed it up on purpose.

"It was nice to meet you," Sebastian says, without any inflection that would indicate he actually means it.

"Yeah, yeah, you too."

Sebastian turns away from my neighbor, and - with an arm around my waist - pulls me into my apartment. As I close the door, I give Roger a little finger wave. This encounter should end that holier-than-thou attitude of his.

Sebastian's already walking around my apartment, looking at my stuff. He pauses when he spots the kitchen, and a grin spreads across his face.

He glances at me.

"Shut up."

Instead of teasing me, he picks up a pan. "Fork?"

I point to the drawer on the end. He snags a utensil and starts to eat straight from the pan while wandering through my living room. I hear a groan of appreciation, and I know it's for the cinnamon caramel goodness he just put in his mouth.

As before, our silence feels comfortable rather than strained. It's as though being in the same space is all we need to smooth out our recent history.

I watch Sebastian as he takes in my home, while eating my food. As far as two-bedroom apartments in Minneapolis go, mine is a good size. Of course compared to his giant house in the burbs, my place is tiny. Whatever, it is what it is. I like my home, and I almost always keep it clean. I'm just thankful I showered today and am wearing my good leggings.

He stops in front of a large painting in my living room, and I snicker. It's the *flower* painting that Izzy made for me.

Sebastian hums and works his way over to my bookshelf. It's not until now that I notice his slight limp. And the duffle bag that he dropped on the floor.

"Shouldn't you be taking it easy?" I ask.

"Yeah," he says, moving towards my couch.

Using a hand on the armrest he lowers himself carefully, but I still catch the wince.

I sit down next to him, turning my body to face him. "How are you feeling?"

"Better." He reaches out and drags a finger down my cheek. "A lot better."

"Good." I catch his hand and hold it in my lap. "What's with the bag?" I nod towards the duffle.

He uses his free hand to scoop up another bite. "I'm staying over."

I raise one eyebrow. "Oh, really?"

"Yep." Taking another bite, he slowly pulls the fork free from between his lips.

"Hmmm." I can't stop staring at his mouth. "What if I were still mad at you?"

"I was willing to risk it. Plus, I can be very persuasive."

"I bet you can." Without meaning to, I lean further in to him with each word.

He licks his lips. "This tastes amazing."

"Glad you like it."

"But it doesn't taste as good as the baker herself."

My mouth pulls into a smile before we close the distance between us.

When our lips meet I swear I hear my soul sigh. His mouth tastes like sugar and sweetness and Sebastian.

Too soon, he breaks the kiss. "I'm so sorry, Baby. I never

meant to hurt you. I want to blame it all on Anna, but I should've told you. Right away."

I push the hood off his head and run my fingers through his hair. "I get it. I mean yeah, it would've been better if you told me sooner. But I get why you waited. And honestly, I get why Anna did it. I can't even say that I wouldn't've done the same thing if our positions were reversed."

Sebastian releases a large breath. "I don't deserve you."

I bite my lip and shrug, earning me the smile I was hoping for.

He grabs the pan from his lap and starts to lean forward to set it on the coffee table, but I can tell the motion pains him, so I take it from his grasp.

"Come here," he pats his lap.

"Umm... " I eye him. "Are you sure that's a good idea? I don't want to hurt you."

He tips his head down to give me *the look*. "Baby, get on my lap."

I stand in front of him and slowly place a knee on either side of his thighs. I don't care what he says, I'm going to be gentle. I don't want to cause him pain.

Once I'm lowered completely, Sebastian takes my face in his hands. "I need you to listen to me. Okay?"

"Okay."

"I love you."

Holy shit!

My breath catches.

"You hear me, little Banshee? I love you. I love your feistiness. I love the attitude you give me. I love the tough exterior you show the world. I love your fight, and your humor, and your kisses. I've never met anyone like you. I love everything about you. And I love how you make me feel." His thumbs brush across my cheeks. "You make me feel like a whole person. Like someone worthy of love. You make me a better man. Like I could take on the world and win."

And just like that, every one of my insecurities float away. I believe him. He means it. He loves me.

I don't even realize I'm crying until his thumbs wipe across my cheeks, again, catching wetness.

He gives me a soft smile. "I've wanted you, wanted to get to know you, since the moment we met. Ever since that damn high-five."

"What?! - " my voice cracks as my brain tries to connect the words that he's saying. High-five? We didn't high-five at the haunted house.

"You see, there was this girl last year. She asked Jackson if the team could give her high-fives when they went out onto the ice."

"Oh my god," I whisper.

His smile broadens. "I thought it was cute, so I agreed. But then I saw her... I saw this little spitfire of a goddess. She was a vision of joy and chaos, and she was hot-as-hell. And when my hand connected with hers, I knew I had to meet her. It took longer than I wanted, but I finally got my wish." My tears are falling freely now. I had no idea. "So you see, when I told this girl that I didn't want a relationship, that was my fear talking. I was afraid that a girlfriend would distract me, affect my game, take my focus. But I was wrong. Loving you doesn't make me weaker, it makes me stronger. I'm done pretending that I don't need you, because I do. I need you, Baby. I need you in my life. By my side." He trails a fingertip along the bottom of my jaw. "You remember the pictures you took at the museum, the selfies from when I scared you?" I give him a shaky nod. "I sent them all to myself. I look at them every night. You're my girl. You have been for a while. And you don't have to say any-"

"I love you!" I nearly shout it, startling us both. I say it again, quieter - "I love you, too."

With my hands on Sebastian's chest, I can feel the shudder that runs through his body. He lets out a long exhale as his eyes become glassy with unshed tears. And it's the most beautiful thing I've ever seen.

I bring my lips close enough so they brush against his when I say it again. "I love you, Sebastian. I have for a long time."

His breath mingles with mine as his hands slide around to the back of my head. He pulls me in at the same time I lean in to his lips.

Each kiss with Sebastian is new. Every kiss has been wonderful. But this one, this one is my favorite.

With our hands tangled in each other's hair, we let our lips take over.

I can feel his emotions as they pour from his mouth. He's all-in. And he trusted me enough to tell me.

I press my body tighter against his, and I feel his hardening cock beneath my ass.

I moan and grind against him.

I feel his hips rise up to meet me, then he groans and stills. Only it isn't a sexy groan, it's a painful groan.

I break the kiss and freeze - "Oh my god, I'm so sorry!"

"Nope, not you. I shouldn't have done that."

I grimace and wait for him to open his eyes. "You're supposed to be resting."

"That's why I brought my bag. I am resting. Here."

"Right. But I'm going to go out on a limb and guess that you can't do any *thrusting* anytime soon."

He drops his head against the back of the couch. "Unfortunately no. Doctor's orders."

"Hmm." I slide off his lap. "You'll just have to hold still then."

He slowly raises his head back up to look at me, as I sink to my knees in front of him.

I slide my hands up his thighs. "I seem to recall an unfinished demonstration of my oral skills."

He opens his mouth, maybe to protest, but thinks better of it.

As I pull down the top of his sweatpants and I see he's not wearing anything underneath. With a smile, I tug them down just enough to free his wonderfully-hard cock.

"Hi, big guy," I say to his dick, as I wrap my fingers around the length.

My lips are an inch away from the prize when there's a knock at the door.

"Go the fuck away!" Sebastian shouts.

I jump up. "No!"

"No? Banshee, you'd better get your sweet lips back over here and around my dick before I strain my groin, even more, by fucking you against your front door."

I know he's serious, and I'm seriously turned on, but the indignant look on his face has me bent over in laughter. "Just hold on."

I hold up a hand as I look for the cash I set down earlier.

There's another knock at the door. This one much more tentative than the first. From experience, I know how thin these doors are. The delivery guy probably heard a lot more of Sebastian's threat than he wanted to.

Snagging the cash, I pull the door open just far enough to grab the bag of food and hand off the money.

"Thanks, bye!" I slam the door, lock it, set the food on the floor, and spin back to Sebastian.

Only he's not where I left him. I spin in a quick circle but he's not here.

A smile tugs at my lips.

Heading down the short hall, I find Sebastian in my bedroom. Laying in the middle of my bed. Pants halfway down his thighs. He's using a hand to stroke himself, and doesn't stop when I enter the room.

"I see you found the bed," I say, pretending that watching him touch himself isn't dropping my IQ straight to the floor.

"It's a nice bed. Now get over here and take off your pants."

I step closer, but shake my head. "No sex, Sebastian. I'm not going to be party to your reckless behavior."

He smirks. "I believe you were about to give me the second half of that blow job."

"I can do that with pants on," I deadpan.

"Sure, if you're sitting on the floor."

"Right, which is..."

"But I want you to sit on my face."

My brain flickers like a half lit neon sign, and the honey badger in my chest drops dead from joy.

Epilogue

Meghan

THE SOUND of the rain stick announces my arrival.

Benny pops up from behind the counter. "Well, lookie who's here!"

"Hey, Benny."

He bows. "Greetings, Mrs. LeBlanc."

I roll my eyes. "Don't be an idiot."

"Hmm, I'd've thought two weeks of sun and sex would put you in a better mood."

I purse my lips and narrow my eyes. "Something looks different. What did you change?"

Benny's right, it's been two weeks since I've seen him.

Things moved kind of quick after the playoffs. Sebastian's recovery took longer than he hoped, so he didn't get to play in any more games last season. He was bummed about it, but he's more than ready to start the new season next week.

As for us, well... Sebastian moved in with me after about a month of officially dating. *I know, right? My place?* He'd bought his house as an investment and said he didn't want to stay there. Not one to half-ass anything, he sold it a week after moving in with me.

Not long after that, he asked me to marry him. It was wildly inappropriate, and not a story we can tell the grandparents, but it was perfect for us. He was balls deep, and I was a heartbeat away from an orgasm, when he asked. Obviously, I said yes. And since he did it in the museum after hours, we even got it on tape.

Sebastian didn't want to wait, and I didn't want to plan my own wedding, so we got hitched at the courthouse, then flew to a glorious little resort in Hawaii to honeymoon.

We just got home, and I've never been happier.

Izzy's still grumpy that I tied the knot before her, but - as her wedding planner - I can tell you it's going to be killer.

Benny clears his throat and tips his head to the side.

I was right, something is different.

"Give me a hint," I tell him, stepping closer to the counter.

The rain stick starts up again.

"Hey, Benny." Sebastian's deep voice fills the coffee shop.

"Hey."

Sebastian stops next to me, draping his arm over my shoulder. "Sweet tat."

"Huh?" I look back and forth between them.

"Thanks!" Benny beams. "It means *Life*."

He looks at me and points to the side of his neck.

Just below his ear is a newly tattooed pair of Chinese symbols, inked in black.

I look closer and bite my lip.

"What?" he asks, eyes wide. When I don't say anything, he opens his eyes wider. "What!"

"Uh, remember that Calligraphy conference I did?"

"Yeah..." His face fills with dread. "It doesn't mean Life, does it?"

I shake my head.

"What does it mean?" Benny asks.

I smirk. "*Kitten.*"

Epilogue II

Luke

PUSHING my way out the doors of Atom's Gym, I curse Jackson under my breath. "Go to Atom's Gym, he says. It'll be fun, he says. It's a no-nonsense place to sweat and workout and not be bothered, he says."

Annoyed, I kick a rock across the sidewalk as I stride through the summer heat towards my car.

It's not Jackson's fault that the big motherfucker who goes to this gym just so happened to be loving up his wife by the front desk when I arrived this morning. And it's not Jackson's fault that I've become the freaking 7th wheel when he and Zach and Ash invite me to tag along with them and their wives.

I pull open my car door and just stand there, letting the heat waft out.

No, it's not Jackson's fault. But he did tip the first domino when he hitched his wagon to Katelyn's star. And now my best friend is living his best life, enjoying the off season, and me? I'm becoming a miserable bastard.

Sleet Banshee

I need a woman. I need to find a wife.
I mean, if Ash can do it, how hard could it be?

Bonus Epilogue

Meghan

"What's taking so long?" I call out, loud enough for Sebastian to hear me through the door.

There's a grunt. And a curse. Followed by a thump as something hits the wall.

"Just give me a minute!" he shouts back.

I roll my eyes and adjust the fabric draping across my chest, making sure it's secured correctly under the golden ropes tied around my waist. "You've had several minutes already."

There's another grunt, and what sounds like him jumping up and down.

"Who's fucking idea was it to dress up in Halloween costumes in the middle of the summer?"

I grin, thinking about the outfit he's putting on. "Would you really rather wear that in October?"

He scoffs, "And freeze my damn nuts off? I don't think so."

"See? Could've been worse." I lean against the wall, waiting for him to finish getting ready. "Plus, it's for a good cause."

"Sounds expensive," my husband grumbles, making my grin grow wider.

"Speaking of expensive, I heard Luke's leaving tomorrow for some family wedding in Mexico."

Another thump.

"How do you even know that?" he sounds exasperated, but I can't tell if it's because of the topic, or the leather he's dealing with.

I reach up and twirl a curl around my finger. "I heard it from Izzy. Who heard it from Katelyn. Who heard it from Jackson. Who, I'm assuming, heard it from Luke."

"Well, next time you get invited to some charity costume whatever-the-fuck this is, let's just send them a check and then go to Mexico instead."

There's a final grunt, and then the handle to the bedroom door is finally opening.

I hadn't told Sebastian what we were wearing, so he hasn't seen my flowy, rather revealing, Grecian goddess dress yet.

But now... now he's seeing it.

Seeing me.

And the look on his face tells me that he likes it.

A lot.

But then he's stepping out of the bedroom, and every complete sentence in my brain fizzles into a random pile of letters. Because standing before me is a half-naked, tattooed and sculpted Sebastian LeBlanc.

The dark brown leather skirt hits him just above the knees. And the sandals that shouldn't be so sexy on him, are. They really, truly, are.

But it's the top half.

Dear god, the top half.

The crisscrossing leather straps molded to his chest have my mouth watering.

"Holy shit." My whispered expletive is drowned out by Sebastian's, "Holy fuck!"

Moving towards me, eyes racing up and down my form, Sebastian drops the Roman shield on the ground. "We're not going."

Closing the rest of the distance between us, I wrap my fingers around the leather and pull him against me. "We're going late."

Acknowledgments

This has been a whirlwind publishing spree and I have so many people to thank. Someone (cough-cough the amazing and wonderful Jaymin Eve) convinced me to publish all 5 of my books consecutively, one month apart. So here we are, we've made it. We started with Vincent and Sasha. Then we met Beth when she paired up with Angelo. And now we've completed the Sleet Series... or have we...?

Thank you, Mom, for being all the things a mom could possibly be. Thank you for being an unpaid editor. Thank you for your constant feedback and support. Thank you for promoting the hell out of my books and for putting them in your library. Your town is lucky to have you as a librarian, and I'm lucky to have you as a mom. I love you.

Thank you, Mander Pants. I love how much you love my books and I love you.

Thank you, M. Penna. You are goddamn rockstar editor and I can't imagine ever letting anyone else touch my books. Please don't ever tire of my writing because I'll never tire of your commentary. *dun dun dun* I love you!

Thank you, James Adkinson. You are so amazingly talented. You've created the most beautiful covers for me, and I can never thank you enough. You see my visions better than I do. And you're just a good fucking person and I love you.

Thank you to all my family. Dad, Roxie, Goofhead. My cousins, my siblings, my aunts and great-aunts. I'm so crazy-lucky to have such an amazing support system. Not everyone has that, and I love all of you.

Thank you to all my girlfriends. My bitches. My besties. You know who you are. And if you're reading this and wondering if I'm talking about you, the answer is Fucking Duh! Life is hard, but it's so much easier with friends like you. I love you guys so much.

Thank you to every booktoker and bookstagrammer who read-reviewed-shared-recommended my books. Your hard work has made such a huge impact on me. Without you all I have no idea where my books would be right now. So thank you. From the bottom of my twisted heart, thank you. I love you.

Thank you, husband. Thank you for always standing with me and behind me and in front of me when I need it. Life would be so damn boring without you. And I love you most of all.

About the Author - S.J. Tilly

S.J. Tilly lives in Minnesota with her husband and their herd of boxers. She spends an unhealthy amount of time with her face buried in books, reading and writing. If she's not nose-deep in text, or harassing her dogs, she's probably playing with her plants, pretending she knows how to garden. You can find her stumbling around online on all the platforms. www.sjtilly.com

Books By This Author

Sin Series
Romantic Suspense

Mr. Sin

I should have run the other way. Paid my tab and gone back to my room. But he was there. And he was... everything. I figured what's the harm in letting passion rule my decisions for one night? So what if he looks like the Devil in a suit. I'd be leaving in the morning. Flying home, back to my pleasant but predictable life. I'd never see him again.

Except I do. In the last place I expected. And now everything I've worked so hard for is in jeopardy.

We can't stop what we've started, but this is bigger than the two of us.

And when his past comes back to haunt him, love might not be enough to save me.

Sin Too
Beth
It started with tragedy.
And secrets.
Hidden truths that refused to stay buried have come out to chase me. Now I'm on the run, living under a blanket of constant fear, pretending to be someone I'm not. And if I'm not really me, how am I supposed to know what's real?
Angelo
Watch the girl.
It was supposed to be a simple assignment. But like everything else in this family, there's nothing simple about it. Not my task. Not her fake name. And not my feelings for her.
But Beth is mine now.
So when the monsters from her past come out to play, they'll have to get through me first.

Miss Sin
I'm so sick of watching the world spin by. Of letting people think I'm plain and boring, too afraid to just be myself.
Then I see *him*.
John.
He's strength and fury, and unapologetic.
He's everything I want. And everything I wish I was.
He won't want me, but that doesn't matter. The sight of him is all the inspiration I need to finally shatter this glass house I've build around myself.
Only he does want me. And when our worlds collide, details we can't see become tangled, twisting together, ensnaring us in an invisible trap.
When it all goes wrong, I don't know if I'll be able to break free of the chains binding us, or if I'll suffocate in the process.

Sleet Series
Romantic Comedy

Sleet Kitten

There are a few things that life doesn't prepare you for. Like what to do when a super-hot guy catches you sneaking around in his basement. Or what to do when a mysterious package shows up with tickets to a hockey game, because apparently, he's a professional athlete. Or how to handle it when you get to the game and realize he's freaking famous since half of the 20,000 people in the stands are wearing his jersey.

I thought I was a well-adjusted adult, reasonably prepared for life. But one date with Jackson Wilder, a viral video, and a "I didn't know she was your mom" incident, and I'm suddenly questioning everything I thought I knew.

But he's fun. And great. And I think I might be falling for him. But I don't know if he's falling for me too, or if he's as much of a player off the ice as on.

Sleet Sugar

My friends have convinced me. No more hockey players.

With a dad who is the Head Coach for the Minnesota Sleet, it seemed like an easy decision.

My friends have also convinced me that the best way to boost my fragile self-esteem is through a one-night stand.

A dating App. A hotel bar. A sexy-as-hell man, who's sweet, and funny, and did I mention, sexy-as-hell... I fortified my courage and invited myself up to his room.

Assumptions. There's a rule about them.

I assumed he was passing through town. I assumed he was a businessman, or maybe an investor, or accountant, or literally anything other than a professional hockey player. I assumed I'd never see him again.

I assumed wrong.

Sleet Banshee

Mother-freaking hockey players. My friends found their happily-ever-afters with a couple of sweet, doting, over-the-top in-love athletes. They got nicknames like *Kitten* and *Sugar*. But me? I got stuck with a dickhead who riles me up on purpose and calls me *Banshee*. Yeah, he might have a voice made specifically for wet dreams. And he might have a body and face carved by the gods. And he might have a level of Alpha-hole that gets me all hot and bothered.

But when he presses my buttons, he presses ALL of my buttons. And I'm not the type of girl who takes things sitting down. And I only got caught on my knees that one time. In the museum.

But when one of my decisions get one of my friends hurt... I can't stop blaming myself. And him.

Except he can't take a hint. And I can't keep my panties on.

Darling Series
Contemporary Small Town Romance

Smoky Darling
Elouise
I fell in love with Beckett when I was 7.
He broke my heart when I was 15.
When I was 18, I promised myself I'd forget about him.
And I did. For a dozen years.
But now he's back home. Here. In Darling Lake. And I don't know if I should give in to the temptation swirling between us or run the other way.
Beckett
She had a crush on me when she was a kid. But she was my brother's best friend's little sister. I didn't see her like that. And even if I had, she was too young. Our age difference was too great.
But now I'm back home. And she's here. And she's all the way grown up.
It wouldn't have worked back then. But I'll be damned if I won't get a taste of her now.

Latte Darling

I have a nice life - living in my hometown, owning the coffee shop I've worked at since I was 16.

It's comfortable.

On paper.

But I'm tired of doing everything by myself. Tired of being in charge of every decision in my life.

I want someone to lean on. Someone to spend time with. Sit with. Hug.

And I really don't want to go to my best friend's wedding alone.

So, I signed up for a dating app, and agreed to meet with the first guy that messaged me.

And now here I am, at the bar.

Only it's not my date that just sat down in the chair across from me. It's his dad.

And holy hell, he's the definition of Silver Fox. If a Silver Fox can be thick as a house, have piercing blue eyes and tattoos from his neck down to his fingertips.

He's giving me Big Bad Wolf vibes. Only instead of running, I'm blushing. And he looks like he might just want to eat me whole.

Tilly World Holiday Novellas

Second Bite

When a holiday baking competition goes incredibly wrong. Or right...

Michael -

I'm starting to think I've been doing this for too long. The screaming fans. The constant media attention. The fat paychecks. None of it brings me the happiness I yearn for.

Yet here I am. Another year. Another holiday special. Another Christmas spent alone in a hotel room.

But then the lights go up. And I see *her*.

Alice -

It's an honor to be a contestant, I know that. But right now it feels a little like punishment. Because any second Chef Michael Kesso, the man I've been in love with for years, the man who doesn't even know I exist, is going to walk onto the set, and it will be a miracle if I don't pass out at the sight of him.

But the time for doubts is over. Because Second Bite is about to start - "in three... two... one..."

Printed in Great Britain
by Amazon